WHITEFISH

A NOVEL BY

RUSSELL MYERS

WHITEFISH
Copyright © 2022 by Russell Myers
All rights reserved. No part of this book may be used or reproduced in any manner whatsoever without written permission from the author. For information address Russell Myers at russellmyersauthor@gmail.com.

ISBN: 979-8-406-85849-3

Printed in the United States
Cover photo adapted from Brad Behrent's Collection
Map created by Stan Sovern and Russell Myers

WHITEFISH is a work of fiction. Certain persons, businesses, and government organizations are mentioned in the novel, and some of the events described may resemble actual events or places. Where real-life figures, businesses, or government organizations are mentioned, the situations, incidents, and dialogs concerning those persons, businesses, or agencies are entirely fictional. In all other respects, any resemblance to actual persons, businesses, or organizations is entirely coincidental.

Alaska

Location of Detail

Kodiak Island

Afognak Island

Kodiak
Airport
Coast Guard Base
Trident Basin

Larsen Bay
Uyak Bay
Walt's Bear Camp
Westbrook Lodge

0 N 50
Miles

ONE

The last thing Samuel Boggs saw was the evil grin on his killer's face.

A bright flash of searing heat ripped through his skull, shattering bone and obliterating brain matter. Then nothing but darkness.

Boggs hadn't expected to die this way, shot point blank in the head by some stranger. Yet there he lay, his blood oozing out onto a blanket of rotting leaves and dried pine needles.

Minutes earlier, Boggs had congratulated himself on the choice of lodging he'd made. A rustic log cabin in the Montana wilderness with a small creek nearby. He'd get a taste of nature up close, even if it was only for one night. The owner of the *Trout Creek Cabin* had advertised its remote setting as having "so much more!"

For Boggs, the cabin promised to have so much less. There would be no neighbors with barking dogs, no guests in adjoining rooms, and no traffic noises. The motel he stayed at in Whitefish the night before had been situated right next to an onramp for U.S. Route 93. The sound of long-haulers coming and going from a nearby truck stop had been constant throughout the night. In the cabin, he'd finally have some peace and quiet. At least, that was the idea.

The owner lit a fire to warm up the place before Boggs arrived. The smell of seasoned firewood, burning in an old cast iron wood stove, had permeated into every crack and crevice of the dwelling. She left plenty of extra wood, too, stacked crisscross on a black metal storage rack next to the stove. *That was nice of her,* he thought. He wished he could've stayed in places like this more often.

It was easy for Boggs to imagine the sorts of people who must have rented the cabin. Cross-country skiers in their bright, shiny snowsuits. Weary backpackers, returning from a trek through the mountains. Camouflaged warriors in heavy boots. He'd read somewhere that during 2010, Montana planned to issue the same number of hunting licenses as the total number of residents.

Aside from a thick bearskin rug sprawled out on the wooden floor, there were no other signs of the struggle between man and beast. No elk or deer antlers, no taxidermy trophies, and no photos of fishermen hanging on the walls.

A queen-sized bed took up most of the loft, and a tattered sleeper sofa was wedged between two lodge poles in the main living area. There wasn't much space, but the cabin had a certain coziness that appealed to a traveler like Boggs. Maybe he'd come back with his wife sometime and they could spend a long weekend exploring the area.

He sat on the rug's soft fur, stretched his sore back against the sofa, and listened to the hypnotic sound of the crackling fire. His socks were so loose they were neither on nor off, but he wasn't quite ready to remove them all the way. For Boggs, less had indeed been so much more.

But then came the knock at the door.

He smiled. The owner must have forgotten something. Not twenty minutes earlier, she had given him the key. "Just put it under the mat when you go," she'd said. She seemed friendly. As he rolled onto his hands and knees and stood up, he looked at the clock on the wall. Nine forty-five. It was getting late. She probably just came back to confirm what time he'd be leaving the following day.

When Boggs opened the door, he realized he'd been caught off guard. That wasn't like Boggs. He was usually careful, but not this time. No, the man who stood in front of him wasn't the owner. And he wasn't friendly.

"Who da ya work for?" the man slurred. His eyes were narrow and glassy, and his head tilted to the side like a curious pit bull.

Boggs was more focused on the gun that was pointed at his face. His heart pounded and beads of sweat gathered on his forehead. He'd seen a Colt .357 magnum before, but never from that angle. The shorter barrel wasn't very accurate at a distance, but from two feet away the man couldn't miss. Even if he was drunk.

He looked at the man more closely. He remembered talking with him earlier that night in the run-down tavern that served the nearest town. Boggs had spoken to a few people while he was there, but he hadn't given them much thought. This man looked to be in his mid-twenties, scruffy face, denim jacket, blue jeans, and a worn-out cap. He looked like he'd be more comfortable in the woods than in town. He certainly knew how to hold a weapon. He looked like he knew how to pull a trigger too.

Back in the tavern, the man seemed annoyed when Boggs had questioned him about how long he'd lived in the area. That was normal. People in small towns didn't like answering questions from strangers. Still, why did the man follow him back to the cabin and why on earth was he pointing a gun at him? Boggs didn't have a clue.

"I said who da ya work for!?" The man barked. His patience was running thin.

The doorway was a bad place to stand. For Boggs it felt like purgatory. He could feel the warmth on his back and a chill from the air outside at the same time. If he could get back into the room, he still had a chance. A 9mm Glock was in his bag, locked and loaded. He just needed some time. Time he didn't have at the moment.

"I work for myself," Boggs said, trying to stay calm. "We're searching for a man named Tony Ferguson and you just happened to look like him. That's why I asked you those questions earlier."

The man squinted. "Who's *we*?" he asked. "You said 'we're searchin.' That don't sound like you work for yourself."

The man may have been drunk, but he was still listening.

"I meant my company," Boggs said. "We have an office in Boise. I have three employees."

The man shook his head. "No, you know who I am. How did ya find me?" The man glanced inside the cabin. "Who else is here?"

Boggs could try to make a run for it if he got the chance. The porch light wasn't very bright. If he reached the trees, maybe he could hide in the darkness.

"I'm telling you the truth," Boggs said. "I didn't come here looking for you and nobody else is with me. Up until two months ago, this Ferguson guy rented a place up in Whitefish. I think he lives somewhere around here now. He's been trying to get out of paying child support. His wife, or I should say his ex-wife, hired me to chase after him."

"I don't have time for your shit," the man said. He steadied the gun with both hands and closed one eye.

"Wait!" Boggs pleaded. "Let's talk about this."

"Then talk!" the man growled. "Why are they still after me? It's been six years."

Boggs knew he'd never make it to the trees, and even if he did it probably wouldn't matter. He took a deep breath, then let it out slowly. He'd learned the technique during a training workshop the agency had organized several years earlier. He hadn't used the breathing exercise in a stressful situation before, but this moment seemed like a good time to start.

"Listen," Boggs tried to reason, "you followed me here. If I was after you, we wouldn't be standing on this porch."

Sweat trickled down the side of Boggs's face. He wasn't sure what else to say. The agency had trained him to keep his mouth shut. It was bad enough if he were killed by some drunk stranger but getting killed for telling the *truth* didn't sit well with him.

The man staggered slightly, lowered the gun, then raised it back up. He was trying to think but he was having trouble. The cold outside could be seen with every breath he took. His eyes drifted.

Boggs continued. "Ferguson had his mail forwarded to a post office box in Thompson Falls. I booked this cabin for one night, then I'm heading over there tomorrow. I don't know who's looking for you or what you've done, and I don't care."

"What I've done?" the man asked. His grip tightened. "What do you know about it, asshole?"

"I'm sorry," Boggs said. "I don't know anything about you. I just came here to find Tony Ferguson." He shifted his gaze downward. He didn't want to eyeball the man. Men like him didn't like being eyeballed. The guy was obviously wanted by someone for something, and Boggs felt confident it wasn't for child support.

"You're not a very good liar," the man said. His slurred speech made him even more threatening. He snickered and wiped his mouth on his sleeve. Then he got a sober look on his face. "Really, I wanna know, how did ya find me?"

The sound of the creek seemed louder than before. If Boggs tried to move, he wouldn't get far. Nobody would hear the gunshots. The cabin he'd rented was too remote. *I should have stayed in town*, he thought. A good handler would have rented a nice place in town. *I should've spent a few extra dollars*. Dammit! He didn't see any way out of the mess he was in. Maybe if he was stronger and quicker, he could go for the gun. He still had hope. The man hadn't shot him… yet. Maybe the guy would eventually realize it was all just a misunderstanding. They'd go inside, sit down, and talk about it. Have some laughs.

"Like I said, I'm not after you," Boggs repeated. "You just looked like the guy, that's all. Sometimes I ask too many questions."

"Bullshit!" the man exclaimed. "Somebody told you where I was, and I wanna know who."

The man winced, then he clenched his teeth together. He was obviously frustrated by the lack of cooperation he was getting. Either that or he was going to puke. Boggs wished the man would've had a few more drinks before he left the tavern. Even one more might have made a difference. He thought about what the psychologist had said during the workshop. He wished he would have paid more attention, but it hadn't seemed important to him at the time. He did remember something about making yourself seem more human to a person who threatened you. Not to act like a victim.

"My name is Samuel Boggs," he said, "but my friends just call me Boggs. Like I told you, I came here to locate a guy named Tony Ferguson. I get paid to locate and serve people. My wife, Emily, and I have two kids, sixteen and ten. They're..."

"Shut up!" the man yelled. "Did Lacy tell ya where to find me?"

"I don't know a Lacy," Boggs replied. He glanced over at his Jeep Cherokee that was parked on the gravel driveway. *Too far*, he thought, and his keys were inside the cabin, on the table.

"I don't see your car," Boggs said. "I can give you a ride. We could go back to the tavern if you'd like."

The man chuckled and shook his head. "You're really somethin'. You think this is funny?"

Boggs widened his stance to gain more balance. The gun followed his every move. "Hey, it's my mistake. I'm sorry. I'll buy you a couple of beers if you want. I'm just trying to earn a paycheck. My wife likes to spend money and raising kids is expensive. You know how it is."

The man looked around like he was trying to figure things out. Probably how he'd escape or how he'd dispose of the body. Boggs wasn't sure which one, but he figured there still might be an opportunity if he was patient.

"Listen," Boggs continued, "this is your show. You've got the gun. Why don't we just go inside, warm up, and talk for a while?"

"I said shut the fuck up!"

The man looked directly at Boggs. He wasn't interested in asking questions anymore. That was a bad sign. His frustrated look disappeared. The situation wasn't going to end well, and Boggs knew it. There would be no more talking. Boggs had to think quickly.

"Wait," Boggs said. "I have some notes."

Boggs opened his jacket slowly so the man could see. "They're in my pocket."

As Boggs began to reach inside, the man yelled, "Stop!" Then he paused. "I'll get 'em."

When he extended his left hand toward the pocket of Boggs's jacket, the gun he held in his right hand lowered slightly, so it no longer pointed at Boggs. It was only for an instant, but an instant was what Boggs was waiting for. He lunged at the man with every ounce of force he had.

The man's body slouched and crashed backward, then both men went flying off the porch, down the steps, and onto the ground. The weight of Boggs landing on top of the man took the man's breath away for a moment, but he held onto the gun. Boggs reached for the weapon, but his hand only grabbed the wrist of the man before they began to roll. Boggs struggled to get his other hand on the gun's barrel as they fought for position. Boggs was underneath the man, but he gripped the man's wrist like a vise and began prying the weapon free. Neither had the advantage.

A shot rang out, but it was lost in the darkness. The smell of gunpowder, sweat, and stale alcohol filled the air between the two men as they struggled.

Boggs tried to roll again on the damp ground, but the man's weight and strength prevented it. Boggs's smaller stature began to take its toll as they continued to struggle. He felt his hands weakening.

"No, wait!" Boggs cried out.

Another shot echoed through the night air and the struggle was over.

Samuel Boggs was dead.

TWO

12 years later…

My name is Brad Keller, and I've owned and operated Keller Construction for the past twenty-nine years. I build decks and fences, throughout most of Clark County, Washington, and I do quite a bit of remodel work, too.

Most of the county's residents have seen me driving my work van at one time or another. It's all black with a white logo on the side: *Keller Construction—Whether it's nailed or screwed—I'm the dude.* I thought it was a catchy slogan when I was in my twenties. Still do.

Keller Construction only has one employee—me. I'm the dude, or at least I'd like to be the dude. I'm pretty good with my hands, so I can build just about anything. The only construction jobs I don't like to do are projects that involve a lot of plumbing work. I'm not sure why, but a plumber once told me, "There are two things to remember about plumbing: Leaks don't get better, and shit runs downhill." I guess leaks and shit just never appealed to me.

On Tuesday, I stopped by *The Old Country Bar and Grill* and ordered a sausage biscuit with egg to go, and a coffee that I needed to have refilled before my biscuit was ready. In the fall, I always know when it's Tuesday morning because the bar and grill serves nickel beers with every order of nachos during Monday Night Football, and they always wait until Tuesday morning to wash the carpets. The chairs get turned upside down on top of the tables, and the place smells like rug cleaner. It was a Tuesday morning. I could tell.

Sal Martin, the bar and grill's owner and head cook, brought out my breakfast in a white paper sack and set it down on the table in front of me. He refilled my coffee again and brought me a sippy lid, which I firmly pressed down on my cup and made sure it was on tight.

"You're running late this morning," he said.

"I spent all night working on the van's timing chain," I said. "I finally got everything put back together this morning."

We looked out the window of the bar and grill where my van was parked. "How many miles does it have on it?"

"Two hundred and eighty-six thousand," I said. "It runs like crap, but what am I supposed to do? If I get a new work van, I might not have enough money to come in here and buy breakfast anymore."

Sal didn't seem too concerned about losing my business. "You should talk to Shafer," he said. "He has that lot on Saint John's Blvd, but I heard he's selling out and moving to Arizona. He might give you a deal on a newer one."

"I bought this one from Shafer," I said. "Of course, that was fifteen years ago. It's been a good vehicle so I can't complain about it breaking down…" I took a sip of coffee. "…but I will anyway."

***

It was nearly nine o'clock by the time I left the bar and grill. I was already two hours behind schedule, and even with all the coffee I'd consumed I wasn't entirely awake yet. Whenever I worked on my van at night, I usually tried to sleep in for an extra hour or two in the morning; but Tuesday was different because I was in the process of building a cedar fence for a friend of mine, Lefty Walker, who lives in Ridgefield, about fifteen minutes from my place.

"I'll let you drive the Zamboni if you get the fence finished and stained before Cheyenne Rose and I go on vacation," Lefty had said to me.

Hey, I'd always wanted to drive the Zamboni. Lefty had been the surface engineer at *Rinky Dink's Skating World* since the place opened, and he was regarded as one of the fastest "ice-sheet resurfacers" south of the Canadian border. He even accomplished a full throttle "fill and chill" during one televised commercial break at the sixteenth annual "Winter Solstice on Ice" event in Portland a few years ago.

"Driving the Zamboni isn't about speed," Lefty would say, "but how smooth the ice surface is when you're done."

For Lefty and Cheyenne Rose, I would've tried to squeeze it in between some of the other jobs I'd been working on anyway. Rearranging my work schedule isn't unusual. Whether I'm waiting for concrete to set, ordering materials, or dealing with bad weather, I always try to have two or three jobs going at the same time to eliminate the possibility of any downtime.

Lefty and I had been friends since high school, but back then we called him Nate "Sky" Walker. Even at five foot nine and a quarter inch, he could dunk a basketball with either hand, and he would've certainly gotten a scholarship to play at a small college or university if it hadn't been for a bet which he made during his senior year with some guy who, like Lefty, had more dollars than sense.

"Five big ones say you can't dunk two volleyballs at the same time," the guy had said to him. Back in my high school, five big ones meant five dollars.

The guy's challenge had happened after school, in the parking lot, and Lefty wasn't ready when they went back into the gym. Not only had he not stretched his legs properly, but he'd forgotten to take the gold band off the ring finger of his right hand.

Still, he soared in the air with those two volleyballs, and he almost accomplished the feat; but the second ball didn't go into the hoop, and in what Lefty later described as a "moment of idiotic determination," he made the mistake of trying to grab the rim on his way down. By the time he landed, not only had he not won the five big ones, but he no longer had a ring finger on his right hand.

Looking back, it might have been a blessing in disguise, because the day Lefty lost his finger was the day he met Cheyenne Rose.

Being a candy-striper at Southwest Washington Memorial Hospital wasn't exactly what Cheyenne Rose, the newly crowned Miss Cut and Loop of the floor covering installers union— the local 196—had in mind for her future career. Still, she liked volunteering at the hospital, and they were willing to work around her cheerleading schedule, along with her family's annual spring vacation to the Circus Circus Hotel & Resort, in Reno.

Cheyenne Rose had been placed at the information desk, near the trauma center, on the day Lefty came in because the hospital had been short-staffed, and even more importantly, because people screaming in pain and the sight of blood didn't seem to bother her.

A nurse who had been tending to a man's broken hip asked Cheyenne Rose to assist with Lefty.

"Five nine, a hundred and forty-two pounds," Cheyenne Rose said after looking at the scale. She wrote down the information on a sheet of paper which was attached to a clipboard. "Can you really dunk a basketball?" she asked Lefty.

"My finger!" Lefty exclaimed. "Can the doctor reattach it?"

"What high school do you go to?"

"I go to Prairie," Lefty replied. "My finger! I just can't believe it!"

"I go to River, and last fall I was a cheerleader for the boys varsity basketball team," she said.

"Do you think my finger will heal?" he asked her. "I mean if they reattach it?"

"I dated one of the players and he was six two, and he used to try to dunk a basketball, but he couldn't jump very high, and I think he might have done it with a volleyball once, but..."

"This can't be happening!" lefty cried out in pain.

Cheyenne Rose held Lefty's detached finger in the air to inspect it. "I heard somewhere that shorter athletes can jump higher, I mean in proportion to their height."

"You're holding my finger," Lefty sputtered, "my finger!"

"In science class, we learned that fleas are able to jump a hundred times their height," she said. "They must have really strong legs." She looked at Lefty more closely. "You have strong legs too, so you must exercise a lot. Have you ever done any long distance running?"

"What's taking the doctor so long?" Lefty pleaded.

"I did the Delta Park Fun Run last summer," Cheyenne Rose said. "It wasn't too bad. I think I'd be able to run a marathon if I trained for it, but I don't want my legs to get too muscley." She turned her calf outward for Lefty to see.

"They don't look too muscley," Lefty said. "You have nice legs."

"Thanks," she replied, then looked at the finger again and shook her head. "I feel sad about your finger."

By the time the doctor arrived, Nate Walker was well on his way to becoming Lefty Walker, along with Cheyenne Rose's new boyfriend. Nearly forty years later, they were still together, happily married, with two children and four grandchildren.

***

Since Lefty and Cheyenne Rose were leaving on Saturday, I intended to have the fence finished and stained by Thursday, or Friday at the latest. I really wanted to drive the Zamboni, so I gave myself a day's cushion, just in case something came up.

After picking up thirty-two bags of concrete from Home Depot, I arrived at Lefty and Cheyenne Rose's house a little after ten. A few showers on Monday evening had left the ground damp, but the sky was clear, and the caffeine had finally entered my bloodstream. I was ready to roll.

September is my favorite time of the year to work outside when the cool mornings are followed by warmer afternoons. Even with an occasional shower, there's plenty of daylight still and I don't have to worry about the summer heat or the heavier rains that come later in the fall. I can work from sun-up to sun-down, or as long as my body will hold up. At fifty-six years old, I can still put in a full day's work, but my sore muscles don't recover as fast as they used to.

I took a deep breath and watched two hummingbirds as they playfully moved from the tops of the trees down to a honeysuckle bush that wove its vines through a small trellis attached to the Walker's house. The birds didn't pay much attention to me as I rolled up the rear door of my work van; just an occasional redirection when I got too close. I'd seen them the last time I was there, too, so maybe they were a couple. I'd heard somewhere that hummingbirds mate for life.

I enjoy seeing animals in the wild, but I didn't have time to keep watching those birds that morning. I had other things on my mind, like keeping my customers happy. People had been calling me for bids, but I already had jobs lined up for several weeks. In Clark County, everybody scrambles at the end of September to get their projects done before the weather changes.

Just as I was putting on my gloves, the sound of an incoming text interrupted my thoughts. I dug out the phone from my back pocket and tapped the screen. The message had three words: *Agency protocol seven.*

THREE

I was surprised the agency had sent me a message. They must have made a mistake. I hadn't worked for them since 2012, but I remembered the protocols. There were twenty-three of them and they had been tattooed onto my brain. Protocol seven meant I needed to make a return call to the same number as soon as I had an opportunity.

I knew I'd have to respond, but I still needed to make a living. It was going to get warmer and more humid in the afternoon, then showers were forecast for several days.

I glanced up. Thirty-two wooden posts were sitting above thirty-two holes in the ground. The fence wasn't going to build itself, and if I wanted to stay on schedule, those posts needed to be set in concrete before I went home that evening. I looked at my phone again then turned it off. The agency would have to wait.

I pulled a wheelbarrow out of my van, then grabbed a small shovel and a large bucket. As I took a drink of water, I looked at all the wooden posts on the ground again. There was no way I'd be able to finish before dark. "Crap."

Working by myself meant I didn't have to worry about keeping employees busy or dealing with their problems every day. But not having employees had always been a trade-off. Some construction jobs are far easier with an extra set of hands. At times, when I had a large project, or if the job required using materials that were too heavy for me to handle alone, I had a few people who I could call on to help me. One of those friends was a man named Don Gustafson.

Don lives in a small trailer on his family's farm in Woodland, Washington, just north of Clark County. Don isn't the sharpest tool in the shed and everybody, including Don, knows it. He scrapes together a meager existence by working on the farm and by doing odd jobs for contractors and other people who need someone strong and reliable. Don is stronger than he looks, and he looks strong. His hands are like baseball mitts. At a height of 6'6" he carries his 290 pounds well. If Don would have been born a tree, he would've been a sequoia.

Don's only physical flaw is that he can't run. He had an infection in his left leg when he was twelve years old, and it had stunted the leg's growth. Not only does it have less muscle, but it's also two inches shorter than his right leg. He had platform shoes built to allow for the difference, but his running days ended when he was twelve.

Apart from the slight hobble, Don never let the disability affect his work. Throughout his 34 years of existence, I don't think he ever considered doing anything else. He's always been content with his life, doing odd jobs and working on the farm. In his free time, Don enjoys his hobbies, which are fishing, trapping moles, and collecting calendars. Out of the three, collecting calendars is, by far, where he has found the most success.

I thought if I called him that morning, maybe I'd get lucky.

He answered, "Hello?"

"Hey Donny," I said. "Are you busy?"

"Nah," he said. "I got a mole going in all directions and he keeps digging right next to the trap."

I chuckled, picturing him down on his hands and knees, leaning over a dirt mound, sweat pouring from his brow. Maybe even a steer or two in the field keeping their eyes on him.

"I could use some help today," I said. "I'm setting fence posts in concrete, and I'd like to finish up this afternoon. Can you spare a few hours?"

"Yeah," he sighed, "I need to reset my traps and move some hay, but I can be there after lunch. Just text me the address."

I was relieved. Don could mix the concrete while I set the posts. Some contractors dry-packed the concrete, but I've seen concrete crumble after it had been dry-packed, and I liked to do a good job. People expected it, and there's nothing wrong with a person who takes pride in their work.

By the time Don arrived at one o'clock, there were twenty-four holes left to fill and I was tired from my lack of sleep. With both of us working hard, the posts were all plumb and set in concrete by 4:15 p.m. There's no way I could have finished the job by myself.

Near the driveway, some cedar fencing and wood rails had been delivered and were stacked on several pallets.

"Do you need any help with the rails and fencing?" Don asked. He was still raring to go.

"Maybe," I replied. "How busy are you this week?"

"I've got nothing," he said. "I just finished splittin and stackin all the firewood for the Hansons yesterday. It took me four days with the splitter. They've got forty cord for sale. Two hundred a cord. That's good money."

"You split and stacked forty cords, all by yourself?"

Don nodded. I just shook my head in awe. Don Gustafson is the only person I know who could split and stack forty cords of wood in four days.

"Why are they getting into that business?"

"Dean says it's just extra. They're using the logs from the trees they cut down for people during the summer."

"What did they pay you?"

Don looked down for a moment, then back up at me. "They gave me two cord, plus all the scraps I wanted for kindlin'. And Dean bought me lunch every day."

"Long days, I'll bet."

"I didn't mind," Don said. "My mom can use the wood this winter."

I reached in my pocket and pulled out some bills. "Well, you deserve more. Here's a hundred for helping me out this afternoon and an extra twenty for the short notice. I'll call you later and let you know about tomorrow.

Don smiled. "Thanks! Yeah, I'm free, just let me know!"

After I cleaned up and put away my tools, I closed the sliding door of the van and sat inside. It wasn't very warm out, but the air conditioning still took a while to cool down the cab area. I wiped my head and neck with a towel, downed a Bevo fitness drink, and looked at my phone.

I hadn't heard from the agency in ten years. There was only one way to find out what they wanted. I called the number.

"Operator," a woman's voice answered.
I didn't hesitate. "This is BK-643."
"Code?"
"Bravo."
"One moment."
I waited until a man's voice came on the line.
"BK-643?"
"Yeah."
"We have a job for you and it's urgent."

FOUR

Typical. The agency liked to label everything "urgent." I just smiled and shook my head.

I started working for the agency in 2008, at a time when the construction industry in Clark County had taken a nosedive. People didn't want to spend extra money fixing up their place if they thought it might go back to the bank, so some of my business dried up overnight. Luckily, I met Samuel Boggs in Alaska that summer and he helped get me a job with the agency. We became good friends.

I had several lengthy interviews and twelve weeks of training in Sedro Wooley, Washington before I was officially hired as a PFT.

PFT is short for pathfinder and tracker. The job description was straightforward—find someone who doesn't want to be found. From 2008 through 2012, I completed over twenty missions for the agency, but my last one was in 2012. I would've bet the man on the phone didn't realize I hadn't worked for them in ten years.

"Who am I speaking to and what do you want?" I asked him. There was no reason to beat around the bush.

"I'm Cobra-14, and the agency needs a PFT in southwest Alaska."

Typical again. Guys with the agency always liked to use Cobra, Hawk, or Eagle for their call signs.

Southern Alaska was my territory when I worked for the agency. I tracked down people who were hiding out, mostly in Anchorage or other cities, but sometimes out in the bush. I was pretty good at it, too. I'd locate the targets, then place GPS tracking chips on nearly everything they owned—house, car, boat, snowmobile.

The chips were designed to look like the round, three-volt batteries that are used in watches and other small electronic devices. They were easy to place, and one side had a thin, sticky substance on it that smelled like tree pitch. It might have been tree pitch for all I know. Once I peeled off the plastic backing, they would stick to just about anything, including my fingers. They had the words 3V and Lithium written on the face, just like the batteries you'd find in a store. The signal lasted about twelve weeks, depending on conditions, but that was plenty of time for the agency to do whatever they needed to do.

"I don't do that work anymore," I said.

"Take a look at the packet before you decide."

"OK," I said. I smiled. "I'll look at the packet, but I'm going to say no."

"We have a courier standing by," Cobra-14 said. "He'll be at your location in a few minutes."

I paused. "What? He's on his way here?"

"Yes."

"To my jobsite?"

"That's correct. The courier has been instructed to hand you the packet directly."

I was shocked. I'd never had a packet delivered to one of my jobsites before. I didn't like being tracked either, especially while I was at work.

The agency was created in the aftermath of 9/11. I'm sure it had a more formal name, or some fancy acronym, but they never told me what it was, and I never asked. I just referred to it as the agency. After the Department of Homeland Security was formed, the agency's operation got buried deep within a division called *Critical Infrastructure Sector Partnerships*.

On my first day of training, I learned about the partnerships, or lack thereof, together with a long list of legal disclosures and security protocols that I swore, under oath, to follow. Most of them had to do with keeping my mouth shut. I was OK with that.

Rumor had it that the only reason the agency was listed under Homeland Security was to get their budget through congressional appropriations. Whenever lawmakers spent tax dollars on infrastructure, nobody ever questioned where the money went. In fact, just making the announcement was a great way for politicians who were already in power to get re-elected.

The agency might have been called a partnership, and the government may have funded the operations, but the missions we performed never had any political oversight. The U.S. Marshals and the FBI stayed out of our way too. I don't think any law enforcement officials who dealt with the agency ever knew where their orders came from. The organizational structure had been deliberately designed that way to make it impossible to know who was in charge. It's called *plausible deniability*. I spent four years as a PFT and I didn't have a clue who made the decisions. The policy was, "Don't ask, don't ask." I was OK with that, too.

I stayed on the phone with Cobra-14 as a silver Camry slowed down and pulled into the Lefty and Cheyenne Rose's driveway. The agency must have had this guy standing by for hours, waiting for me to call them back. That, and the fact I hadn't worked for the agency for such a long time, made me feel a little suspicious.

"Who's the delivery boy?" I asked.

"Nobody in particular," Cobra-14 said. "He isn't part of the mission. If you accept the job, your handler will meet you in Anchorage."

I watched the man get out of his car about twenty feet from where I was parked. He looked like a bean counter. He was short in stature, had thick glasses with black rims, and he was dressed in a navy-blue suit. He wore a white shirt with a blue and green striped tie. Maybe he was a Seahawks fan, who knows? He held up a large envelope as he approached my van.

When I raised my hand, the bean counter stopped.

"What's this all about?" I asked Cobra-14. "Why are you calling me after all these years?

"Take a look at the packet, BK. You'll understand the reason we've contacted you after you see the information."

The agency was certainly going out of their way to show me something, but I didn't like the presentation. Something didn't seem right.

"If I accept the job, I want CH-163 to be my handler," I insisted.

There was a long pause before Cobra-14 responded. "We can't do that."

"Then you can tell your accountant to turn around and get back into his car. I don't need to see the packet."

There was another long pause. "Take the packet," he said. "We'll talk to you later about CH-163."

***

After the bean counter drove away, I sat in my van and looked over the material. I was a little confused. The agency wanted this guy found, and they said it was urgent. But there was nothing in the packet to give me a reason for their rush to locate him. What had he done? Why was he so important to the suits in the corner offices who made all the decisions? And why me?

On the first page of the packet, a dollar amount was included for completion of the job, and all my expenses would be covered, regardless of the outcome. It was always non-negotiable. I looked at the offer several times. Wages had gone up in ten years. The agency would pay me $30,000 to locate a man named Kyle Westbrook, plus I'd get another $15,000 up front to cover my expenses for up to two weeks. I was stunned. That was over three times what I used to get.

The Westbrooks claimed to be part native Alutiiq, and Kyle had two brothers and several relatives who lived on Kodiak Island. He was an avid outdoorsman, and he knew his way around the wilderness, even the harsh Alaskan wilderness. He had relatives all over southern Alaska, so I knew he'd be a challenge; but guys like him usually made costly mistakes. They'd stay in touch with family or friends, or they'd fall into routines.

He'd probably gotten sloppy because the packet said he'd been off the grid for eighteen years. With only a little bit of information, a trained PFT could locate targets in no time if they lived in a city. In remote areas, it took longer, but that was my specialty.

I was pretty sure Kyle Westbrook was in some remote location. For the money they were offering to pay me, I knew it wasn't going to be easy. The packet said the agency planned to send me to Kodiak for a week, but they didn't have a clue if Westbrook was on the island or not. With about 1.9 million acres of wildlife refuge, a person like him could get lost for quite a while if he felt like he was being followed.

Suddenly, I noticed something in the packet I hadn't seen earlier. It was written on a note, taped to the back of the last page. It all came back to me as I sat there in my van. Things began to make sense. It was the real reason I had been offered the contract to find Westbrook.

I called the number I'd been given. Cobra-14 spoke before I could say anything.

"If CH-163 wants to be your handler, we'll allow it this time. Have you seen the note?"

"Yep."

"Do you want to talk to CH-163 or shall we?" he asked.

"No, I'll talk to her. Get the equipment delivered as soon as you can."

"It's on its way. We've booked your flight from Portland to Anchorage at 9:20 tonight. The handler we originally chose for you will meet you in Anchorage, but if CH-163 agrees to the contract, she can take over the operation after you reach Kodiak. Have her contact us for confirmation, and we'll deliver the contract to her shortly. Good luck."

"Thanks."

I looked at the note again and shook my head. After twelve years, they finally found out who the bastard was.

The note simply stated, *"Kyle Westbrook is Whitefish."*

FIVE

Twelve years ago, Samuel Boggs, was killed in Montana. It was on October 8, 2010. I'll never forget the date because it was the same day I stumbled upon a bank robbery in Kelso, Washington. It was, by far, the worst day of my life, and I've had some pretty bad days.

The morning didn't start off lousy. In fact, everything was fine until that afternoon. I had just spent an entire week helping a friend build a deck for his two-story home overlooking Mayfield Lake. Even though it's only about an hour and a half north of where I live, the job allowed me the time to relax and take a break from the daily grind. As it turned out, I should have left sooner or stayed longer because the timing of my departure couldn't have been worse.

I pulled into a Handy Mart near the lake to get some snacks for the drive home. I ordered a burrito "combo meal" but I should've gotten it *a la carte* because the rest of the *meal* ended up being a small bag of flamin' hot potato chips and a Coke. By the time I reached the interstate, my stomach had already convinced my brain that my culinary decision had been a mistake, and no matter how much I drank, I couldn't get the flamin' taste out of my mouth.

Boggs called me while I was driving.

"You're breaking up," I said.

"I…w…ill…pu...ll...o...ver." His garbled voice was hard to understand. I stayed on the line. "Can you hear me now?" he asked.

"Loud and clear. Where are you?"

"I just left Whitefish, Montana. I've got a good lead on a deadbeat dad who's lived in three different places in the last eight months. Sometimes I think these guys go out of their way to make themselves miserable."

The job had been for his own company, Private Eyedaho, which was based in Boise, where Boggs and his family lived. Quite a few of the PFTs had their own private detective companies and the agency didn't mind, as long as their work didn't interfere with agency business.

"Where to now?" I asked.

"Thompson Falls," he replied. "I've got a PO Box number, and a nasty note from his former landlord."

"I don't know how you do it," I said.

"Business is booming," he said. "You should come to Idaho. You'd fit right in, and the money isn't bad if you don't mind the work."

"What, sitting in a car, waiting for husbands or wives to cheat on their spouses?"

"It pays the bills."

"No, thanks!" I said. "I'd rather re-plumb an old house, and you know how much I like doing that."

He laughed. "You wouldn't believe all the new neighborhoods that have been built around Boise."

"Things are still slow around here but they're getting better. Someday I'll go back to my construction business full time."

"The agency will miss you," he said, "but I can understand." He paused. "Oh, I forgot. Emily wanted me to ask you how the Julie situation was going. I can tell her to mind her own business if you want."

The Julie situation.

My wife, Julie, and I had been having a difficult time, and it had only gotten worse. We made plans to celebrate our fifteenth anniversary in December of 2010, but it had been hard for either of us to imagine growing old together. We started living separate lives, and we'd stopped asking each other about how our days went, our plans, our dreams. We grew apart.

"She's in Boston visiting friends for a couple of weeks," I said. "Tell your lovely and curious wife that I'm doing fine."

"Emily worries about you," he said. "You should come visit. She'd love to see you again, and she has a few projects for you."

I smiled. "What, has your honey-do list gotten too long?"

Boggs laughed. "Longer every day. I'm definitely not the dude."

I laughed. "Alright, I'm getting ready to exit. Give her a kiss for me."

"Will do."

***

A few minutes after our call, I took the Kelso exit. My plan had been to cash a check, stop by Hair Jordan's, then drive home and cook up some of the fish I'd caught at the lake that morning. I was looking forward to getting home—watching a ball game, eating fresh trout—but most of all, sleeping in my own bed.

Jordan Sheridan, a friend of mine, was the owner of Hair Jordan's, and I made the forty-minute drive up to his barber shop in Kelso about twice a month to get my flattop trimmed. I had thick, dark brown hair, with a touch of gray on the sides, and Jordan would use a straight blade with warm lotion to shave my face and neck. My skin was so smooth afterward, and he did it all for ten bucks—the same amount he'd charged me for years. Of course, anytime he wanted help with a project, or something built, I always did it for free or gave him a great deal.

I never made it to Hair Jordan's that afternoon, and the baseball playoff game I wanted to see was finished by the time I got home. I still ate my trout, but I wasn't very hungry after what had happened earlier at the bank.

Fate had decided it, really, or maybe it was just bad luck. As I got off the exit in Kelso, onto Allen Street, I looked at my gas gauge, which showed a quarter tank. It was enough to get me home, but I never like to have less than a quarter tank of fuel when I'm driving. There were several cars lined up at the gas station, so I decided to cash my check first. That decision led to a series of events, namely me being at the bank when the robbery occurred instead of having a full tank of gas and a trim.

I was at one of the teller windows, leaning against the counter, when the guy walked in. I remember it was busy, even for a Friday afternoon.

"May I have your driver's license, birth certificate, social security number, passport, and what is your mother's maiden name?"

I don't recall exactly what information the teller had asked me to provide, but it was something like that. It's more common for me to notice and remember things that are out of the ordinary.

As far as the guy who came into the bank, he was looking around, checking things out, suspicious as hell, so he got my attention. I found out later his name was

Joe Bernard, an ex-con from Gresham, Oregon. He looked like a bank robber—shifty eyes, unshaved, Yankees hat. He might as well have been wearing those fake glasses with the large nose and mustache, or better yet, a nylon stocking over his face.

I cashed my check and walked out the front door while he was still in line. I could still taste the remnants of the flamin' hot potato chips, and there was a girl sitting in the waiting area who was dressed in one of those skimpy cosplay outfits. She was more distracting for me than Joe Bernard, who I saw holding a gun inside his jacket pocket. Nobody else seemed to notice, but I could see his right hand gripping the stock of the revolver as I walked past him.

Hey, I figured it wasn't my rodeo. I wasn't going to call 911 because some guy had a gun in his pocket. I figured he was up to no good, but I just left the bank and didn't plan on looking back. If his buddy hadn't backed up their Mustang in the parking space right next to my work van, I would've been at the gas station or Hair Jordan's by the time the robbery occurred. I'm not a very big guy—five ten, a buck seventy-five—but there's no way I could've squeezed through the space he left between the two vehicles.

I didn't even get a very good look at the driver at first because I tried not to stare, and I've got bad peripheral vision. I figured the guy was probably nervous. I wasn't going to get a bullet in the head, by mistake, just because I was parked next to him, so I kept walking, right past the vehicles, to the far end of the parking lot like nothing was happening.

Joe Bernard was in the bank for a long time. Too long. After the robbery, he just stood near the front entrance and looked out the glass doors toward the

Mustang. Then he scanned the rest of the parking lot. Maybe he thought the cops were already there. Who knows? The police were certainly on their way by then. I figured maybe another three or four minutes before they'd come tearing down the street, lights blaring and sirens screaming. Then Joe Bernard looked in my direction. *Crap!*

The Chevy Impala I was hiding behind was a big car, so he never saw me. It was a 1975 model. I owned one when I was in high school, so I recognized the year. Mine was black too, but it was in better shape. I used to wash it every few days and I waxed it at least once a month. It shined. I spent so much money on that car: wheels, paint, the sound system. It had a huge trunk, and we'd pile four or five people in the back seat. Guys, girls, you name it. I was thinking about the Impala and some of the good times we had in high school, but then Joe Bernard walked out through the doors and started coming my way. He moved quickly, right past the Mustang. What the hell?

I was squatting on the driver's side, looking through the Impala's window. It was the last car in the parking lot, so why was he still coming toward me? *Crap!* I realized; the guy in the Mustang wasn't his buddy after all. If the Impala was his car, I was in trouble.

He hadn't seen me. He was still looking around as he hurried in my direction. Maybe that was his Corolla, or maybe he owned the Ford truck. There was a landscaped area behind me, but a chain link fence was on the other side, so I wasn't going anywhere. *Dammit!* No way did he own the Corolla. He kept coming. It was either the truck or the Impala.

Crap!

SIX

"Operator," a woman's voice answered.
"This is BK-643," I said.
"Code?"
"Bravo."
"One moment."

I heard the sirens wailing in the distance. I sat there, on the asphalt, and leaned against the Impala's bumper. I had less than a minute before the cops would get there.

A man from the agency came on the line. "BK-643?"

"Yeah," I said. "I'm involved in a situation. I'm at a bank right now and it was robbed a few minutes ago. I was just a bystander, but I ended up getting caught in the middle of it. Long story short, I smashed the robber's head in with a decorative stone I found in the landscaped area near the parking lot."

I paused and listened as the sirens were getting closer.

"Self-defense, mostly," I continued. "There are cameras around, but I'm wearing tinted glasses and a hoodie, so I don't think I've been identified yet. The police are on their way."

"Location?" the man asked.

"Kelso, Washington. Northwest Federal on Tam O'Shanter Way."

"Kelso?"

"Yes!" I said, "Kelso. K-E-L-S-O."

"Outside?"

"Yes, outside the bank. In the parking lot."

"Copy your situation BK. Are you injured?"

"No, I'm fine."

"Was anyone else with you?" he asked.

"No, I'm alone."

The man on the phone paused before continuing. "Are there any other injuries or fatalities?"

"No, just the one. The bank robber. He's dead. Wait! I don't know about inside the bank. I wasn't inside during the robbery."

"So, he had already robbed the bank?" the man asked.

"Yes. He robbed the bank. And he's dead."

"And you killed him in self-defense?"

"Yes!" I said, "with a decorative stone!"

"One moment," the man responded.

The sirens were getting louder. Lots of them. People gathered outside the front doors of the bank as I sat there and waited. The guy in the Mustang had rolled down his window. His eyes were fixed in my direction and his mouth was wide open. Aside from his strange look, I could only think of one thing: The bastard needed to learn how to park.

I felt like the bank's employees and bystanders were all gawking at me. They certainly kept their distance. I had to remind myself they were probably more interested in the dead bank robber who was lying there in front of me. They probably just thought I was calling 911.

Then I looked at Joe Bernard again. I could see some money coming out of his bag. What could he have gotten, a few thousand dollars? What a waste. I remembered seeing him put the gun back in his jacket after he came out of the bank. I shielded myself from the others, reached inside his pocket, grabbed the gun, and tossed it a couple of feet away. Some of the onlookers had their phones out, but my glasses and jacket helped conceal my face.

"BK-643," the man on the phone said, "Robert Crest will be your attorney. I'll text you his information to give to the police. Nothing else from you is required. Act like you're in shock. Let Robert take care of this. He's standing by. He'll follow up with you after he speaks to the police. Are you OK?"

"Yeah," I said. "I'm fine."

I stood up, put the phone in my back pocket, leaned against the Impala's hood, and waited. I could tell by the interior it wasn't the car I'd owned in high school. Wouldn't that have been something?

When the first officer arrived, he stopped his cruiser right in front of Joe Bernard's body. I just stood there, pointing toward the gun and the decorative stone. I never said a word. Still, within a minute, there were ten or fifteen cops, and I was on the ground, my face pressed against the asphalt, with two of them on top of me. Kelso cops.

After the police identified Joe Bernard, I found out he had robbed that same branch less than two weeks earlier. He was wanted for twelve bank robberies in the Kelso and Longview area. He was just some low life career criminal, and now he was dead. Maybe he deserved it.

Once I was released, I called Boggs. He didn't think he'd have good reception at his cabin, so he sat in a tavern and talked with me for over an hour. He made me feel better. It wasn't like I regretted what I'd done, but it was the first time I'd ever killed anyone, and I was a little shaken. Boggs knew just what to say. The agency offered me some counseling, but a few hours later I was ready to move on. Then, the next day, I found out Boggs had been murdered. Like I said, the worst day of my life.

After the bank robbery, some smartass at the agency started calling me "Kelso," and it stuck. They made jokes about me. "Where does Kelso Brad buy his ammunition? The Kelso Quarry." "Ha, Ha, Ha," I'd tell them. Hilarious. A bunch of comedians. The jokes went from bad to worse. They included parked vans, Impalas, decorative stones, and the small town of Kelso, which is located right off Interstate 5 in southwest Washington.

Screw them! I figured. I liked the name and I've used it ever since. It reminds me of that day, and I think Boggs would have liked it, too. Keller is my real name, but when I'm working for the agency, I'm Brad Kelso.

I've thought about that day a lot over the last twelve years; the bank robbery, the phone call, my friend getting killed. But as I sat there in my work van and looked through the packet, it was *all* I could think about. *Why?* Because the agency's note said Kyle Westbrook was *Whitefish*.

That meant it was Kyle Westbrook who killed Boggs.

SEVEN

On Saturday morning, October 9, 2010, a man from the agency using the call sign *Eagle-6* notified me about Boggs's murder. I packed a suitcase and drove for eight straight hours from Clark County, Washington, to Thompson Falls, Montana.

Del Simpson, a colleague of Boggs's and mine, flew from Alaska to Montana and met me at the *Trout Creek Tavern* that night. Del worked as a PFT in northern Alaska and out on the Aleutian Islands. We'd bump into each other occasionally, but each of us had our own territories and the agency didn't like to commingle resources. I suppose it made sense. If one field agent became compromised, they didn't want another one to be exposed as well. Still, there were certain times, especially in Alaska, when having an extra person in your corner or watching your back never hurt, especially out in the bush.

I arrived at the tavern first. It was seven thirty and there were no seats left at the bar. I spotted a table that had some empty drinks on it, and nobody seemed to be using the two chairs, so I walked over and sat down. A waitress came over a few minutes later, just after Del walked through the door.

I stood up and shook hands with Del. He was a few years younger than me, had chiseled features, and stayed in good shape. He had large hands and a powerful grip. Under the circumstances, neither of us were very happy to see each other.

"I'll have a bottle of Bud and a hamburger," I said to the waitress.

"Do you want fries with that?"

"Sure."

"Make it two," Del said. We sat down and the waitress left.

Del looked around the bar. "So, this is the place?" he asked.

"This is it," I said. "Boggs was sitting in this tavern when I talked to him twenty-four hours ago. The agency is pulling phone records, but his killer would have likely been someone he met here. The owner of the cabin he rented said he was all alone at nine o'clock. Eagle-6 told me he still had three hundred dollars in his wallet, and a postcard was left on top of his body."

"Then it obviously wasn't a robbery," Del said. "Have they checked the postcard for prints?"

"They're checking but you know how that usually goes."

I handed Del a recent photo of Boggs to show people. "I spoke to Emily today. She's not doing very well."

Del shook his head. "I wish I had more than one night to help you, but I have to be back in Alaska tomorrow."

"Hey," I said. "I'm glad you're here. Thanks for coming." I paused. "Are you ready?"

"Yep."

We spent the next two hours interviewing dozens of people at the tavern who lived in the area. We didn't find any good leads, but everyone seemed willing to talk to us. They had all heard about Boggs's murder. They just didn't know anything.

"It was busy last night," one of the bartenders said. "I remember him 'cause he was talkin' on the phone when he ordered."

"Do you recall what he had?" I asked.

"Nope...wait... he was drinkin' beer and he had me get him some malt vinegar. Yeah, he was eatin' the fish and chips. Now I remember. He didn't stay at the bar very long though. I think he left and sat down at one of the tables near the back. He probably had to wait until one of them opened up. I don't remember seeing him after that, but like I say, it was busy."

"Do you recall if he talked to anyone, or maybe he got into an argument with somebody?"

"I didn't notice him talkin' with anyone here at the bar. Like I said, he was on his phone for a while. Maybe you can find out who he was talkin' to on the phone."

Yep, everybody's an investigator.

A couple of the regulars remembered Boggs too.

"He was on his phone the whole time," they said. "He might have spoken to a few people before he left, but he didn't stay here very long after his phone call."

The consensus was that we should be investigating whoever was on the telephone with him; but like I thought, after the agency pulled his phone records, the only two people he had talked with were Emily and me.

The tavern didn't have any surveillance cameras and nobody we questioned recalled anything out of the ordinary, just that the place was busy. The agency sent in a team, and they looked at all the credit card and debit card receipts the tavern had processed; but after going through each one of them, we still didn't find anything useful. The tavern was a dead end.

Sadly, the night we interviewed all those people was the last night I saw Del alive. I talked with him several times on the phone, but Del died in a plane crash the following spring when the Piper Cub he was flying from Stebbins to Nome crashed in Norton Sound. Del and I weren't as close as Boggs and I were, but it was still difficult for me to lose two friends within six months. For me, the *Trout Creek Tavern* had bad mojo.

The following day, I traveled all the way up to Whitefish and back, but still didn't find any clues. Boggs had mentioned to me that he was going to the post office in Thompson Falls the following day. He never made it there, and I interviewed several people around the town to find out if they'd seen Boggs, or anything they could remember that might have seemed suspicious that evening. Nothing. Even the deadbeat dad had an alibi.

Boggs getting killed had been a shock, not only for me, but for just about everyone who knew him. He wasn't the type of guy who liked to take risks or get into dangerous situations. He didn't carry much money with him when he traveled, and most of his friends couldn't recall him ever arguing with anyone—even the people he'd been hired to locate.

The only real clue to his murder was that stamped postcard, which was found on top of his body. It had no writing or address, which was odd, since it had already been stamped. They eventually found three fingerprints on it that didn't belong to Boggs, but all three were dismissed. They came from one gift shop employee and two tourists who had looked at the card sometime before Boggs had purchased it in Whitefish on the day he was killed. The photo on the card was of

Whitefish Lake. Several partial prints were discovered too, but they couldn't be identified.

Emily mentioned that Boggs would sometimes carry stamped postcards in his breast pocket and would mail them to her when he traveled. That way, he could just write a quick note and drop them off in any mailbox, wherever he was, without making a special trip to a post office during the day.

It made sense that Boggs would have the postcard with him, but the investigators knew there was no way it could have randomly ended up on top of his body after he was dead. In fact, they determined that whoever had murdered him probably took the postcard from Boggs's jacket and tossed it onto his chest. They could never figure out why.

A murderer checking pockets wasn't out of the ordinary, but the $300 in cash that had been untouched in Boggs's wallet made the investigators, and everyone else at the agency, even more curious about the postcard. For that reason, all the agents started calling the killer—*Whitefish*.

EIGHT

I kept ruminating about the past as I drove home from work. I'm not usually vindictive, but the thought of revenge consumed me. The feelings of anger that had been locked up inside of me for twelve years began to resurface.

One thing was certain: I didn't have any intention of finding the man who murdered my friend only to let someone else finish him off. I would do it myself, and I would do it for Boggs. I could even save the agency a few bucks in the process. Maybe the bean counters had already thought about it. It could be the reason why they contacted me in the first place—to save money. I wouldn't have put it past them.

They might not have realized it, but if they would have just asked me, I would've tracked down and killed Kyle Westbrook for free. Of course, when I worked for the agency, information was always given on a need-to-know basis. The fact that I would've located Westbrook without getting paid was something the agency didn't need to know. Besides, I could really use the money.

I live in a three-bedroom, two-bath bungalow on a couple of acres of land in what's considered rural Clark County. My large, detached shop can easily hold four or five vehicles, and I built a room inside of it with a couch and a couple of chairs, and a big screen TV where friends can come over and watch Seahawk games on Sundays. It's a man-cave on steroids, complete with a large tool room, weight machines, and a bar area with a sink and refrigerator. It even has a wood burning stove for when it gets cold outside.

I pulled into my driveway, parked in front of my shop, and called an old friend.

"Hello?" she answered.

"Hi Chris," I said. "How have you been?"

She paused. "Brad?"

"Yeah, it's me." I hadn't talked to her in several years, so I knew she'd be surprised to hear from me.

She scoffed. "I should have known it was you. What now?"

"What do you mean, 'what now'?"

"A package was delivered to me about fifteen minutes ago," she said. "Actually, it's packages. Three of them to be precise. Funny thing is, I never ordered a new computer. One of the boxes had two new satellite phones, some cold weather gear, and what looks like two pounds of gummy bears."

Crap, I thought. I had some explaining to do, and fast.

"I don't know who sent you the gummy bears," I said.

She was silent for a moment. I pictured her with her arms crossed and that irritated look she used to get when she didn't approve of something I did, which happened far too often back in the day. Her father came from northern Germany and her mother's family was Bavarian, which gave her blonde hair and blue eyes, and no appetite for foolishness. She could also outdrink me.

"The computer is pretty nice," she said. "What's going on, Brad? The delivery driver didn't know anything, of course. What are you trying to drag me into?"

"Listen Chris…"

"Don't listen Chris me!" she exclaimed. "If this is what I think it is, you can just start calling me CH-163 again. Tell me why the agency is sending me new equipment."

"They offered me a job. I told them I wouldn't take the assignment unless you could be my handler."

"What job, Brad? We've been out of that business for ten years."

"I know, I know, and we agreed not to discuss our time with the agency, but you need to know something. They found out who killed Boggs."

"Sam?" Chris asked. "They've got Sam's killer?"

"They haven't got him yet. They know who he is now, and they think he's in Alaska, but they need a PFT to locate him.

"So, why you? And why me? Don't they have people up there?"

"They didn't say. They delivered a packet to me less than an hour ago. The agency left me a message this morning and had a guy standing by until I called them back. He came right to my jobsite."

Chris sounded concerned. "That's unusual. Why did you say yes, and what have I got to do with it? What makes you think I'll just drop everything and handle a mission for you?"

"I'm sorry, Chris," I said. "I just don't trust anybody else to be my handler."

Chris Hoffman, before she became Chris Malinowski, had been well known throughout the agency as one of the best handlers in the business. What that really meant was that her PFTs located their targets, didn't get into trouble, and she kept costs down. An agent's handler was critical to the success of any mission. They provided information, equipment, and organized whatever logistics a PFT needed to complete their assignment. They took care of the tedious work so the agents wouldn't be distracted by the details.

Alaska was one of the worst places a PFT could work, and their handlers had it even worse. Winters were brutal and they seemed to last forever. Even during the summer months, weather almost always played a factor in how missions were planned and executed.

Some of the areas were so remote, the fugitives never showed up on the grid, and the vast areas a PFT had to travel provided all sorts of complications. Getting equipment and supplies to them was difficult and sometimes impossible. PFTs in Alaska used single engine airplanes like agents in the lower forty-eight used taxis. Expenses often climbed through the roof, and it always took longer than expected to locate the targets.

A PFT might have a broken SAT phone and no cell reception. He could be tracking a fugitive in a blizzard, with icy roads, in temperatures so cold tires would freeze flat. An agent might have forgotten his wife's birthday or ran out of clean underwear. Too often, several things happened, all at the same time, and needed to be dealt with immediately. When a PFT needed assistance, they had one person to call. Handlers did exactly what their job title said. They handled things.

Handlers were underpaid, overworked, and rarely appreciated. Real life wasn't like TV or the movies where a government agent might be tracking down a bad guy through the wilderness in a tuxedo or standing on the rail of a helicopter as they swooped in for the kill. No, for the most part, PFTs were flakey, demanding, and moody. Some of them had trouble locating their targets, and many of them would stumble back to their hotel rooms late at night from the nearest watering hole.

Keeping agents in line took special skills, and Chris Hoffman had special skills. Chris Malinowski? Ten years earlier, she quit working as a handler to become 64-year-old John Malinowski's younger wife.

"I was sorry to hear about John," I said.

Chris sighed. "Yeah, I got your card. The fact that you wrote 'many condolences for the family' was a nice touch."

"What was I supposed to say? I'm sorry about your husband but I never liked him anyway?"

"Don't start with that again," she said. "It's only been a year since he passed away and you never knew him. He was a kind man."

"Kind-of-old," I mumbled. I didn't think she'd heard me.

"What?"

Crap. "What?"

"Do you still think I married him for his money?"

I had originally thought it, but two weeks before their wedding, she found out his entire estate was going to his kids. The whole family, along with their attorneys, presented her with a two-inch-thick prenuptial agreement. She still married him, probably for the security, but she should have gotten a better deal. I was still married at the time, but I cared about Chris more than I should have. What was I supposed to tell her? Congratulations?

"You're right," I said. "I'm sorry. I never knew him. The fact that he was twenty-three years older than you never crossed my mind."

"If memory serves me, you were still married."

"I was married to a woman who didn't love me," I said. "By the time I got divorced you were already married."

"Well, La-Di-Da. It wasn't like you were contacting divorce attorneys when I was single."

I had to tell myself to refocus. This conversation wasn't going anywhere, and I had plenty to do before I left.

"I didn't call to argue with you about what happened ten years ago. Did the agency send you a contract?"

"Not yet, but I don't think I can do it anymore. And why would they want someone like you?"

Chris had been the handler for about half of my missions with the agency and we worked well together, until we didn't. In Chris's world, the trains always ran on time, and she didn't let anyone, or anything, stand in her way. If she agreed to take the job, I knew we could find Kyle Westbrook in no time. I also figured she might need the money. I doubted the Malinowski family was very generous after John died. But it really came down to only one reason why I wanted Chris to be my handler: I trusted her with my life.

"Someone like me?"

She sighed. "I mean your age, Brad. Are you ready to chase down someone who may be out in the bush? Are you even in shape?"

"Is that a proposition?"

"Don't even try it, old man. I might be a widow, but I haven't got time for any of your nonsense. What's the agency paying these days?"

Yep, I knew it. She needed the money. She would've just said no if she didn't need the money. She would've turned down the job immediately. She had been working as the purchasing manager at a local library, so her salary must have been less than she deserved.

"The contract said your cut will be $15,000, plus an additional $7,500 bonus if we find him in the first two weeks. And you get to keep the computer."

I was expecting a moment of silence and that's exactly what I got. Then she started asking questions. "For that much money, who's the target?"

"A guy named Kyle Westbrook. Most of his family lives on Kodiak Island."

"How much are they paying you?"

It was common for agents and handlers who worked together to discuss wages. It was an unwritten rule to be open about it, like all of us were rooting for each other to get paid as much money as we could. Handlers generally made about half of what a good agent made, but they didn't take the same type of risks.

"$30,000 plus expenses," I answered.

"Why is the agency willing to pay us so much to find this target? You said his name is Kyle Westbrook?"

I didn't know what to say, mainly because I had the same question. "Does it matter?"

"It might," she said. "He's not famous or related to someone important, is he?"

I hadn't considered it until Chris said it. I must have had blinders on before. I was more worried about revenging Boggs's murder than trying to find out who Westbrook was, or the real reason why the agency would pay us so much.

"You don't know, do you?" she asked. "It never crossed your mind that this guy might have connections?"

"All I know is that he killed Boggs. I don't care who he's connected to. Our job will be to locate him. That's all. We can let the agency figure out what to do with him." I paused. "This guy killed Sam, Chris. He deserves what's coming to him."

I needed Chris on this one. I was out of practice, and she was the one person who could keep me focused.

"You probably already know this, but I moved back to Camas a few months ago," she said.

"Yeah, I heard."

Camas was about a thirty-minute drive from where I lived. She had grown up in the small mill town that became more of a suburban sprawl over the past twenty years. Housing projects littered the landscape now, but her place overlooked a corner of Lacamas Lake that still had a pretty nice view. She'd kept the house after her parents died, even though she and John had lived on the eastern side of the state.

"Do you still have the place in Spokane?" I asked.

"No," she answered. "That went to the kids, but they gave me plenty of time to move out. I like being back here anyway." She paused. "Why did the agency send me cold-weather clothing, and why was I sent the gummy bears? You're the one who used to eat gummies."

"They obviously messed up. I haven't received anything yet, so they must have figured we'd see each other. They told me I'd be getting my gear in Anchorage tonight."

"Tonight!" she exclaimed.

"Yeah," I said. "The flight leaves at nine-twenty. I need to contact my customers and figure out what I'm going to do about the current jobs I've been working on. The agency told me they would send you a contract, and if you agreed to it, they'd have you take over tomorrow when I get to Kodiak."

After a long pause, she sighed. "Brad Kelso," she said, "I can't believe we'll be working together again. Go ahead and make your calls. I'll start setting things up in my office."

NINE

"Thanks for watching Jenny while I'm gone," I told Chris. The Siberian husky jumped out of my Bronco when I opened the door. "I think she remembers you."

"She's so big," Chris said, kneeling on the ground. The dog was loving on her. "She was just a puppy the last time I saw her. She and Forrest should get along fine."

"Forrest?"

"John and I got him a few years ago."

I looked toward the side of Chris's house, a single level ranch-style place on about an acre of land. The large, fenced backyard sloped downward toward the lake. I'd been there years earlier, before she was married. The place was surrounded by county property, which included some lowlands and a higher, wooded area near the house with Douglas fir, oak, and maple trees. Her property sat back about fifty feet from the street and had a large, graveled area for parking. Watching us through the chain link was Forrest, another Siberian husky.

"There's plenty of space for them to run," Chris said.

Jenny bolted toward Forrest, who was pacing around behind a gate.

"They seem to get along," I said. "You named him Forrest?"

Chris smiled. "You don't own the rights to the name. Besides, it was *my* favorite movie, if you recall."

"Yeah, don't you remember, you taught me how to climb, and I showed you how to dangle."

"You're a dork," she said.

***

We only had a few minutes at Chris's house to go over the information in the packet, and we didn't have enough time to create any type of strategic plan before she drove me to the airport. I didn't even know where I'd be staying that night, if the agency had booked a hotel in Anchorage, or if they planned to fly me to Kodiak.

We received several messages on our way to PDX, along with our digital IDs and a short outline of a cover story the agency had chosen for me. Chris scrolled through several texts after we arrived in the short-term parking garage. We walked quickly toward the terminal. "The original handler will meet you in Anchorage," she said. "Her name is Cassandra Carmichael." Chris paused. "I guess she doesn't have a call sign."

"That's strange," I said. "Are they just using actual names these days?"

Chris laughed. "You're probably the one who started that. They started calling you Kelso instead of BK-643."

"I like the name, Kelso," I said. We crossed the walking bridge, went through the revolving doors, and headed toward security. "Have they mentioned anything about a photography website? I want my cover story to be solid before I start asking people questions."

"They haven't said anything about it yet, but it's on my list. Wherever they have you staying tonight or tomorrow, you need to wait until everything gets set up. We'll compare notes after we both get some sleep. If Westbrook has been on the run for eighteen years, one day won't make a difference."

The TSA agents waved us through security after we showed them our digital IDs. I asked Chris to go to the gate with me, which gave us a few more minutes to discuss the mission. Plus, it was nice to see her and talk with her again. She looked good.

"I'm concerned because the agency hasn't given us much to go on yet," she said. "All we know is that someone will meet you in Anchorage after you arrive. I don't like it. They should be providing us more information."

"Don't worry," I said. "Once I get to Alaska, things will settle down, I'll get some sleep, and like you said, we can make a plan. I'm too tired to do anything right now."

Chris and I stood in the aisle near the gate and looked at each other. I was flooded with so many emotions, and not just about finding Boggs's killer. Being with her felt so comfortable, like we'd never been apart. It was strange. I was tired and I was leaving on a mission, and even after all these years, I still cared about her. I could tell she felt the same way. It had been so long. Chris and I had never officially dated, but there was one time…

"Boarding now open for all passengers on Alaska flight 155 to Anchorage," a gate agent announced over the loudspeaker.

I smiled. "I guess that's me." We hugged each other, longer than we needed to.

"It's good to see you," I said.

Chris nodded then handed me my boarding pass. "I'll do some preliminary searches of Westbrook and his family," she said. "I'll finish setting up my office and get the agency's data linked to my computer." She paused. "You should get some sleep. You look like hell."

I turned toward the gate, walked a few steps, then looked back. "Love you too."

***

It was twenty minutes past midnight when I arrived at Ted Stevens International Airport in Anchorage. "Landed" was all I wrote when I texted Chris.

She texted back, so I knew she wasn't getting any rest. "The agency has you traveling to Kodiak tonight," she wrote. "Use the encrypted files and the other cell phone from now on."

I felt bad for getting her involved, but I wasn't sorry to be working with her again, and maybe the money would really help her out. If I would have kept the original handler, things might have been easier, but having Chris onboard gave me comfort. I knew she had my back.

The airport was easy to navigate, and I already knew where I was going after I exited the tunnel; but it was late, and even after sleeping on the plane, I couldn't stop yawning. As I walked through the terminal toward baggage claim, the scent of coffee, fast food, and perfume still lingered, but most of the shops were closed. The peanuts they'd provided on the plane hadn't satisfied my hunger. I realized I hadn't eaten any dinner before I left. A woman was standing just beyond the secured area. I stopped before I reached her.

"What, no sign?" I asked.

The woman smirked. "I didn't think I'd need one."

We started walking, side by side, but she was leading the way. She was in her early thirties with dark brown hair pulled back into a ponytail. I could tell by her confident demeanor that she knew what she was doing, like she was more used to giving orders than taking them. Her athletic build led me to believe that she could handle herself too.

"Do you have a name?" I asked.

"I'm Special Agent Cassandra Carmichael," she said. "And you're Brad Kelso. I've seen your profile."

I smiled. "Can I call you Cass?"

"No."

"You've read my file, but I don't know anything about you," I said. "Do you live up here?"

"Let's try to keep this professional," she said. She handed me a folded piece of paper with a list of about twenty items on it. "This is the equipment we'll be providing to you before the flight."

"What flight?"

"The flight to Kodiak. You'll need to sign for everything. If you want something else from Anchorage, CH-163 should contact me directly. Our pilot will stay here on standby because we won't be assisting you on the island. He might be able to fly you to a location once or twice, but you'll need to use the local resources as much as possible. If you want transportation from us, we'll need some lead time."

I looked at the list. "I don't need the laptop," I said. "I'll just use my phone. Does the handgun come with a silencer?"

"Yes. It's a 9mm Glock, standard issuance, and it comes with a 6.8-inch suppressor."

"Why so long?" I asked. "Don't you have anything under six inches?"

"Sorry," she said, "that's all we had."

We continued down an escalator. "You were sent a SAT phone, correct?"

"CH-163 and I each have one. Mine is in my checked luggage."

"I'll make sure it's working properly before we leave. We've had some trouble with the battery life of these new satellite phones the agency ordered. Do you want an extra cell phone? You won't have any cell service on most of the island, but you can use it in town.

"Thanks, but I already have an extra phone," I said. "I'll give you the number, and CH-163 should have the tracking software linked to the agency's network already."

We kept walking toward baggage claim and stopped when we reached carousel number two.

"So, Cass, how long have you been with the agency?"

"Listen, Kelso, my job is just to get you to Kodiak. And don't call me Cass. It's Special Agent Carmichael, or Chief to you."

"What do your friends call you?"

She seemed irritated. Maybe she didn't have any friends. "OK," I continued, "Chief it is. You can call me *Brad*, or *Kelso*, or *Brad Kelso*, or *Special Agent Brad Kelso*. But I also like to be called *Gummy Bear* if it's said with affection."

"You've been away for too long," she said. "You need to take a few training classes on harassment and etiquette in the workplace."

"OK, I get it. Just trying to be friendly."

She grabbed a small leather folding wallet and passport from her bag and handed them to me. I looked inside the wallet. It was full of cash, maybe three thousand dollars, but I didn't count it. There was a driver's license, a passport, and two credit cards in the name of Brad Kelso. Both the license and the passport were scuffed, like they'd been used for a while. "That's not a very good photo of me," I said.

The chief was surprised. "It's the same one that's on your real license."

"I know, it's just not a very good photo of me."

She held back a smile. "The notes said you had a strange sense of humor. But it's not so strange. More annoying than anything."

I laughed. "Look at the chief, making jokes. Since we're friends now, can I call you Cass?"

"No."

After I picked up my bags from the conveyor and put them on a cart, the chief and I continued outside, then we walked past the taxis toward the far end of the terminal.

"The driver's license and passport are under the Kelso name," she said, "but the numbers and addresses have been changed since you retired, or whatever. If anybody tries to look them up, they'll get the cover story, and we'll get a notification."

"Retired? I didn't retire. I left."

She didn't seem to care. "I just do what I'm told," she said. "I'm not even sure why they sent you here. My team has already done most of the work. The agency usually has a reason, but in this case, I have no idea what it is."

I grabbed her arm to turn her toward me. "This mission is personal for me. The guy I'm tracking killed my friend."

"Personal?" she asked. She freed her arm. "All I know is that you didn't want me to be your handler. The agency told me to check your gear, get you to Kodiak, and then leave you alone. If something happens to you after we get to Kodiak, it's not on me."

"We?" I asked. "You're flying to Kodiak?"

"I'm responsible for you and all the gear until we land," she said. "Yeah, I'm going."

"I think that's a bad idea," I said. "Kodiak is a small airport and a small town."

"Don't worry," she said. "I won't tarnish your reputation. Once we land and unload the gear, you're on your own. We'll be flying right back. I'll confirm your story if someone calls." She pulled out several business cards from a purse in her handbag and handed them to me. They said *Northern Exposures & Framing* with an Anchorage address and phone number. "If you need anything, call me; or better yet, tell your handler to call."

I chuckled. "Framing?"

"Do you understand your cover?"

"Yeah, I'm a freelance photographer," I said. "Wildlife and the colors of fall. I know the routine."

"The website we've set up has a link to Northern Exposures in Anchorage and Seattle. You're on the staff in Seattle, but the Kodiak job will be considered freelance."

A minivan was parked alongside the curb, waiting for us. The chief opened the passenger door and got inside, so I opened the hatch and filled the back of the van with my gear. Then I slid open the door and sat in the second row of seats. She turned and looked toward me.

"This is Driver," she said. "He's taking us to the plane we're flying to Kodiak."

"That should be easy to remember," I said. "When do I meet 'Pilot'?"

Driver chuckled, but the chief was serious. "Bob is the name of the pilot. He and the two of us are the only ones in Alaska, at least for now, who know you're working for the agency. If there are any questions, stick to the cover story."

"Has everything been sent to CH-163?" I asked.

"She'll have everything she needs tonight or tomorrow morning," she said. "Listen, we've worked on our covers for months. I'm not sure why the agency is letting you use Northern Exposures, but if you mess this up, it puts us all at risk."

"I understand."

"Just making sure," she said. "I know it's been a while."

"Yeah," I said. I looked out the window as we drove off. "It's been a while."

TEN

We were still in the hangar when Pilot Bob asked Chief Carmichael how much my gear weighed. I didn't know why, until a few minutes later when I saw all the other bags and boxes that had been stuffed into the rear of the aircraft. The plane was smaller than I'd expected; a single-engine Cessna 185 that had been customized with only three seats so it could have room for extra cargo.

"Four hundred pounds, including Kelso," she said. Apparently, the combined weight wasn't too much for the Cessna because Pilot Bob just nodded.

"What's the food service like onboard," I asked. "I'm hungry."

The chief dug out a protein bar and a bottle of water from her bag and handed them to me. "This will have to do."

"Thanks! You've got everything in that bag of yours," I told her. "You're like Mary Poppins!"

She wasn't amused, so I didn't say anything else. I ate the bar quickly and finished the water before we boarded the plane. Chief Carmichael sat in the passenger's seat and let me have the back to myself.

"We might have to adjust that weight to four hundred and one pounds now, Chief," I said.

She just sighed, but Pilot Bob was more pragmatic.

"Don't worry," he said. "We have over two-hundred pounds to spare. With the extra equipment onboard, I just wanted to know our total weight before we took off."

Pilot Bob seemed thorough and safety conscious. I was glad because a mixture of rain and sleet pelted the windshield of the airplane as we taxied toward the runway. Nobody said anything about the weather or the visibility which was, on a scale of one to ten, close to zero.

I supposed pilots in Alaska were used to flying in bad weather, and I'd certainly had my fair share of rough flights, but the darkness added to my overall concern about our safety. I adjusted my headset and leaned forward.

"Pilot Bob, shouldn't we wait a while, at least until the weather clears?"

"It's soupy right now but it should get better soon," he said. He looked at the chief.

She turned around toward me. "We have to drop you off and get back here this morning," she said, "so I decided not to wait."

"Great. Sounds like a smart idea," I said sarcastically. A gust of wind shook the small plane. "Maybe we'll miss the heavy stuff."

At least there wasn't any thunder and lightning, and the headset muffled most of the other noises. I was so tired that even if we would've flown upside down, I probably could have fallen asleep. I needed the rest, but I wanted to talk to the chief and gather as much information about the agency's current operations in Alaska before we landed on Kodiak. The flight might have been my only opportunity. Pilot Bob hadn't spoken more than a few words to me since I'd met him, and it was obvious he was taking orders from Chief Carmichael. I knew any information I was going to get would come from her.

As we lifted off, we banked to the right and I was able to see the glow of the lights coming through the clouds over Anchorage. The air inside the cabin was damp and stuffy, and even though I had the back to myself, it was still cramped with all the equipment and luggage. I probably overpacked, but I knew it would be difficult to get things sent to me once I was on the island. Getting caught in Alaska without the proper gear can be disastrous.

A minute after takeoff, the plane leveled out and headed away from the city. Even after the rain diminished, the only thing ahead of us were varying degrees of darkness. I was glad because the turbulence, which was only a few small bumps and dips that came and went, was less than I'd expected. I knew I wouldn't stay awake very long with the hum of the engine, so I decided to interrupt the silence.

"How did the agency figure out Kyle Westbrook was Whitefish?" I asked.

Chief Carmichael looked back at me and didn't say anything at first, like I was wasting her time. Then she sighed and started talking, probably an involuntary reaction of professional courtesy.

"The agency has a new machine that can piece together partial fingerprints, and even smudges. Someone in Colorado was going through old case files and found partial prints on an old postcard that was found at the crime scene. The machine matched them up to Kyle Westbrook."

She looked forward again, adjusted her seatbelt, and leaned back. Was that it? I guess she was finished, having given me as much information as she had planned to give. Either that or she didn't know anything else.

I still had questions. "You didn't answer me before; how long have you worked for the agency?"

She looked back at me like I was asking for her social security number and mother's maiden name. I smiled. "You know, we're on the same side," I assured her.

"The same side," she mumbled. She faced forward and pulled out a yellow note pad from her black leather satchel and began to write, either not wanting to talk anymore or just wanting to ignore me. It didn't work.

"Boggs and I were good friends," I said. "He recruited me to work for the agency, and he mentored me. I even spoke to him on the day he died."

Chief Carmichael sighed and stopped writing as she continued to look forward. She was done being professionally courteous. "I understand how you feel, but that was twelve years ago," she said. "The photo we have of Kyle Westbrook was taken this summer by Nick Pulte, one of our DEA agents. I worked with Agent Pulte. He vanished, along with most of his equipment. We were able to get his photos from the cloud, but we have no idea where he's at. He's officially missing, but he's probably dead, and we haven't been able to tie the Westbrooks to his disappearance.

We've been following Pete Westbrook, Kyle's brother, for months, and we almost have enough evidence to convict him of distributing fentanyl, but now we'd like to find out who killed Agent Pulte, too. We know it wasn't Pete because we know where he was when Agent Pulte disappeared. Right now, that's our top priority."

She shook her head, looked back at me, then continued. "Listen, we had no idea the guy in the photo was Kyle until this week. As far as Agent Pulte's murder, now Kyle's our main suspect, but we haven't been able to locate him. I know that's why you're here, but it's only been a few days. Our team hasn't been given enough time to find him. If you want the truth, we don't need a washed-up PFT getting in our way and messing things up."

She certainly wasn't pulling any punches or giving me a vote of confidence, but what did the DEA have to do with it?

"You're DEA?" I asked.

"I split time between the agency and drug enforcement," she said. "There just aren't enough agents in Alaska to handle everything, so Homeland Security combined some of the departments." She paused. "I'm the lead agent in Anchorage now for both offices."

"You're in charge of the operation and they wanted you to be my handler?" I asked. "That doesn't make sense."

"Someone in D.C. felt my team needed assistance and it would take too much of our time if we tried to find Kyle Westbrook, so they decided to bring in a PFT to help us locate him. You should be working directly under me, but the agency said we'd be better off letting you find him, using your own handler. I think it's a mistake, but it's not my call."

I smiled. For once, I thought the agency was right.

"If Pulte was a photographer, why did the agency give me the same cover?"

"No, Agent Pulte was working as a deckhand on the Westbrook's barge. All the photos taken by Agent Pulte were from his phone. The barge business is run by Pete's brother, Jason. It was the closest we could get to Pete at the time. Agent Pulte was able to make contact with Pete on several occasions, and he was even scheduled to start working for him; but like I said, he disappeared.

The barge was docked in Kodiak and Pete was out of town. That's what threw us off, so we started looking at Jason and some of the other deckhands." She paused. "Jason runs the barge operations, but we don't have any evidence yet that he's involved with the fentanyl distribution. Agent Pulte had already confirmed the barge business was legitimate. The fishing operations are what Pete Westbrook has been using to launder the money. Our forensic accounting team has studied Westbrook Holdings, and they say the numbers don't add up. By quite a bit."

"So," I asked, "Pete's dealing drugs, and now you think Kyle killed Pulte?"

"That's where we're at," she said. "I hope you and your handler are ready for this mission. I'll need to be updated continually about your progress, location, and who you're talking to. We have an informant on Kodiak, and we don't want that cover to be compromised."

"Is the informant working for the Westbrooks?"

"The informant is only providing information, not active pursuit. It won't affect your job."

"My job is to find Kyle, but I'd like to gather as much information as I can before I start risking my neck. If you think Kyle killed Pulte, that is certainly something I needed to know."

"We suspect Kyle Westbrook killed Agent Pulte, but we don't have any evidence yet. Like I said, we're close to being able to prosecute Pete Westbrook for distributing fentanyl, and if he was involved in Agent

Pulte's murder, we'd like to hold him accountable for that, too. We'd also like to find out who Pete's supplier is. We don't know if the fentanyl is being imported or produced locally. We'll give you all the information you need to know but having you on the island could compromise our operation and we've already lost one agent. Look, we've spent a lot of manpower and spilled a lot of blood to put these guys away, and we don't want all that effort to have been wasted because some old agent is trying to settle an old score."

She obviously wasn't very fond of me being there. "What did you say?" I asked. "I can't pick up everything through the headset when I don't have my hearing aids in."

She didn't appreciate the humor, so I stopped trying to be funny. "You've been here for how long?" I asked. "And you're saying you don't have enough evidence? It sounds like your main problem is a bunch of agents who are too full of themselves to ask for help. You want to blame me on the first day I get here, but I'm not the problem. I haven't done anything yet. Maybe that's why the agency sent me here, to clean up your mess!"

I wasn't scoring any brownie points, but I was tired and done taking crap from her. We both just looked the other way and didn't say anything for the rest of the flight. Of course, I was asleep during most of it.

Aside from a few short radio calls, Pilot Bob stayed silent until we got closer to Kodiak. We hit a few bumps as we descended, and a blanket of low clouds covered most of the area around the airport. I looked at my phone. It was 3:00 a.m. and it felt like 3:00 a.m., no longer nighttime and not yet morning. We drifted as a few wind gusts blew us sideways during the last few hundred yards. Pilot Bob hit the throttle just before the plane sat down on the wet runway—by all accounts, a near perfect landing. I felt like clapping.

"Nice landing, Bob," I said.

He looked over his shoulder at me and smiled.

"Thanks."

It turned out to be the last thing Pilot Bob said to me.

ELEVEN

After we landed, we taxied directly to the northwest end of Kodiak's airport, where ten or twelve small aircraft were parked. Two vehicles were in front of a rental car company, a short distance from the planes. One of them, a Jeep Wrangler, had been reserved for me under the name Brad Kelso. Even in the dim light, I could see the bright orange glow of the Jeep, and the word *Rubicon*, written on the hood.

"Are you kidding me?"

"It was either that or the minivan," Carmichael said. "The car rental market up here is crazy right now, and we didn't want you to use any vehicles from the Coast Guard base since you're working undercover."

"Brilliant," I said. "And by that, I mean the color."

She shrugged.

After I filled the Jeep Jack-O-Lantern with my gear, Chief Carmichael and Pilot Bob flew back to Anchorage, and I went to my hotel, less than a two-minute drive from the airport. It wasn't even enough time to defrost the windshield.

The Buskin Hotel had clean rooms, good WiFi, firm beds, and a nice breakfast buffet in the morning. At least that's what the chief told me before she left. I parked the Jeep in front of the hotel and walked inside. The lobby was spacious and clean but nothing fancy. A sectional sofa and two chairs had been placed around a fake fireplace in the center of the room. A smaller area between two room dividers, called the *Business Center,* had a computer and a printer, and was situated on the opposite side of the front desk. A set of double doors, which were open, led to the main hallway. The clock on the wall, behind the check-in counter, showed 3:30 am.

I walked around the lobby, but didn't see anybody or hear anything, not even in the hallway. Instead of waking up someone that early in the morning, I went out and sat inside my Jeep and put the seat back down as far as it would go.

The fog thickened as the wind died down, and moisture began to form on the Jeep's windows. I wasn't cold with my jacket on, but I had an eerie feeling as I laid there with my arms crossed in the dark. I needed to get my bearings. It had been so long since I'd been hired to locate anybody, so I felt somewhat out of place, like I didn't belong there. It was the first time I thought I might have bit off more than I could chew. I certainly wasn't going to get any support from Anchorage. The chief had made that clear. It was just Chris and I, together, trying to find one man—the man who killed Boggs. I closed my eyes and began to drift. I smiled. Alaska was where I met Boggs for the first time. I remembered the day like it was yesterday.

Three buddies and I from Washington State, had gone up to fish on the Situk River which flows into Yakutat Bay, about two hundred miles north of Juneau. Alaska is a great place to fish when the salmon are running. The four of us would go up to Yakutat for five or six days almost every summer. We'd spend most of our time wading upriver, catching sockeye on the Situk, and then one of the days we'd usually take a charter out to where the bay meets the ocean to fish for coho, lingcod, sea bass, king salmon, and halibut.

We'd rent a small cabin, fish all morning, then drink beer and tell lies for the rest of the day. Good times.

I overheard Boggs late one morning in the general store asking Nina, the store's owner, some questions while I was trying to get a corn dog out of the food warmer. The broken tongs I had been using weren't working, so I just reached in and grabbed the corndog with my hand. I burned my fingers a little bit, but I can't resist the smell of a good corn dog while I'm on vacation. It's really the only time I eat them.

"Use the tongs," Nina mumbled.

"They won't close," I said. I held them up so she could see the broken handle. Boggs stood at the counter and chuckled. He was medium height, medium build, and was dressed like he'd just gotten off a subway after work. He wore a dark sport coat with slacks and shoes that needed shining. He didn't have a tie on, but he was certainly out of place in Yakutat. I figured maybe he was a tourist and had just gotten into town.

Nina scoffed and grabbed another pair of tongs and set them on the warming case.

"Serves me right," I said.

Boggs had been asking Nina questions about a guy named Butch who lived in Yakutat. I knew who he was referring to, and of course Nina did too, but she wouldn't give Boggs any answers. Heck, I heard she'd dated Butch for a while before she was married, so she certainly knew him. Yakutat is a small fishing village, maybe five or six hundred residents, so everybody who lived within a hundred miles knew who Butch was.

"Do you mean Butch Adams?" I asked. I set my corn dog and some other snacks on the counter.

"Probably," he said. "I wasn't given his last name, but I know he works as a fishing guide around here."

"I saw him this morning," I said. "He's heading upriver."

Nina glared at me like Boggs was a spy and I was committing treason by divulging national secrets. She was a nice gal, married to some guy who worked on the north slope, so he was never around during the summer. At least we never saw him. She was native to Alaska, with dark hair and round features, and she spoke softly, almost like she was whispering. Her lips barely moved. I had to lean in toward her just to hear what she was saying.

Most people just nodded when she asked them a question. She wasn't shy or anything, she just mumbled and was hard to understand. I liked to joke around with her, which meant I told jokes and she stared at me until I was finished. I don't recall her ever laughing at them. I used to tell her, "Smile! Smile! Like the way Mr. Roark said it on *Fantasy Island.* She'd grin for a moment, but her smile would never last for more than a few seconds.

"Was he alone?" Boggs asked me.

"No," I said. "He's guiding someone today. Are you looking for a guide?"

"Maybe," Boggs said. "How much do you charge?"

I laughed. "I'm not a guide. I just came here to fish with some friends. If you bring some beer, you could come out with us."

"Thanks for the offer," Boggs said, "but I can't today. Do you recall if the man he was guiding was named John?

"Yeah, John was his name. You know him?"

"Not personally," Boggs said, "but if you tell me where they're staying, I'll buy you a six pack. Next time we'll go out fishing. It sounds like fun."

Boggs smiled and seemed friendly, but Nina was pacing around behind the counter, so I paid for my snacks, and the two of us walked outside.

"Where are you from?" I asked.

"Idaho," he answered. My name is Samuel Boggs."

"Brad Keller," I said as we shook hands. "You should know something, Sam, beer is expensive up here. Don't make promises you can't keep."

Boggs laughed. "I never do. And my friends just call me Boggs."

I smiled. "So, Boggs, you don't know Butch's last name, you're not here to fish, and you'll buy me beer if I tell you where they're staying. Is that the deal?"

Boggs just stood there for a moment. Then he smiled. "That about sums it up."

"You're not fishing, so you must be hunting."

"Searching is more like it."

"For Butch or John?"

"John," he said.

"That's good," I said. "I like Butch. He's a good guy. Great fisherman, too."

Boggs smiled. "I'm more concerned about finding out where John is staying."

"I don't know John," I said. "I just met him this morning. I'll tell you where he's staying, though. He's out at the Bear Claw Lodge on Lost River Road. Butch normally takes people out in his boat, but John wanted to take the four-wheelers out this morning, then hike upriver and do some fly fishing. They'll probably be back at the lodge later this afternoon." I paused. "Is Butch safe with him?"

"He should be fine. Now that I know where John is staying, I'll check it out and relay the information. I'm not here to cause any trouble. I'm just trying to locate him, that's all." He paused. "You seem to know your way around."

"Yeah," I said. "I love Alaska. I've lived in a few different places throughout the state, but I like to fish around here."

Boggs reached in his pocket and pulled out a card. "If you're ever interested in doing some PI work, we might be able to use you."

I looked at the card. *Samuel Boggs, Private Eyedaho.* "You're from Boise?"

"Yes," he replied, "but I work for an agency that does some business up here, too. Locating people mainly. Various reasons. To tell you the truth, I'd just as soon stay down south, close to my family." He smiled. "The agency likes to hire guys around our age. I guess we don't cause too many problems like some of the younger private eyes." He paused. "Think it over. With a little training, I think you'd be a natural."

I looked at the card again. *A private eye*, I thought. *Wouldn't that be something?*

"It's not as glamorous as people think," he said. "Look at me, I'm no Magnum."

I laughed. I couldn't recall ever meeting an actual private eye before, but Boggs was certainly nothing like what I'd expected. "How long are you staying in Yakutat?" I asked.

"I don't plan on staying," he said. "If everything goes well, I'll be leaving this evening. I guess I should buy you those beers."

"I'll tell you what," I said as I pointed down the road. "There's a place a few blocks from here, on Boat Harbor Road, called *Nellie's*. You can't leave Yakutat without having one of Nellie's chicken pot pies and I haven't had one since last year. I'll be back in town this afternoon, so I could meet you there at, let's say four o'clock, and you can buy me that beer."

"That's a deal," Boggs said, "but if you see Butch and John…"

"We already limited this morning, so I won't be seeing them today. It's not my rodeo, anyway. As long as Butch is safe with him, I won't say anything."

"I'd appreciate that. Like I said, you're a natural."

***

I guess Boggs thought I'd make a good PFT from the start. After I got home from the trip, I gave him a call. That's when he helped me get the job with the agency. I took over Boggs's territory and he went back home to focus on his own business. He still did a few jobs for the agency in Idaho and Montana, and every once-in-a-while I'd visit him and his family in Boise. Mostly, I just talked with him on the phone. We were good buddies. I would've done anything for him.

Just before I fell asleep in the Jeep, I realized it had been eight years since I'd gone fishing in Yakutat. It's funny how time goes by. I missed fishing with my friends on the Situk, and I missed talking with Boggs, too. I knew this trip to Kodiak wasn't going to be with friends, and it certainly wasn't a fishing trip. I really couldn't call it *searching*, either. No, it could only be described as one thing…I was *hunting*.

TWELVE

It was still dark outside when I woke up. I raised the seat, rubbed my tired eyes, and yawned. The windows of the Jeep were so frosty I couldn't see anything except the glimmer of light coming from the Buskin Hotel through the rear windshield. I heard a few voices and some car doors opening and closing, so I knew people were getting up and going to wherever the heck hotel guests go so early in the morning. My phone said 5:30 a.m., and I had quite a few messages, but it was dark, cold, and damp, and I was groggy. I didn't feel like reading them until after I went inside and warmed up.

Judging from the cars in the parking lot, the hotel seemed about half full, and checking in early didn't seem to be a problem for the woman at the front desk. I probably looked exhausted so maybe she just pitied me.

"Do you mind being on the first floor?" she asked.

"Does it have a bed?"

She smiled. "Actually, it has two queens, but if you'd prefer to stay in one of our king rooms, you could wait until one is available before you check in."

"The first floor sounds perfect."

She typed away on her keyboard and looked out toward the parking lot. "Is that your Jeep parked outside."

"Yeah, I didn't choose the color."

She laughed. "I've seen it before. You rented it from Emerald, didn't you?"

"I suppose. I'm a photographer, and the company I work for took care of it. They said it was either the orange Jeep or a minivan. I'm starting to think I should've gone with the minivan.

She laughed. "I like the bright color. We get a lot of fog, so you'll always be able to find it."

Great job, Chief, I thought. I'd be spotted wherever I went, even at the hotel, and even in the fog. I had to remind myself that this was a "hiding in plain sight" mission, whether I wanted it to be or not.

"I came in earlier, but nobody was at the front desk, so I slept in the Jeep for a couple of hours. I can tell you from experience, it makes a better glow stick than a bed."

She laughed, then handed me a keycard. "You're in Room 112, and I can tell you from experience, your bed will be more comfortable than sleeping in the Jeep."

I was too tired to ask her about her experiences on the queen beds in Room 112, but even the floor sounded better than the Jeep. I started rolling my suitcase toward the hall. "What time is breakfast?"

"Six to nine," she said. "Would you like a wake-up call?"

I looked back and saw her smiling. "I think I can stay awake for a half hour," I said, "but if you don't see me passing by here on my way to breakfast, don't call." She laughed.

When I got into my room, I didn't even turn on the light at first. With my feet on the floor, I laid back on one of the queen beds and looked at my messages. A batch of encrypted files, which included a more thorough dossier on Kyle Westbrook, along with information about some of the members of his extended family had been sent to me.

The agency only gave me the one photo of Westbrook, which had been taken on a boat a couple of months earlier. The bean counters had determined the location to be Kodiak Island, so I couldn't think of a better place to start my search than right where I was, on one of the queen beds in Room 112 at the Buskin Hotel. I didn't have enough energy to move once I laid down.

I sighed, then rolled onto the edge of the bed. Then I wiped my eyes again and chuckled to myself. *If Kyle Westbrook could see me now*, I thought, *he wouldn't be worried at all.*

The agency confirmed that both Pete and Jason Westbrook, Kyle's brothers, lived in their family's remote lodge on Uyak Bay. A few of their relatives lived in the city of Kodiak, which gave me some hope that I'd find Kyle quickly, but it didn't seem likely. Kyle was what the agency liked to call a *ghost*, a person who's been off the grid for a long time, in this case eighteen years. That meant he had been a ghost for almost six years before he killed Boggs.

When my job was to track down ghosts, information was always critical. Friends and family might hide the truth, even for a long time, but they usually weren't very good at it. It always amazed me how people had different ways to conceal what they knew. "I haven't seen him in years," they'd say, or "We weren't very close, but he always talked about moving to Argentina."

The family members, or at least some of them, certainly knew where he was. I was sure of it. Kodiak island is big, with a landmass larger than the states of

Delaware and Rhode Island combined, but there are only about thirteen thousand residents, and over half of them live in the city of Kodiak. Some people think living in remote areas, or *the bush*, is all about isolation, but when your nearest neighbor is more than a few miles away, you become dependent on others for supplies and other resources.

I'd worked on the island as a PFT before, twice in 2012, but on both occasions my cover story had been that I was a construction worker who had been hired to build bathrooms out at the launch complex. The complex is in a remote area of Kodiak Island that's a little over an hour from Kodiak's airport. I located the first target in two days. Easy-peasy. He had been using a fake ID to gain access to the Coast Guard base. I had no idea what nefarious activities he'd been trying to get away with, but once I was able to identify him and track his movements, the agency put a kibosh to his plans.

The second target took me three days because he worked as a greenhorn on a fishing boat, and I had to wait until they came back into port. Mostly, I stayed out of sight on both occasions to avoid having to answer questions since the targets were so easy to find.

I thought my cover story was better this time around. Residents of Kodiak are used to tourists and visitors, and even professional photographers. Plus, I didn't have to do any rough framing, concrete work, and even more importantly, no plumbing.

On Kodiak, taking photos was a great excuse to go just about anywhere on the island, and a message came through during the night that the photography website we were using for my cover story was up and running. All I needed was a waffle, some bacon and eggs, and a couple of hours of sleep, and I'd be ready to start my search.

I knew I had to be convincing as a photographer, but most people don't question what someone does for a living. They just accept whatever they're told. Criminals are different, especially career criminals. They're suspicious by nature because they're always hiding something. They become paranoid of everybody they meet, and when a trained agent notices it, it's like an alarm bell goes off.

A criminal might ask a question like, "Why did you come to Kodiak to take photos?" instead of "What kind of photos do you take?" People who are hiding something are always more interested in why you're there, at first, instead of what you're doing. It doesn't take long for an agent to figure out who the bad guys are just by the questions they ask or the answers they give.

After reading my messages, I decided to take a shower first, then hit the breakfast buffet and take a short nap before going to Kodiak's harbor, about six miles from the hotel. Since the photo showed Westbrook on a boat, I figured Kodiak's harbor was a good place to start. Plus, I wanted to visit an old friend.

THIRTEEN

I strolled along the wooden planks of Saint Herman Harbor, carrying a six-pack cooler filled with Budweiser in one hand and a duffle bag in the other. The salty air and smell of diesel engines seemed familiar, but it'd been years since I'd been to the harbor, a place where hundreds of vessels, both commercial and private, were moored.

I meandered my way toward the far end of the docks and stopped when I saw the stern of the *Northern Sky*, an 86-foot steel-hulled fishing boat, which had been tied down in its slip for over 25 years. The owner, Skip Thorson, had captained the vessel's last voyage when he spread the ashes of his beloved wife, Anne, a hundred miles southwest of Kodiak Island, in the waters directly above the Aleutian Trench.

"Take me out to a place where the water is as deep as the mountains," Anne had struggled to tell Skip from her hospital bed only hours before the cancer had taken her final breath. "I've loved you and only you in my life," she whispered, "and the sea has been my witness."

With his best friend, fishing partner, and the love of his life deceased, the Norseman retired from commercial fishing, and vowed he'd never again take the *Northern Sky* out to the open waters until he saw the bright, soothing colors of a rainbow bridge that would guide him to the afterlife.

Skip was sitting on a folding chair, his arms resting on a round metal table near the center of the ship's deck. The sound of seagulls squawking in the distance along with gentle waves splashing against the pillars concealed my arrival. Skip's eyes were focused on the object in his hands.

"Ahoy!" I yelled.

Skip looked up, but he didn't say anything at first. Then he took off his reading glasses as I got closer. "Brad Kelso," he said. "I'll be damned."

"Tell me something I don't know, old man," I called out. "Permission to come aboard?"

Skip chuckled. "Granted, that is if you can solve a riddle."

"A riddle?"

Skip looked frustrated. "How do I delete an app on this new iPhone?"

I laughed. "You have to hold your finger on the icon for a couple of seconds, then release it. When it says *remove app,* you touch that. Just make sure you really want to delete it."

Skip deleted the app. "You have proven yourself worthy to come aboard."

"You painted her," I said as I climbed over the edge of the boat.

Skip stood up and came over to meet me. "I take her out of the water occasionally to give her a good makeover. I had the hull painted black five years ago. I did the red stripe myself this summer. What do you think?"

I dropped my duffle bag, and we shook hands. "Looks great. When are we going to take her out?"

Skip sighed. "You know better than to ask that." He raised his arms toward the heavens. "I'm waiting for the Lord almighty to give me a sign!" He looked back at me. "The next time this boat goes out to sea will be its last." He paused. "Unless the new harbormaster gets his way."

"The harbormaster?"

"He says I shouldn't be living on her when she's moored here. I told him if he looks at the code, it says, and I quote: 'Any vessel which is not in use for the purposes for which it is normally operated, and which has remained moored to the boat harbor facilities continuously for a period of 90 days or more, may not be occupied, except that one person may occupy the vessel if serving in the capacity of a caretaker.' Well, I told him—I'm the caretaker."

I chuckled. "Did you memorize that?"

"You damned right I did! I give them plenty of business, too, and I watch out for things around here. They should be paying me to stick around."

"I believe that."

Skip pointed toward the inner harbor where the harbormaster's office was located. "We've had four harbormasters in the past twelve years, and they all say the same thing, at least for a while." He smiled, then backhanded me on the shoulder. "You see what you did? You got me started."

I laughed. "It didn't take much."

I grabbed two beers from the cooler and set them on the table. "Good," Skip said, "you brought bottles. I prefer bottles."

"I remember."

Skip grabbed a beer, twisted off the cap, and took a drink. "Ahh, that hit the spot." He smiled, then rubbed his shaggy gray beard. "So, what brings Brad Kelso back to Kodiak?"

"I'm doing some freelance work now, and I'm here for about a week to take some photos for a guy who's writing an article. It's a feature piece about how the Kodiak brown bears get so big."

"Hell, there's no secret to that. Plenty of food, and lots of space."

"Well, by that logic, you should be a giant by now, living all alone on this yacht."

"Yacht?" Skip laughed. "Brad, you've been on dry land too long." We sat down on the deck chairs and relaxed. "I'm kind of glad to see you actually," he said. "Each time you came into town something crazy happened. I'm ready for a little crazy."

"I wouldn't go spreading that around," I said.

"None of my business, but photos? Really?"

"The guy writing the article is looking for someone who can help him with another story or two in the future. He's interested in contacting people or families who might live in remote lodges near Uyak Bay." I pulled out the photo of Kyle Westbrook and showed it to Skip. "Have you ever seen this guy?"

Skip grabbed his glasses off the table and put them back on. "Can't say that I have. How old is this?"

"It was taken this summer."

"What's his name?"

"Kyle Westbrook."

Skip put the photo down and had a serious look on his face. "*The* Kyle Westbrook?"

"Do you know him?"

"I never knew him personally," Skip said. "He has some cousins who live in town, and the brothers stay out at their old lodge. Brad, I'm not sure if that's the family you should contact about an article. You know about the murders, don't you?"

"I read something about Kyle, but it didn't say anything about a murder."

"He killed two brothers near the Larsen Bay Cannery maybe, what, about eighteen years ago I suppose."

"How long was he in jail?"

"Not a day," Skip said. "They couldn't find him. He just disappeared. Everybody knew he probably killed the Beverley boys, but he took off, probably out to the bush or down to the lower forty-eight. They didn't have much evidence on him, at least from what people said. I think the FBI was called in too. We don't get too many murders on the island, so it was big news. The father of the boys was fit to be tied. Threatened to kill the whole Westbrook family. Word had it that he put out a contract on Kyle and kept it out there for years."

Skip picked up the photo again and looked at it closer. "He doesn't look the same. He could've had some work done. Course, he's not young anymore and he's got the beard. Westward Ho," he mumbled. "Yep, no doubt about it. You say this photo was taken this summer?"

"Yeah, what do you mean by Westward Ho?"

"That's the boat he's standing on in the photo. Look at that railing." He paused. "I can't tell if they're in a harbor or out to sea, though."

I took the photo from Skip. "You've seen the boat?" I asked.

Skip stood up and walked to the starboard side of the *Northern Sky*. I followed him. He pointed toward a large fishing boat that was in a slip toward the other end of the dock. "There she is," he said, "The *Westward Ho*."

I looked at the photo again, then back at the boat. There was no doubt about it; the photo had been taken on that boat."

"Do you have any other photos of Kyle Westbrook?" Skip asked.

"No," I said, "just this one."

"Well, if he's on the island, I don't know where he's staying, but my guess would be out on Uyak Bay with his brothers. Of course, it's a big island. I haven't seen him around here."

"So, I hear he's part native, Alutiiq," I said.

"Yeah, right," Skip said. "They've tried to claim that for years. That family is whiter than me."

I laughed. "I said part. And nobody is whiter than you."

Skip laughed. "That might be true, but you can't say anything about the color of somebody's skin these days, not even in a good way. Back in the day, a gal might have wanted to go out with a guy who was tall, dark, and handsome. Maybe she had milky white skin, and a fair complexion. Hell, say that now and you're a racist."

I laughed. "You're still reading those old romance novels, aren't you?"

"I like my romance novels!" Skip said. He scoffed. "I'm not that old yet. Besides, what's wrong with a little love and romance?"

I smiled. "Nothing. We could all use more of it."

Skip sighed. "I've been listening to my books on tape because my eyesight isn't as good as it used to be. A gal named Anna Wheeler narrates one of the books on my list. Ever heard of her?"

"No."

He looked sheepishly at me. "If I can get this new library app downloaded, I'll be able to listen to it on my new phone."

"OK," I said, "I can take a hint. I'll help you download it, just let me finish this beer."

Skip smiled and raised his bottle. "Here's to friendship and to those who deserve it."

"I'll drink to that," I said. The bottles clanked together, and we took a drink.

"That boat where you used to stay isn't docked here anymore," he said. "Do you have a place?"

"I'm over at the Buskin."

"All the way over there? You should've said something. I could fix you up a bed here if you'd like. It'd be nice to have some company."

"Thanks for the offer, but the magazine is paying for the room. Besides, if I remember correctly, you snore like a freight train."

Skip laughed. "Well, there is that."

"So," I said, "this Westbrook might have killed two brothers, huh? Where does the Beverley family live?"

"Old man died maybe eight or nine years ago. The wife left him after the murders. Heard tell she moved to Florida, got involved with a Coast Guard captain from the base." Skip shook his head. "If Kyle Westbrook is on Kodiak Island, he must be using a different name. I haven't heard a damned thing about it. Course, the Westbrooks keep to themselves for the most part. Aside from fishing, the older brother, Jason, runs a transport business between here and Anchorage. Heavy stuff. Things that won't fit on a plane. He's in port every couple of weeks. Just barges stuff back and forth."

"How many workers or crew members do they have?"

"Ten or twelve total if you count the barge. Less now, until crab season starts back up. Pete Westbrook runs the fishing operation, and he takes the boat out to Dutch Harbor sometimes. They stay busy all year long. In the summer, some of them live on the compound."

"Compound?"

"The old lodge. They've got some cabins and a warehouse on what, maybe five acres. When the parents were alive, they used to do scenic tours along with fishing and hunting trips over there. The kids helped too, but that was years ago. I don't know if compound is the right word, but that's what some people call it." Skip squinted. "That might be a good place to hide if nobody was looking."

"It sounds like a good place to hide, even if people *were* looking," I said.

Skip nodded. "Larsen Bay is the closest airport to Uyak Bay, but the whole area is pretty remote where the Westbrook's live. I know they have a floatplane, and both Jason and Pete are pilots."

"Can you keep this between us?" I asked. "Oh, and can you keep this duffle bag somewhere safe for a few days?"

Skip looked at the bag. "What's inside?"

"It's legal, but something I don't want a curious hotel maid getting their hands on."

Skip shook his head and wiped his brow. "You need to be careful, especially if you're dealing with the Westbrooks. And you shouldn't be poking around, asking people about Kyle." He paused. "You better get your story straight, too. You say a friend of yours wants to contact him about brown bears and people who live near Uyak Bay? My ass! What are you really doing here?"

FOURTEEN

It was just before noon when I arrived at the Kodiak Harbormaster's Office. The building was situated at the east end of the inner harbor, about a ten-minute walk from where I'd left Skip Thorson on the *Northern Sky*.

To get some exercise, I left the Jeep parked in the southern bay's lot and strolled along the connecting road for about half a mile until I reached the inner harbor's boardwalk. When Chris dropped me off at the airport, she gave me a look like I was old and out of shape, and she was right. Maybe I could lose a few pounds while I was on the island. When I grabbed the skin on my waist, I could easily pinch an inch and I didn't want to go back home flabby.

Outside of the harbormaster's office, the smell of fresh paint lingered from the building's recent remodel. As a contractor, I always noticed the work of other contractors, and most of the time I wasn't very impressed. In this case, however, the new metal roofing and the exterior siding job had been finished by someone who knew what they were doing. I wouldn't have gone with the drab blue-gray exterior, but who was I to judge? A small bell jingled when I opened the door.

A man and woman were working in the office area situated behind a long counter. The man was sitting in a swivel chair with a phone to his ear, and the woman was helping two gentlemen with their fees and permits.

"It gives you four hours on the wash pad," the man told the person on the phone. He paused. "Uh huh. Uh huh. I get it, but if it takes you longer, we'll still have to charge you for the extra time."

He didn't notice me when I walked in, but the woman smiled.

"That's it, gentlemen," she said. "You're all set." The two men she was helping thanked her, then left as the bell jingled again.

"What can we do for you?" the woman asked me.

"Hi. My name is Brad Kelso and I'm doing some freelance photography work around Kodiak. Mainly wildlife and the last of the fall colors, but I was wondering if it'd be OK if I took a few photos around the harbor."

"Sure," she said. "It's a public space, but if you want any close-ups of the boats, you should get permission from the owners. And we don't allow any trespassing."

"Actually, that's why I'm here. I was just over at the south harbor, and I saw a boat there that I'd like to use for a photo spread. I was wondering if you could tell me who the owner is."

"What boat?" she asked.

"It's called *Westward Ho*."

The man, still on his call, walked over to the counter. "You say you're a photographer?"

"That's right."

He raised his index finger toward me. "Hang on, give me a minute," he said, then went back to his desk to finish his call.

"What kind of photos do you plan to take?" the woman asked.

"Here, take a look."

I took the camera strap off my shoulder and held the Nikon D750 on the counter in front of her so she could see the viewing screen. She leaned forward and I was able to smell the flowery fragrance of her perfume. Our heads nearly touched. She smiled as I scrolled through the photos. "I took some shots of this guy on his fishing boat earlier. He told me to come in here and talk to the harbormaster about the other boat."

She looked at the photos. "Skip Thorson," she said, then laughed.

The man finished his call, then came over to the counter. I stood back up. I didn't want to smell whatever fragrance he was wearing.

"Skip told you to come talk to me?"

"Are you Curtis Hightower, the harbormaster?"

"Yeah, but I wouldn't believe anything that old man says. You can take photos around the harbor, but we can't give you permission to publish any of them until we see them. The boat owners expect a reasonable amount of privacy."

"I understand. I'm not here to break any privacy rules. What I'd like is a few photos of the entire harbor, but there might be a boat or two I'd like to use in a spread, so I'd like to be able to contact the owners to see if they'd be interested in talking to me about it."

"Who did you say you worked for?"

"I'm here doing some freelance work for a company that writes articles for National Geographic. They want to do a story about Kodiak, and they sent me here ahead of time to take some photos. A journalist will be coming in a couple of weeks to write the story. Can we count on you two for interviews?"

The woman smiled. "Sure, we..."

Hightower interrupted. "They can interview me when they come," he said. He pointed toward the woman. "Lacy can set it up, or she can put it on my schedule. We get busy around here, so whoever comes from the magazine should try to call ahead of time." He grinned. "National Geographic, huh?"

I pulled out two cards from my pocket and handed one to Hightower. "I'll pass it on that you're the person to talk to. I wrote my private number on the back. Here's one for you too, Lacy."

Lacy took the card and looked at my number. "Brad Kelso," she said. "Your name sounds familiar. Where are you from?"

"I live in Washington State now. I don't think we've ever met, but about ten years ago a company I worked for did some construction work on the island, mostly out near the launch complex. I built a restroom in a building where they didn't have water service. I'll give you some free advice too. Never buy one of those no flush, incinerating toilets." Lacy and Hightower smiled. "Let's just say I tried it out when I finished putting it in, and you don't want one." They laughed.

"So, you work for the government?" Lacy asked.

"No," I said, "but throughout Alaska most of the construction work we did were government jobs. Airports, communications facilities, you name it. I just showed up to work every day."

"Sounds like a lot of shit," Lacy said. We laughed.

"If you want to talk to any of the owners, let us know and we'll have them call you," Hightower said. "Lacy will set it up." He drifted back toward his desk but reiterated to me, "Like I said, when you finish taking photos of the harbor, come back in so we can look through them."

"OK, I will."

"You said something about the *Westward Ho*?" Lacy asked.

"Yeah, I'd like to contact the owner about doing a photo spread using their boat. Maybe talk to them about the article."

"Well, I know the owners, so I can tell you for sure that they won't like it if someone is out near their boat, especially someone who's taking photos.

"Oh, really, why is that?"

"They're just private, that's all."

"Well, let them know I'm interested, or maybe I can talk to them directly. Do they live around here?"

Lacy looked at the card again. "I'll let them know." She smiled. "Brad Kelso. Are you sure we haven't met before?"

"Not that I can recall, and I think I'd remember that."

She smiled again. "Well, just remember what I said about the *Westward Ho*."

"I will."

After I left, I figured the Westbrooks would get a call that day from either Lacy or Hightower, most likely Lacy, because she seemed to know the family. At least she knew them well enough to know they didn't like people hanging around their boat. I also knew how being patient was a virtue when tracking someone in a small town or in a remote setting.

Friends and relatives tend to react to strangers asking questions, and sometimes the surrogates of the target would attempt to contact me first, like linemen on a football team trying to protect their quarterback. The trick to finding a quarterback is locating the *pocket* of protection. The whole process usually saved me countless hours of snooping around, looking for needles in haystacks, and the last thing I wanted to do was snoop around and look for needles.

Even worse, Private eyes, and some PFTs for that matter, are often paid to just sit at various locations and do nothing. They call it a "stakeout," which is just a fancy word for waiting. Sure, the time can be spent listening to a ballgame, or reading a novel, but I can't recall the last time I was on a stakeout when I didn't wish I was doing something else.

For the agency, there was no getting around it; stakeouts were a necessary evil, but at least they didn't involve cheating spouses. The stakeouts I did were all about finding people who didn't want to be found, and some of the time they provided valuable information. It was also a great way to get comfortable using the latest technology.

One of the items the agency had sent with me to Kodiak was a long-range listening device called a parabolic microphone. It was six inches long, wireless, and looked like a cigar from a distance. The new design didn't have a dish attached to it, which was a big improvement over the old technology. It had a small chip that could record conversations for up to eight hours, and it had a great built-in noise-reduction feature, too. It was the sleekest design I'd ever seen, and if it was pointed in the right direction it could pick up a whisper from a hundred yards away. The earpiece didn't fit very well, but it stayed in as long as I didn't move around too much. All the engineering must have gone into the microphone because the earpiece was annoying.

I also had a pair of glasses with me that had a zoom lens. They were only 2x, but in a situation where I wanted to see something clearer from a short distance, they came in handy. I had some time, so I sat on a bench a few hundred feet from the harbormaster's office and waited. I was on a stakeout. To my delight, I didn't have to wait long.

Lacy came out through the front door a few minutes after twelve, probably on her lunch break. She looked around, grabbed a pack of cigarettes from her jacket, and lit one up. She didn't seem interested in eating anything, but the more I thought about her not eating, the hungrier I started to get.

It looked like she was texting on her phone, which didn't help me. The agency didn't give us access to text messages unless we could get a court approval, which took several days. Of course, it would have been handy to know what she was writing and who she was messaging, but I didn't have time to wait.

She leaned back against a blue Subaru Forester. After a few minutes, she flicked her cigarette into the air and tiny sparks shot up from the ground when it bounced. A small plume began to rise, but after one twist with the bottom of her shoe, the butt was smashed into the asphalt. She blew out the remaining smoke from her lungs, then smiled when she looked at her phone. Someone called her.

I raised up the microphone like I was smoking it.

"Hey," she answered.

Filling in the blanks when I listened to people on phone calls was not a talent that I possessed, but I usually got the gist of the conversations.

"Like I said, a guy came in and was asking questions about the Ho," she said.

As Lacy listened to the person she was talking to, she looked around the parking lot.

"His name is Brad Kelso," she said, "and he's a photographer. He said he wants to take some photos around the harbor, including the *Westward Ho*, and maybe some of the other boats. He said it's for National Geographic. He asked me who the owner was."

This was the call I'd hoped for, but I was still guessing who was on the other end of it.

"Nothing," she said. "I told him I knew the owners and they wouldn't want some guy hanging around their boat taking photos."

Another short pause. Lacy seemed comfortable with whomever she was talking to.

"No, he just wanted me to ask your family about taking the photos. He seemed friendly. It's probably nothing, but I thought you should know."

She must have been talking to a Westbrook. There were only three of them.

"Washington State, but he said he did some construction work on the island, too. He seemed to know his way around. I've never seen him before, but his name sounds familiar."

I began to wonder if she'd heard my name somewhere from my last two missions on Kodiak. I stayed on a boat in the harbor, but Skip was the only one I spent time with. I didn't remember seeing her or anybody else who worked in the operations center.

"Yeah, but I didn't have much time," she said. "He has a website with some of his work, and a short bio. He left me his number, so I'll text it to you."

She had already looked me up. *Interesting*. She pulled out a card, probably the card I'd given her.

"Yeah, he's at the Buskin. Sheryl said he's staying in Room 112."

Lacy sounded like she was proud of her detective work. It was always exciting and yet unnerving for me to listen to people talk about me when they didn't know I was listening. I just never knew what I was going to hear or what information I'd be able to pick up.

"Who am I meeting?" she asked.

A meeting? My ears perked up even more.

"Should I call Pete?"

That eliminated Pete. It was either Kyle or Jason on the phone.

"No, that's just what he was asking," she said.

One more name is all I needed. Either way, Lacy obviously knew the family, even better than I'd previously thought.

"Yeah, but I think he's just a photographer."

It's a noble profession. What does she mean by "just?"

"OK, I'll call him during my next break. Don't worry, I think he'll come. He seemed nice."

Nice? I was in the friend zone.

"You know me too well," she said. "Bye."

Maybe I wasn't in the friend zone, but it sounded like I was getting invited somewhere. I needed to find out more about Lacy. She wasn't suspicious of me yet, but by listening to her part of the phone call, I knew the Westbrooks were suspicious of everyone. She said she planned to call me during her next break, so I had some time. I got up and walked back to the Jeep and drove it to the hotel. I needed to relax, take a short nap, and get ready. Things were starting to happen.

FIFTEEN

Just as I was getting back to the Buskin Hotel, I received a call from Don Gustafson.

"Hey Donny, what's up?"

"Did Mr. Walker call you?"

"No, why would he call me, Donny?"

"Well, it's about the fence boards. We're supposed to make them all level, right?"

"You mean the tops?" I asked.

"Yeah, the tops are all supposed to be level, right?"

"No, Donny, we're sloping them on this job, the same slope as the ground. That way the boards are all the same length. Did you cut down some of the boards?"

"A few."

"How many?"

"About twenty-eight."

I swiped my keycard and entered the hotel room. I placed the *do not disturb* sign on the outside handle, then leaned against the door after it was closed. "How many have you put up so far?"

"About thirty-five."

I sighed, then paused to think. "That's pretty level ground, Donny. How many inches did you cut off the boards?"

"Are you mad?"

"Just tell me, Donny, how many inches did you cut off the boards?"

"Well, the first few I barely had to cut, but the last ones, maybe three inches."

I sat down on one of the queen beds and closed my eyes. "Are the rails all level?"

"Uh, let me see. Uh, no. They slope with the ground. I see what I did now."

"Just take down the boards you cut and use new ones," I said. "Keep all the cut ones in a separate pile. I'll be able to use them somewhere else."

"I started at the gate, like you told me. You know where it slopes up—right before the maple tree?"

"It's OK, Donny. Don't worry. It isn't that many boards."

"Are you mad?"

"Quit asking me that. I'm not mad. I'm always happy with the work you do, and we all make mistakes. I'm glad you called."

"It was Mr. Walker who came out and told me I needed to call you." Don paused. "Wait a second, he and his wife just came outside again. I think he wants to talk to you."

I heard Lefty say something to Don before he got on the phone. "Brad?" Lefty asked.

"Yeah," I said, "it's me."

"Hang on, let me put this on speaker," he said. "It's me, Cheyenne Rose, and Don here. Can you hear us?"

"Hi Brad," Cheyenne Rose called out. "Are you still out of town?"

"Yeah, I can hear you," I said, "and I'm still in Alaska."

"We've got a problem with the fence," Lefty said. "Don cut some of the boards."

"Is it cold there?" Cheyenne Rose asked.

"Don told me about the boards, Lefty, and we'll take care of it right away. It isn't very cold here yet,

Cheyenne Rose, but they say a storm might be coming in this week."

"Are you still going to be finished by Friday?" Lefty asked.

"Are you catching lots of fish?" Cheyenne Rose asked.

"I've just been helping a friend, so I'm not fishing on this trip. Don should be finished with the fence tomorrow, Lefty, then he'll stain it for you on Friday. Have you picked out the stain color yet?"

"Hang on," Lefty said. "Honey, do you have that color chart?"

"Are you still there, Donny," I asked.

"Yeah."

"We might have enough fence boards to finish," I said, "but if you need more, just go buy them using my account."

"OK."

"We're looking at the chart now," Lefty said. "I like the browns. I don't like those reds or that whitewash gray. Maybe the natural or even a darker brown like the walnut."

"Do you need a passport to go to Alaska?" Cheyenne Rose asked.

"Honey," Lefty said. "We're talking about stain colors. Which one do you like?"

"I like the cedar look," she said.

"I just use my driver's license when I go to Alaska," I said, "but you can use a passport, too. If you drive up through Canada, you need to have a passport. As far as the colors, it sounds like you want something between the natural cedar tone and a clove brown. Both of those stains will give you the cedar look Cheyenne Rose is after, and they don't have the reddish tint. I'll have

Don get a sample of each of them and he can stain two of the boards he cut. That'll give you a better idea of how it'll look on the entire fence. Then you can decide tomorrow."

"Sounds good," Lefty replied.

"Have fun!" Cheyenne Rose said, "and stay warm!"

"Donny, count the boards and then go get the stain samples for the Walkers. Text me when you finish working today to let me know how far you got."

"OK, I will."

***

After the phone call, I turned on the TV and laid back on the pillows. It was hard to be away from my construction business. I was lucky Don was free to help me out while I was gone. My mind seemed to be going in so many directions and I was still tired. I had to remind myself that I was getting paid good money to locate Kyle Westbrook, and Chris was counting on me too. I thought I'd rest my eyes for a few minutes, but I fell asleep and was startled when my phone buzzed an hour later.

"Hey, what's up?" I rasped.

"Are you sleeping?"

"No, just resting my eyes, Chris."

"The agency called," she said. "They got a few hits on the photography website and the Brad Kelso searches all lead to one networking site. There's been activity so you must be doing something right."

I stood up and stretched my back. "I hear Kyle Westbrook was wanted in connection to two murders here eighteen years ago. It sounds like he might have been a person of interest, and that was almost six years before Boggs was murdered. Why wasn't that information in the packet?"

Chris paused. "Who told you that?"

"Skip Thorson."

"That's the old guy who lives in the harbor, right?"

"Skip would tell you he's not that old," I said. "Besides, he knew who the Westbrooks were, and he's the one who recognized the *Westward Ho* from the photo. He said Kyle was a suspect in the death of two brothers. Their last name was Beverley. See if you can get any information about those murders. Like I said, he told me it happened about eighteen years ago."

"Brad, you need to be careful. The agency isn't giving me much information, not like they used to. I looked up the *Westward Ho*, like you asked, and they couldn't tell me anything besides licensing information and ownership records. They said a different division of Homeland Security has taken over the data center and I'm supposed to fill out digital request forms every time I want to know information not directly related to the mission. How am I supposed to know if information is related to the mission before it starts?"

"Don't get all worked up, Chris. Just send me what you have. Oh, and find out what you can on a Lacy. She works in the harbormaster's office. I don't know her last name, but she seems to know the Westbrook family. And get me everything you can on Pete and Jason Westbrook. The agency's file doesn't give us much to go on. The way Carmichael sounded; they're involved in some type of narcotics distribution."

Chris scoffed. "Maybe that's the reason for the big payday. They think you might provide them with information that would lead to a big drug bust."

"I don't think Carmichael believes that. She didn't want me anywhere near the Westbrooks."

"It's probably above her pay grade," Chris said. "Let me get back to you about the Westbrooks. I'm going to spend the evening filling out digital request forms so we can get whatever we need when we need it. I might even tap some of the other sources the agency has in Alaska."

"Other sources?" I asked.

"You don't need to know."

SIXTEEN

The blue Subaru Forrester was parked directly in front of the Whiskey River Saloon when I arrived. I didn't know how long Lacy had been waiting, but her window was rolled down and she smiled when I waved.

"Hey there," I said as I came around to the driver's side. "Nice to see you again. Are you going inside?"

"Yeah, just having a smoke."

"Thanks for setting this up with Pete. Is he here yet?"

"I don't think so." She looked around. "I don't see his car and he hasn't texted, but he'll be here." Lacy watched as I rubbed my hands together then put them in the pockets of my jacket. I looked up and down the street but didn't see any cars coming.

She smiled. "You should get a real coat."

I laughed. "I have one, but it was warm out this afternoon, so I left it at the hotel. I should've remembered how it seems colder here at night than what the temperature says. It must be the dampness."

Lacy coughed, then cleared her throat as she buried her cigarette into an empty coffee cup. She set the cup back into the front console's holder. "It's supposed to be nice for a couple of days then get iffy on Sunday. Working at the harbormaster's office, we have to constantly keep track of the weather. This time of the year, it's always damp and cold at night. How long are you staying on the island?"

"Probably a week," I said. "I'll travel around and get as many photos as I can, then the magazine will look at them before the writer does his story. I'm staying at the Buskin Hotel near the airport."

Lacy grinned. "I know. Sheryl, the manager, is a friend of mine."

I smiled. "You've been checking up on me. You already knew how long I'd be staying on the island, didn't you?"

Lacy smirked as she turned off the car's engine. The window slowly went up. "Maybe," she teased.

As she grabbed her purse, I startled her by opening the driver's door for her. Before she could say anything, I offered my elbow and arm. "Madam, would you like to accompany me to the festivities?"

She grinned. "Festivities? You've obviously never been to the Whiskey River."

I held her arm, then closed her door before we made our way onto the sidewalk. "Can't say that I have."

"You're definitely not from around here," she said.

I laughed. "If I hold on to you now, maybe if I drink too much, you'll hold on to me later."

She smiled. "I'm not making you any promises yet."

When we arrived at the front door of the saloon she stopped and asked me, "Are you married."

"I'm divorced," I said, "but I do have someone back home who I've been seeing for a while. Nothing serious."

I'd learned a long time ago that people are more suspicious of single, middle-aged men who weren't dating anyone, and I didn't want Lacy to have any suspicions about me whatsoever.

Lacy held out her left hand. "There's no ring on this finger either. I was married once but it didn't take. He was a fisherman and the only thing I regret is that he didn't fall overboard and make me a widow."

"Ouch," I said, then smiled.

"I heard a comedian say that once," Lacy said. "I thought it was the funniest thing at the time, probably because it was true. At least it was for me."

"Do you still see your ex?"

"No, he moved to Juneau, thank God. It's been five years. I don't know if I could take it if he still lived around here."

"No boyfriend? Nobody's going to punch me out when we walk inside, are they?"

She grabbed my arm and smiled again as I opened the door. "Like I said, I'm not promising you anything yet."

***

The Whiskey River Saloon, located in downtown Kodiak, was only a few blocks from the inner harbor. As we walked inside, I scanned the room, a habit I'd picked up during the time I worked for the agency. There were two pool tables, an area for darts, several big screen TVs, and about twelve stools surrounding a circular bar which was situated close to the entrance. It looked like most bars in most towns. There were three booths for seating on one side of the room and several sets of tables and chairs on the other. The place was about half full. *Not bad*, I thought, for a Wednesday night.

Lacy led me by the hand toward the far end of the room. A Willie Nelson song was playing, and I was glad it wasn't too loud. I wanted to have a conversation with Pete without it being too noisy, and I have trouble hearing conversations in bars when the music is too loud. Lacy smiled and said hi to a few people along the way. Eyes kept following us as we paraded our way toward one of the booths. I sat facing the front door like I always tried to do. I'd learned how to position myself, locate threats, and detect where any dangers might come from. It was more tactical training than anything else and Lacy didn't seem to notice. I think she just liked the attention we were getting. Some of the people in the saloon were probably her friends, wondering who I was and why we were together.

She sat opposite of me and smiled as we faced each other. I smiled back but looked right through her toward the entrance. I was still scanning the room. I figured any threat to me would probably be walking through that door soon.

"Nice place," I said. "What's with the dollar bills above the bar?"

Lacy turned her head for a moment, then looked back at me. "It's not complicated. You take a dollar bill, you write on it, then you tape it above the bar."

"Does it have to be something profound?"

Lacy laughed. She looked over her shoulder then leaned in toward me and whispered. "Randy, the manager, tells everybody not to write the word "fuck" on the bills, but that's his only rule." She leaned back. "The bathroom walls are probably more profound, at least the men's bathroom. Give these fishermen a sharpie and some alcohol, and what do you expect?"

"Do you spend much time in there, the men's room?" I asked.

Lacy laughed. "More than I'd care to admit, but less than you think," she said, then laughed even harder.

"Have you ever put a dollar bill up there?"

"Oh yeah," she said. "It has my initials on it too. My last name is Miller, so LM. I'll tell you what, if you find it, I'll buy you a beer."

"That sounds like a challenge. There must be a thousand bills up there."

"At least."

"What does yours say?"

Lacy smiled. "Wouldn't you like to know?"

I laughed. "Well, the only thing I know so far is that it doesn't say fuck and it has the initials LM on it." I paused. "I think I might need another clue."

"You can see it from here," she said, "and that's the last clue you're getting."

"I can't read any of them from here. You must have great eyesight."

She scoffed. "I said you can see it. I didn't say you were close enough to read it."

Two men walked in the front door and looked around. "There they are," Lacy said. "I told you they'd be here."

I felt uneasy as the two men walked toward the booth. I'd been given Pete's bio by the agency and Chris had sent me photos and a few more details about the Westbrooks before I left the hotel. The other guy? I didn't have a clue who he was, and the guy looked like a linebacker. Why would Pete bring muscle with him?

"So, this must be Brad Kelso, the photographer from National Geographic?" Pete asked without introduction.

I nodded, "Well, actually I'm freelancing for them, but a few of my photos should be in the article. You must be Pete." I stood up to shake his hand, but he didn't move.

"So, you're just nobody who wants to be somebody?" Pete said. He laughed, then the guy he brought with him laughed too.

"Well, that's one way to look at it," I said.

"Is there any other way?" Pete smirked.

"Show him some hospitality, Pete!" Lacy said, then looked at me. "You see what I mean about people around here not having any manners?"

"Oh!" Pete cried out. "Well, excuse me, your highness!" He bowed slightly. "May we properly introduce ourselves. I'm Pete Westbrook and this is Tony Lee." He looked at Lacy. "Is that better, bitch?"

Lacy lowered her head and fluttered her eyelashes. "Why yes, it is, asshole!" Pete smiled and Tony chuckled. "This is what I have to put up with," she said to me.

I smiled and sat down. "I guess you've known each other for a while."

"Since we were kids," Lacy said. "Pete and his brothers used to..."

"Lacy!" Pete interrupted. "I'm sure that Brad Kelso here, almost somebody, isn't interested in hearing about our childhood." He looked at me. "Are you?"

"I enjoy a good story, but I suppose Lacy can tell me later."

"Lacy won't be talking about my family at all." He looked at Lacy. "Right?"

Lacy sighed. "I guess not." She put her elbows on the table and leaned toward me. "Like you said, we've known each other for a long time. Anyway, Pete's the guy to talk to about taking photos." She slid out of the booth and stood up. "I'm going outside for a smoke. Anybody want a beer?"

"I'll have a Budweiser," I said, "but let me buy this round." I took out a hundred-dollar bill and gave it to her. "Use that until it runs out."

Lacy looked at Pete. "You see, he's a gentleman," she said, then walked away.

"Two more Buds," Pete hollered before she went outside.

I motioned with my hand. "Have a seat, guys."

Pete slid in on the seat, but Tony took a chair from a nearby table, turned it around backward, and sat down at the end of the booth. I hadn't seen anybody as big as Don Gustafson in a long time, but this guy was close, maybe a few inches shorter and thirty pounds lighter, but still a daunting figure. He just sat there like a brick wall. One thing was certain, I wasn't going anywhere.

"Don't take this personally," Pete said, "but we don't want you anywhere near the *Westward Ho*."

"That's what Lacy thought," I said, "but I still wanted to talk to you about it. The boat is quintessential Alaska. If you let me take some photos of it, one of them might make the cover. I know it'd look great in a photo spread, sitting there in the harbor. I'm sure you have some stories that the writers would love to hear about, too."

Pete shook his head. "I guess you didn't understand me, Mr. Quintessential," he said. Tony chuckled. He asked Tony, "Anthony, was I not clear?"

"Crystal clear," Tony said, then chuckled again.

Pete furrowed his brow as he looked at me. "Tony says I was clear. Not only clear, but crystal clear. Are you saying he's a liar?"

I could feel the tension escalate. I was looking at Pete, but I could sense Tony's readiness to brawl on command. When I was younger, I might have taken the bait, but I was older and had been trained for situations like this. Besides, I didn't want to wind up in the hospital.

"So, let me get this straight," I said. "I come in here to meet you. I tell you that you have a terrific looking fishing boat. Then, I offer to buy you and Tony some beers." I shook my head and smiled. "Why are you breaking my balls?"

Tony chuckled, then Pete laughed and leaned back. "OK," Pete said, "You're right. You haven't done anything. We've just had some bad luck with people who ask a lot of questions about our business. You seem like a nice guy, but the fact remains, we don't want any photos of our boat published in the magazine, online, or anywhere else for that matter."

"OK," I said. "I can appreciate that. No more talking about photos or boats." I noticed Lacy waiting at the bar. "When Lacy gets back over here, we'll drink to it. Like I said, the beers are on me until that hundred runs out. With the price of beer in Alaska, it shouldn't take very long." Pete and Tony nodded in agreement.

I didn't want to discuss *my* business either so I'd planned for some friction, or something that might show me the Westbrook's pecking order. I also wanted to steer the conversation away from photography. Pete might have been one of the owners of the *Westward Ho*, but I was pretty sure he wasn't in charge of the family business. He kept saying "we" too much.

By the time Lacy got to the booth, the tension was gone, and Pete and I were talking about some good fishing spots around the island. Tony got up, grabbed his beer, and walked to the other side of the room to talk to someone else.

Lacy stood at the end of the booth and spoke to Pete. "Randy said he needs to find another dart player for Saturday night's tournament. Can you make it?"

"Nope," Pete said. "I've got plans."

"Without you or Jerry, he doesn't have a fourth player who's any good." She looked at me. "It's a yearly tournament against *The Standing Bear Pub*. Whiskey River will probably lose, so that's why nobody wants to play. Oh, and Randy said he's closing the kitchen in a few minutes. Do you guys want anything?"

"Something smells good," I said. "Is that barbecue?"

"That's the wings," Lacy said. "They're super good. You want an order?"

"Let's get a couple of orders," I said. Pete nodded.

"OK," Lacy said, "two orders of barbecued wings."

"We might as well get a few more beers while you're up," Pete said.

Lacy sighed. "Are you going to give me a tip later."

"Take it out of the hundred," Pete said then laughed.

Lacy put her hands on her hips. "So, I guess the bitch gets to serve everybody now that we're all friends, is that it?"

Pete grabbed his beer and took a drink. "At least until that hundred runs out."

SEVENTEEN

The curtain rods in Room 112 at the Buskin Hotel were poorly installed and no matter how much I tried to shut the drapes, they wouldn't close all the way. In the morning, a beam of sunlight came through the gap and shined directly onto my face. I was still tired and had to squint to read the red digital numbers on the alarm clock—8:23. "Crap!"

After I rolled to the edge of the bed, I picked up my phone. *Good*, I thought, I typed in my notes. It wasn't just a dream. I relaxed and sat there for a moment, trying to collect my thoughts. Pete hadn't provided me very much information at the Whiskey River, but I was confident he believed my cover story. He probably knew where Kyle was staying and I imagined the oldest brother, Jason, did too. Their compound on Uyak Bay was an obvious place to start looking, but I knew it would take some time for me to figure out a plan on how to get out there without them knowing about it.

I made a few calls, one to *Island Tours*, a company that rented floatplanes, and the other calls were to try to find a place that rented small boats, or skiffs, on Uyak Bay.

For PFTs, tracking humans has very little to do with muddy footprints, broken branches on the side of a trail, or whatever else some Hollywood writer's imagination comes up with. No, finding a target is all about getting information from people who might have had contact with them. People fall into habits, especially after a long time, and my job was to figure out Kyle Westbrook's habits.

One of my habits was to pick up my phone and check my messages. I scrolled through them but didn't feel like reading any, so I tapped the phone icon and hit send.

"Hey," Chris answered. "How are things going?"

"I got your text," I rasped, then I cleared my throat.

"Are you just getting out of bed?" she asked.

"Still lying down."

"That's not like you."

"I know! I usually don't wake up so late, but when was the last time I stayed out past midnight?"

"I'd guess it's been ten years," she said. "How did it go last night? Did you get any other good intel after your last text?"

"I don't know. Pete didn't say much about his family, but Lacy was chatty. Did you find out who Tony Lee is?"

"His rap sheet didn't have much," Chris noted, "just two third-degree assaults. He was charged with domestic abuse a couple of years ago, but the case was dropped." She paused. "Nothing's been recorded since then. He's worked for Westbrook Holdings, on and off, for about eight years."

"No surprise there," I said. "He seemed loyal to Pete, but it could be just a local thing. Tony Lee had some other friends at the saloon, but I didn't see anybody else who acted like they were on the Westbrook's payroll."

"Did you find out how many employees they have?" Chris asked.

"Skip Thorson told me ten to twelve, but less now until crab season starts back up. Let's assume Kyle is using a different name if he's working with his brothers. I can't imagine an entire crew keeping quiet if they knew he was on the island, especially if he has a reputation of being a murderer. Can you get me a full list of their employees from the agency? I need to be at the docks on Sunday when the barge arrives. If Kyle's not with Jason, I need the list so I can start checking off names."

"I already asked," Chris said. "They told me they're working on it."

"Working on it?"

"You need to be careful, Brad, because things have changed. They sent me a disclosure notification with over fifty pages of privacy information, and they made me sign it. They're trying to cover their asses in case something goes wrong."

"I need information, Chris. I can't start waving around Kyle's photo to everyone in town. I'll be exposed, and we'll lose him. Or even worse, I'll be the one who gets lost! Kyle Westbrook knows how to get around without being detected. He's been a ghost for eighteen years, and if he's hiding in plain sight, in a place where he grew up, that takes some skill. I think the reason the agency is paying us so much is because they didn't want to risk losing any more agents. Kyle has found a way to stay in the shadows for a long time. The DEA wants their drug bust, and the agency wants their killer, and I'm still not sure which one is more important to whoever's in charge."

"So, what's the plan? Offense or defense?"

"I don't know. Probably a little bit of both. What's the status of the tracking devices?"

"The signal is working on the first three chips," Chris said. "I've got your Jeep listed as number one, the *Westward Ho* as number two, and Lacy Miller's Forrester as number three. Is that right?"

"Yeah, I didn't have a chance to put one on Pete's vehicle. He told me Tony Lee gave him a ride."

"Where did you stick the one on Lacy's car?"

"I tossed it in her driver's side door console last night."

"How did you pull that off?"

"I was being a gentleman," I said. "You'd be proud."

"You opened the door for her, didn't you?" Chris asked. "You're trying to squeeze her, aren't you?"

Chris was right, I was flirting with Lacy to get information. Back in the day, the agency had nicknamed the tactic the "future squeeze play". It worked until it didn't and often ended with an agent establishing a "current squeeze play," which always ended in disaster.

"She might be the one who leads us to Kyle Westbrook. I'm just being nice to her."

"Bullshit!" Chris exclaimed. "I didn't sign up for this project so you could squeeze every girl who knew the Westbrook family."

"You worry too much."

"Don't give me that, Brad. She's not the target! You better remember that."

I paused, wanting to change the subject. "Oh, that reminds me, I got roped into playing in a dart tournament on Saturday."

"Darts?" Chris asked.

"Yeah, Pete Westbrook is pretty good at darts, but he told the owner of the saloon he couldn't make it. We ended up playing a few games and I beat him, so they signed me up. I'm officially competing for the

Whiskey River Saloon in the annual Monie Marie Dart Tournament."

"Maybe all the time you spent tossing darts in your shop will finally pay off. What, or who is Monie Marie?"

"I have no idea. I guess I'll find out Saturday. It's not a money tournament. Randy, the manager of the saloon, said something about a trophy, or a keepsake, or something like that."

Chris seemed irritated. "You do realize this isn't a vacation?"

"Hey, I figured what the hell. There will be people there who know the Westbrooks. I don't know. Maybe it was a bad idea."

"Stick to the script," Chris said. "You know the drill. Locate Kyle Westbrook, place those tracking devices, then get the hell off that island. Let the agency take care of the rest."

"You sound upset."

"This isn't a game, Brad. Kyle Westbrook has probably killed three people already, maybe more. He has his brothers looking out for him, along with who knows how many people who work for the family. It's a big island, but there's not very many people who live there. By the hits we're getting on the website, people have been looking you up. I don't like it."

"Don't worry," I said. "I have everything under control."

"That's what worries me. You're being too arrogant."

I sat up straight. "Listen, Chris, I can't just waltz over to Uyak Bay and start looking for Kyle Westbrook. I'll need to rely on my cover more than I'd like to, but we knew that going in. We don't even know if Kyle is at the lodge, or anywhere on Kodiak for that matter. If he's living on the compound, we'll find him. If he's with his brother, Jason, on the barge, we'll know Sunday morning. I need to be there with a good story when it comes into port. I'm working on it, trust me."

"I know you're working hard, but can't you ever just stay under the radar? Do you have to become everybody's best friend the first day you meet them?"

"Chris, I still need to find a way to get onto the Westbrook's property. At some point, I'll probably need to get dropped off by a helicopter or floatplane and hike in. Going straight to the property by boat will be risky. There aren't any roads over there. Pete and I got along last night, but with his drug business, he'll be suspicious of everyone. I don't see him sending me an invitation."

Chris paused. "How about your squeeze, Lacy. She knows the family?"

I chuckled. "You're jealous! I told you, there's nothing to worry about. She does have a connection to them, and she knows something about Kyle too. I can smell it. She'll be at the dart tournament Saturday night so maybe I'll find out more about her relationship with the family."

"Just don't be smelling her! And don't drink too much on Saturday."

"Don't worry!"

"That's my job," Chris said. "I get paid to worry, and I know you too well. By the way, what's Island Tours? A charge came through from them just now."

"I scheduled a flight from Kodiak to Uyak Bay at ten. I'm renting a skiff too, so I'll be able to take some photos of that section of the island from the water. I don't plan to get very close to the Westbrook's property on this trip, but I'd like to see the area. Basically, I just need to get over there and get my bearings to see what the ridge looks like and if I can hike over it. From the satellite images there's no good access except from the water. If I come down that inlet by boat, they'll see me coming the whole way, but they wouldn't expect anyone to get dropped off by a helicopter or floatplane and hike over the ridge."

I walked toward the bathroom. "Oh, before I forget, didn't we pack my SAT phone in the camera bag? I need that today."

"Yeah, why?"

"It isn't there. I looked all over for it. It isn't in the Jeep either."

Chris was concerned. "Hang on, let me get a locate on it. I'll call you back."

"OK."

A few minutes went by before Chris called back. "You're not going to like this," she said. "Your SAT phone is in Anchorage."

EIGHTEEN

I made my way down the long hallway of the Buskin Hotel with only one thing on my mind: breakfast. As I walked past an open set of double doors which led to the lobby, a familiar face spotted me.

"There he is!" Lacy hollered, as she leaned against the front counter. Sheryl, the manager, smiled from behind the registration desk like the two of them had been waiting for me all morning. I waved but didn't say anything, so Lacy walked over to where I stood. She smiled like she'd just won a bet.

"Hey Lacy," I said. "What brings you to the Buskin?"

"I told you yesterday, Sheryl's a friend of mine." She glanced back at the manager who smiled again. "I hear you booked a flight today."

"I forget just how small Kodiak is," I said. "Yeah, I'm planning to get some photos on the northwest side of the island. Pete said *Island Tours* was a good outfit with some of the best pilots, so I called them this morning."

"Want some company?" she asked.

"I like to work alone," I said, "but thanks for the offer."

Lacy blocked me from going through the doorway to the breakfast area and put her hands on her hips. "I know you're renting a skiff from Walt's Bear Camp," she said. "I already told you, that's close to where I grew up. I know that area like the back of my hand."

I nodded. I knew where the conversation was heading.

"I took the day off, so I can run the skiff and you can take your photos," she said. "I'll take you places you'd never be able to go if you tried to manage the boat and camera all by yourself." She grinned.

I knew it could be a good opportunity. Heck, she might even be able to dock the boat on the Westbrook's compound. She seemed willing, maybe even too willing.

"OK," I said, "but no smoking on the boat."

"Shit, Walt won't care. He's been renting those skiffs out for years. I'll bet the number five boat still leaks."

"Number five boat?"

She laughed. "Yeah, Walt numbered his boats one through five instead of naming them. He only has four rental boats, though, because he doesn't have a number four boat. He says the number four is bad luck."

"That's not very reassuring," I said. "I called around. Walt's Bear Camp was the only place I could find that rented boats, but I don't want one that leaks."

"It doesn't leak that much; besides, there are three other boats to choose from. You should have asked me where to rent one." She paused. "Walt's is probably the best place, though, if you want to stay in Uyak Bay."

"Next time, I'll ask you for sure. I was just following up on something Pete told me, that hunters, photographers, and wildlife viewers travel to Uyak Bay all the time. I figured that was a good place to start taking photos. I asked him, but he didn't seem very interested in talking to me about what the scenery was like near his place."

"Pete's OK," she said. "The Westbrooks don't like people who ask a lot of questions. They're just private, that's all."

"How many Westbrooks are there?"

"Well, three," she said, then she stammered, "but…but one of the brothers moved away a long time ago, so it's just Pete and Jason now." She paused. "When their parents died, the boys took over the lodge, but they decided to close it when Kyle, the other brother, left. Now, Jason runs their transport business between Kodiak and Anchorage, and they have the *Westward Ho*, too. Pete captains the *Ho*."

I smiled. "I guess I shouldn't ask you where their lodge is located. Pete might get mad at you."

"It's no secret," she said. "It's actually only a couple of miles from Walt's place."

"What does the other brother do? You said Kyle, right?"

"Like I said, he moved away. Why do you care?"

The tone of her voice changed abruptly, and I didn't want to lose Lacy as a source. "I don't really care about the Westbrooks," I said. "I'm just impressed by how many people you know and your knowledge about what's happening on the island."

She smiled. "Well, I do know a lot of people. I've lived on the island my whole life, and everybody comes into the office to get their permits and pay their fees."

"Do you like working there?"

"Yeah. Curtis is OK, but he probably won't stick around. None of the harbormasters stay for very long. I think it's because we get so busy, and the job is stressful. They don't get paid very much, either."

"I'm happy about the weather today," I said, changing the subject.

"Don't get too excited," she said. "The weather around Uyak Bay can be completely different than here. It's supposed to be nice, though, but the weather on Kodiak can change fast."

"I wanted to ask you, how many of those hunting and fishing lodges are located over there?"

"Quite a few, why?"

"It could be a great photo spread, an old hunting and fishing lodge on Uyak Bay."

She answered before I had the chance to ask.

"No, we are NOT taking the skiff anywhere near the Westbrook's lodge," she said. "You know how Pete is, and Jason is even worse. They like their privacy. We don't want to be around that area anyway. We can cruise up the shoreline to the north and the east. We'll get plenty of good photo opportunities and there are quite a few lodges up there, too.

It was already "we," I thought. "Is there any cell reception around there?" I asked.

"GCI has reception if you're close to the Larsen Bay Cannery, but none of the other carriers have service in that area. If you want some photos of the cannery, we could go there, but there's not much else to look at. I think we should stay in Uyak Bay and maybe even Spiridon Bay. You won't have any reception there. Do you have GCI?"

"No."

"It won't matter then," she said. "You won't be able to use your phone except for the GPS."

"Do Walt's boats have radios?"

Lacy laughed. "Are you scared to be alone with me?"

I smiled. "No, but you just told me one of the boats has a leak and there's no cell reception. That's not very reassuring."

She laughed. "I'm sure we can still make it to shore, even if we get a leaky boat."

"Then we'll get mauled by a giant bear, I suppose."

"Don't worry, the bears won't bother you unless you're being stupid," she said. "Hopefully we'll see a few of them. It's late in the season, but I know some places that aren't too far away. Maybe we'll get lucky." She grinned.

I chuckled, "I guess I feel lucky already."

"Well, aren't you something," she said. "Is your headache gone from last night?"

"Yeah, I feel fine now." I looked toward the breakfast area where the smell of bacon was drawing me in. "Maybe I just needed some sleep, and something to eat."

"Well, maybe I'm the one who should feel lucky." She smiled.

OK, I thought, Lacy was obviously getting more comfortable. "Do you want a waffle?" I asked. "The hotel has whipped butter and real maple syrup, but you probably knew that already."

"Nah," Lacy said, "you go ahead. I'll just have coffee. We can sit down, and you can tell me more about yourself."

***

After breakfast, Lacy waited in the lobby while I went back to my room. I had one large bag filled with a camera, some lenses, and other photography equipment. Another bag had boots and rain gear, and I had a small suitcase filled with extra clothing. The only thing I was missing was my SAT phone. I called Chris.

"First of all," Chris said, "Just so you know, I've been instructed to address Cassandra Carmichael as *Special Agent Carmichael* or *Chief Carmichael*. Why did you tell me she liked to be called *Cass*?"

"Really? Is that right? I don't know. Maybe she just likes me more."

"That's not the impression I got."

"OK," I said. "From now on, I'll start calling her *Chief* too. I don't want you to get jealous again."

"I'm not jealous!" Chris exclaimed. "Don't be such an ass!"

"What about my SAT phone? Did she say anything?"

"No, Brad, someone named "Driver" called me back and told me they had a reason for not allowing you to take the satellite phone to Kodiak."

"That's a bunch of crap," I said. "She told me she was checking the batteries. How am I supposed to maintain contact with you when I'm on the other side of the island?"

"Maybe that's why they took it. They don't want you over there."

"Did Driver give you a reason?"

"No. He said it was something we didn't need to know."

I had to think for a moment. Not having communication was something I could handle, but I didn't like being lied to, especially by someone who was supposed to be on my side.

"What about InReach?"

"It might take a few days to get you one, but I'll order it."

The more I thought about the chief lying to me, the angrier I got.

"Ask Special Agent Carmichael, or better yet TELL HER, to have Pilot Bob meet me at Trident Basin at seven o'clock on Sunday night! I should be ready to fly to Uyak Bay by then. And tell her I'll need him until Monday morning! If Kyle's at the lodge, we'll get this thing finished. If he isn't staying with his brothers, we might need to start from scratch!"

"Don't blow a gasket," Chris said. "Try to stay focused. You've worked without a SAT phone before. Are you taking a gun with you today?"

"No," I said, "and Lacy's going with me. She said she grew up on that side of the island, so she took the day off to give me a tour."

Chris didn't say anything at first, so I waited for it.

"Well, isn't that nice of her."

NINETEEN

I was still angry about Chief Carmichael taking my SAT phone when I met Lacy in the lobby.

"What happened? she asked. "Did your dog die?"

"Jenny's fine," I said, "but a certain lady friend of mine lied to me, so excuse me for being a little moody."

I was telling the truth— except for the friend part.

"I don't understand why people feel the need to lie," she said, "especially when they don't need to. She doesn't deserve you."

Lacy didn't seem upset about having to console me. "I'll get over it," I said. "I won't let it ruin our day." She smiled—more than she should have.

***

I put my bags into Lacy's Subaru, and she drove us to Trident Basin, a patch of water on the opposite side of Near Island, close to the harbor where floatplanes take off and land. We strolled a short distance from where we parked to a concrete boardwalk where three metal ramps descended onto three wooden docks that had been set up for the planes.

Eighteen planes could be docked there, but there were only eight in the water. I didn't see any sign saying *Island Tours*, but Lacy didn't hesitate as she walked toward the center ramp.

"Island Tours own the black and yellow planes," she said.

Two single-engine De Havilland Beaver DHC-2 aircraft, painted yellow with a black horizontal stripe, were below us. Out of the eight floatplanes, only two of the aircraft were painted yellow and black, and they were both using the center dock, so I followed Lacy as we made our way down the ramp.

"Interesting color choice," I said.

Lacy laughed. "We call them the bumble bees," she said. "You can see and hear them coming from a mile away."

I shook my head and smiled. It didn't matter if we were in a bumble bee plane or not. When I was with Lacy, I was exposed. Hiding in plain sight might be a great way to work undercover but knowing it and doing it are two different things. Being exposed, even with a good cover story, goes against every instinct an agent might have. And lying? That's really what undercover work is all about.

My plan had been to follow Lacy's lead for a couple of hours, then somehow get close enough to the Westbrook compound to see the ridge that surrounded it. But just like being in the bumble bee plane, I knew that whatever we did and wherever we went, we'd be seen coming from a mile away. Lacy would make sure of it. I had hoped having her with me for the afternoon would help me gather more information about Kyle Westbrook and his family, but as we boarded the floatplane, I wasn't so sure. Maybe she and the Westbrooks would gather more information about me.

"Isn't Jim going to take us up," Lacy said to the pilot, a woman named Hannah Jones, who was probably in her early thirties. She had short auburn hair and a cute smile that made her look younger. She wore a leather flight jacket and blue jeans and seemed ready to go.

"Jim's flying for the Westbrooks today because their floatplane has some fuel line issues," Hannah said. She showed Lacy and me where to get our headsets. Then she did her final checks outside the aircraft as we loaded my gear and climbed inside.

"Jim's a better pilot," Lacy told me, loud enough for Hannah to hear. "Instead, we get Hannah Banana." She paused. "Boooring."

"As long as we don't crash," I said, "I'll be happy." Hannah chuckled.

Lacy shrugged. "Take the front seat," she insisted. "You'll have a better view."

***

The distance from Kodiak City to Walt's Bear Camp on Uyak Bay was about fifty miles, but it might as well have been fifty thousand miles for anybody who didn't have a floatplane, helicopter, or a boat. The scenery changed dramatically as we made our way west, then north, toward Uyak Bay.

Aside from the thick vegetation and deciduous trees in the lowlands, patches of brush covered most of the landscape below the rocky mountain tops. It didn't look like there were too many trails on the ridges, but the brush and grass thinned out at the higher elevations, and the mountain peaks were covered in snow. If I needed to hike along the lower ridgeline, the steep slopes would be the hardest to navigate.

As we approached Walt's Bear Camp, Hannah circled around twice before she told Lacy and me to prepare for landing. We drifted down and hit the water smoothly before the floats took over and slowed us down quickly, then we became more of a boat instead of a plane. I'd been a passenger on many floatplanes, and I could tell Hannah was a good pilot just by the landing.

At first, the camp looked deserted. Two small cabins stood out, situated between clusters of trees which had been trimmed down to allow for a better view of the bay. The cabins sat on a narrow plateau, and several outbuildings were above the main lodge, which reminded me of an old general store. A large sign saying, "Walt's Bear Camp" was perched on the roof with a smaller one underneath it that read, "Lodging, Boat Rentals, Food, Beer, Wine, and Adventure!"

As we approached the floatplane dock, a man who looked Asian, probably in his mid-fifties, came down the path from the lodge. He passed by a larger set of wooden docks where four skiffs were tied down.

"There's Walt," Lacy said.

I looked up and down the shoreline and couldn't see any other lodges or residences in either direction. The bay seemed deserted with no boats in sight.

"It really is remote on this side of the island," I noted.

Lacy smiled. "It gets busier in the summer," she said, "but there are still hunters and fishermen around this time of the year."

"Does anybody come here during the winter?"

Lacy pointed toward the bear camp. "Yeah, but Walt has a place in Victoria where he goes every year. He usually leaves by mid-September, but his daughter surprised him and is coming to visit next week. I'm sure he's happy to get your business because I don't think he has anybody else booked this week."

Walt came to the edge of the dock, smiled at us, and helped tie down the plane to secure it before we got out.

"Hey Walt!" Lacy yelled over the plane's engine, before Hannah shut it down.

"Hey Lacy," he said, then looked at me. "Brad Kelso, right?"

"Yes, and you must be Walt."

We all got out and stood on the dock. Lacy and Hannah gave Walt a hug.

"The boat is all ready for you. Number one skiff. Are you going out too?" he asked Hannah

"I'm staying here," she said. "Is the kitchen open?"

"Sure, we'll find something," Walt said.

Hannah looked at Lacy and me. "Four hours, right?"

I looked at my phone, which had no bars, but the time showed 10:45. "How about we plan to go back at three?"

"You're paying for it," Hannah said, "but I need to leave by five at the latest." She grinned "Don't get mauled."

I smiled. She had a point, but I wasn't worried about the bears.

Hannah left and went inside the lodge. I took a few photos of Walt outside the bear camp while Lacy moved my gear from the floatplane to the skiff. Maybe having her along wasn't such a bad idea. The only problem, of course, was that she thought I was a professional photographer, and professional photographers, when they're on assignment, probably spend most of their time taking photos.

I didn't mind a few hours behind the camera, but I started to worry about my cover. Would I need to carry my gear around the entire day just to convince Lacy that photography is what I did for a living? Whenever I said I worked in construction, it seemed more natural. Spending nine or ten hours a day building decks, porches, and she-sheds was business as usual for me. But photography? My goal for the day had been to see the ridge and try to figure out a way to get to the Westbrook's lodge without being seen. I had no desire to spend the afternoon changing lenses or worrying about filters and lighting. I needed a plan.

Lacy moved in and out of the skiff like she'd taken them out her whole life. Maybe she had. Hannah came back outside, and I spent a few more minutes taking photos of her near the floatplane, but after that I was ready to roll.

"Do you need any help?" I asked Lacy.

"No," she said. "I think we're ready. I just need to get my rifle out of the plane, and I don't want anybody else handling my rifle."

"Since I'll be unarmed, will you protect me if we get attacked?" I asked.

She walked over and grabbed her Remington from the back seat of the plane. Then she smiled.

"I don't need to outrun any bears. I just need to outrun you." She smiled.

"I'm faster than I look," I said.

Lacy tilted her head and raised her eyebrows like she didn't believe me.

"On second thought," I said, "maybe I'll just stay in the boat."

"Orcas need to eat, too," she said, "but for tourists, we like to call them *killer whales*."

"I think we need a bigger boat."

"Don't worry," she laughed, "you'll be safe with me."

"Famous last words."

We started out slowly, then Lacy hit the throttle after we got a few hundred feet from the docks. We took off, and I held on tight with each hand, grasping the metal front and side rails for stability. The bow raised up slightly and a salty mist shot in the air as we roared over the water as fast as the skiff would go. We moved with enough speed to pull a water skier, but not quite fast enough to catch any air when we hit the waves.

Lacy had a smile on her face, and I couldn't help but smile, too. I looked at her closer. As she steered the boat near the shoreline, her wind-blown hair flowed straight back. When she closed her eyes, she reminded me of Chris a decade earlier. She seemed more attractive to me when she wasn't talking. The two women were so different yet seeing the look of pure joy on Lacy's face in such a pristine setting was intoxicating.

I grabbed my camera without even thinking about it. "Do you mind?" I asked her.

She looked at me. "What!?" she hollered.

We had to yell over the sound of the wind and the motor to hear each other. "Can I take some photos of you!?"

She smiled and yelled back. "Sure!"

She looked at me and posed. The moment was gone. I shouldn't have said anything. I should have just taken the photo. I guess a real photographer would have just captured the moment digitally, that split second of an emotion that only a person who's paying attention can see or feel. I wrapped the camera's strap around my neck. Next time, I'd remember.

When I originally found out about the Westbrook's lodge, I spent as much time as I could studying maps of Kodiak, especially the ones that showed Uyak Bay.

Now that I was there, I realized the area was even more vast than I'd imagined. The bay is around five miles wide at its mouth and narrows to about a mile wide for most of the thirty-some miles it runs inland. It nearly splits the island in two. The mountains jet up from its shores to a height of up to four thousand feet. From the water, the snow-capped peaks looked even taller.

Luckily, the day turned out to be mostly sunny because I was able to clearly see what the mountains, ridges, and most of the vegetation looked like. There was more of a chill in the air than the day before, probably because of the windy conditions on the water.

Lacy was right when she said she knew where she was going. She would pull the throttle back in some spots, which was a great indicator for me that I needed to take some photos. She must have figured I wanted wildlife shots because anytime we saw an interesting bird or other animal she'd slow down and try to line me up for the best angle. I must admit, she knew how to handle the skiff.

"Oooh, right there," I'd say. Then I'd snap off ten quick ones. "OK, got it." That was her cue to throttle-up again. We were a well-oiled machine after about an hour on the water.

Without saying anything, Lacy guided the skiff toward a small inlet where a creek, about twenty feet wide, was running into the bay. She pointed to where we were going. I think both of us were tired of yelling over the motor, so I just nodded my approval. I'm not sure if it made any difference, but I felt like my nod sealed the deal.

As we got closer to shore, she turned the skiff directly toward a small rocky beach area, about twenty feet from the mouth of the creek. Thick grass littered most of the shoreline, and the area where we were headed was no different. I nearly fell over when I stood up, so I bent down and grabbed a rope which had been attached to a cleat at the front of the skiff. The boat skidded up onto the rocks and I jumped out with the rope in my hand like the two of us had been practicing it for days. Lacy wasn't as excited as I was about me staying dry during our successful landing. I guess she expected it.

"Tie us off!" she yelled, like I was being too slow. She pointed toward a large fallen tree that had somehow washed ashore, its roots clean, but still intact. It had probably only been there since the last storm.

I wrapped the rope around one of the tree's large roots, tied it off, clapped once and showed her my hands like I'd just roped a steer. I looked back at her, but she was too busy raising up the motor to have noticed. My rodeo days were over before they began.

"What now?" I asked.

She looked at me like my IQ had dropped thirty points in a matter of minutes. Then she pointed toward my bags.

"Are you forgetting something?"

Crap! She was right. I was a photographer. I nearly panicked, but then I realized my camera was still wrapped around my neck. I held it up. "I'm only taking this one," I said. "I'll come back if I have to, but I might need to outrun you."

I was relieved because she just laughed. Then she grabbed her gun, a canister of bear spray, and put some snacks and two fitness drinks into a small backpack.

"I'll pack it in, but you're packing it out," she said.

Packing, I thought. We hadn't discussed "packing it in." I was glad, though, because I figured I'd be hiking over a ridge at some point in the next few days and I needed the workout. If I was a gentleman, I would have grabbed the backpack and carried it both ways. I smiled. Maybe I was *just* a photographer.

We walked toward the creek, then headed upstream. The only thing I was thinking about was how to get a better view of the Westbrook's inlet, which was now about four miles from our location.

I should have paid more attention to what we were doing.

TWENTY

When the grass and brush were too thick along the banks, Lacy and I just walked upstream through the shallow water of the creek. Our heavy socks and rubber boots provided plenty of protection from the frigid glacial runoff, but my pants were still damp in spots from the waist down. It had been slow trekking, but we'd already seen two bald eagles, several black-tailed deer, and a river otter in the first thirty minutes, and some late-season salmon were running up the stream or resting in the deeper pools.

A variety of birds were along the banks, and they'd squawk and crow when one of them had a fish, or a worm, or whatever else they were fighting over.

Lacy stayed a short distance behind me and tried not to scare off the wildlife as I "worked." The whole thing was a sham, but I had taken hundreds of photos, and I thought a few of the shots might even be OK; probably not the quality of a decent wildlife photographer, but maybe there'd be one or two of them Chris could photoshop and upload to my online profile.

I had been meandering along, trying to plan out the next few days on the island. It was only Thursday. If I needed to hike over the ridge to get to the Westbrook's property, timing would be critical. I had been trained to spot opportunities when they presented themselves, and for me that opportunity was looking more and more likely to be Sunday night.

Jason was scheduled to arrive on the barge from Anchorage Sunday morning, and while Pete and I were playing darts, he told Lacy that he planned to fly back to the compound Saturday afternoon. I guessed if Kyle was living on Kodiak, he'd be at the lodge Sunday, too. The barge, the *Westward Ho*, and even their floatplane would all be sitting idle for a few days. Where else would he be?

Lacy and I kept up our pace through a section of water where it was a little deeper, and I was trying to stay as dry as I could without having to climb up onto the bank. I was looking down, not paying much attention to anything else. The birds were making noise again as I walked around a sharp bend. The stream widened out again, and the water became shallower.

My mind drifted. I daydreamed about getting back to Walt's, and maybe even sitting down and having some hot chocolate on the lodge's front porch. Somewhere where I wouldn't have to wade through water or listen to the birds. Just a little peace and quiet before we flew back to town. That's when I heard Lacy whisper loudly from about sixty feet behind me.

"Brad!"

I'm not sure what decibel level would be considered *loud* as far as whispers go, but if there was a scale from one to ten, with one being a soft whisper like someone telling their best friend a secret in a quiet room, and a ten being a louder whisper, like parents trying to calm down their rowdy kids in a bouncy house, Lacy's whisper would have pegged the needle at around fifteen.

Loud whispers in that range are never something you want to hear from someone, especially from sixty feet away. Even at close range, like trying to wake up someone in church, with let's say a two, loud whispers can lead to embarrassing or awkward moments, at best.

In the case of Lacy's loud whisper, over the sound of the babbling creek, from sixty feet away, *best* is certainly not the term I would have used to describe the situation that had presented itself.

It shouldn't have been a surprise. After all, we were trudging through the water and walking on game trails for one reason: to spot a bear. So, when Lacy whispered loudly at me, I naturally looked up, and even though I had been prepared for it, I was startled by what I saw.

At that point, I didn't know how many bears surrounded me, because five of them took up the entire limits of my peripheral vision and I didn't want to move my head to see if there were any more. I didn't even know bears liked to hang out together in groups like that, and the five brown bears I saw were of varying degrees of size and color. They surrounded me on three sides.

One of the cubs was on the rocks to my left, and it had a blond streak of fur around its neck. The other cub was slightly smaller and was almost glued to what looked like their mother.

Another medium sized one, with a more reddish coat, maybe close to 250 pounds, was farther upstream and not paying attention to the evolving situation. Judging from its lack of interest, it must have been the teenager. And I guess the one that had given me the most pause, at first, was the one that was closest to me, on my right.

The male bear, or boar, had a thick dark brown coat, and he was lying on his stomach on a patch of round river rocks less than fifteen feet from me. We got a really good look at each other. His huge paws, about twice the size of my skull, were stretched out in front of him and he looked at me almost like he was amused by the fact that I had somehow gotten lost and found myself in the wrong part of town. I know it's ridiculous, but I swear he smiled at me.

I looked back at Lacy, who was still sixty feet behind me, and she waved for me to come back toward her. I don't know if she thought I was happy about my current surroundings, or if I would have some involuntary reaction, being a photographer, and start snapping off photos, but she seemed even more worried about my situation, at least at that moment, than me. The big bear just laid there, fat and happy, probably having had his fill of salmon before I got there. At least that's what I had hoped. I thought if I didn't startle him, maybe he'd let me walk back downstream from where I came without ripping my throat out, which he could have certainly accomplished in seconds.

Lacy had her rifle pointed in the right direction, but the bear controlled the situation. He must have weighed a thousand pounds, probably more, but I've never been good at guessing weight and I didn't want to stare at him too long. If I stayed where I was, he might have looked at me as some type of room service, or food delivery meal, that he'd forgotten he'd ordered.

Since papa bear didn't budge, I slowly backed up and tried not to move my arms, turn around, or make any other sudden gestures. They must have seen me coming up the creek for a while, so I knew they didn't perceive me as a threat. Heck, I didn't perceive me as a threat. I looked back at Lacy again, and she still had her rifle up, but as I moved toward her, she seemed less worried than she had been at first.

After I was about thirty feet away from the large bear, I finally turned away from him. That's when the cub with the blond streak around its neck charged at me.

TWENTY-ONE

I had done some research on Kodiak bears, and over the years I'd seen plenty of black bears in the wild. I even fired my rifle into the air to scare off an angry grizzly once, a couple of hours north of Anchorage, near the Talkeetna River. But I'd never been charged by a bear, and even though the cub's charge was false, fast, and not very aggressive, I'd heard about situations involving bears that had turned from bad to worse.

A "false" charge, or a "bluff," is common for bears to do in the wild, so it probably wasn't unusual given the fact that I had been so close to them. The brown bear population on the island is around three thousand five hundred, which is roughly two bears for every three-square miles of land. There was a good chance that these bears had seen humans before.

The false charge was likely the cub just being uncomfortable with the situation. Maybe he had been trying to scare me away. Who knows? He didn't want any part of me. He probably only weighed eighty or ninety pounds, so one on one, I could have put up a good fight. Even if he kept charging, which I knew he wouldn't, he wasn't the bear that concerned me the most. And at that point, the huge male boar next to the stream, still only thirty feet away from me, didn't concern me either. I had heard stories about male bears killing young bears for a variety of reasons, so I knew he probably wouldn't be very protective of the younger cubs. I imagined he'd already had his fill of salmon, so

I assumed he was just lying there, relaxing, and trying to enjoy the show.

The bear that concerned me the most was the female sow. After the cub had made its false charge at me, I locked eyes with the sow from about forty feet away. Some people say bears aren't very smart, but I can testify to the contrary, because without any words whatsoever, that sow and I came to an understanding: I was no longer welcome in the neighborhood.

There were no chases, no more charging, and nothing else needed to be said. All it had taken was one growl from the mother and she had made it clear: If I wanted any part of her cub with the blond streak around its neck, I'd have to go through her.

I turned around, walked away, and never looked back until I reached a safer distance. Then I snapped off a few photos of the bears, mainly for posterity or credibility, because Chris would never have believed me, and I still needed to act like a photographer around Lacy, who was smiling when I finally reached her.

"I should've had one of your cameras," she said.

"And I should've had one of your cans of bear spray," I said, "or five cans."

"I'm a good shot, but my money would've been on the mama," she said. "You didn't take any close-ups of the big guy. I think he was posing for you."

We started walking downstream. "Sometimes I just like to enjoy nature," I said, "without always thinking about work, work, work."

Lacy laughed. "You call that enjoying nature?"

"Yeah," I said, "maybe the word *enjoying* is a stretch. I think I might have peed a little back there."

Lacy laughed. "You almost won the Darwin Award this year."

I shook my head. "That's reassuring."

"You didn't hear me at first. You just kept walking. I thought you were going to bump right into them. Didn't you see all the birds?"

"I did afterward. Do they just hang out near the bears and wait for scraps?"

"Yeah, the bears don't care," she said. "When they're fishing, it's common to see the birds around."

"I think I'm done for the day. Do you mind if we head back to the skiff?" I looked at my phone. "It's almost two o'clock."

"What, no more enjoying nature?"

I smiled. "Did you see how big he was?"

"Twelve, thirteen hundred pounds," she said. "The only time I've ever seen them gathered like that is when they're fishing. It's rare to see a big boar like that around the young ones."

"I wonder if they considered that some form of entertainment," I said.

She smiled. "I know I did. You seem to be calm now, though. Were you scared?"

"I didn't have time to be scared. And I don't think the sow liked me very much."

"Yeah, she didn't care much for your company. But aren't you glad we came?" She chuckled.

I laughed. "I could be in a shopping mall right now taking photos of crying kids and stressed-out parents. I wouldn't have to worry about bears, killer whales, and leaky boats." I paused. "Yeah, I'm glad we came."

***

My cover seemed intact, but the day had been a bust up to that point because I didn't get a chance to see the layout of the Westbrook property, or what kind of access there was from the ridges around their compound. I looked at the terrain near Walt's Bear Camp one more time before we boarded the plane to go back. Since the Westbrook property wasn't very far away, and was on the same side of the bay, I had a thought.

"Hannah, do you mind if we fly low along the coastline of Uyak Bay for a while on our way back? I noticed some interesting geology to the south as we came in and I'd like to see what it looks like from a lower elevation."

"How far south?" she asked.

"Oh, not more than three or four miles."

"Sure."

Lacy chimed in. "We could fly up to Larsen Bay. It's the other direction, but it's not very far from here and I could show you where I grew up."

"How about we save Larsen Bay for the next trip," I said. "We can take more time, and you can give me a tour that doesn't involve me having to change my pants afterward."

"I don't know," she smiled. "Maybe next time you'll forget to bring an extra pair."

***

Hannah did just as I'd asked. She flew the plane low, but made it clear we needed to keep an eye out for any birds along the shoreline.

"Ninety-nine percent of bird strikes are below 2500 feet," she said, "and I don't want to have to replace a windshield, or worse."

The scenery was amazing from that altitude. We were low enough to see the gentle waves reach the rocky shore of Uyak Bay, and above us the shadowy mountains cast a purple haze below the snowy peaks.

As we came upon the Westbrook's inlet, I could feel Lacy watching me.

"That's an interesting place," I said. "Do you know if that lodge rents out rooms, or if it's a private residence?"

Lacy grinned. "That's where the Westbrooks live," she said. "I told you it wasn't very far from Walt's."

The ridges surrounding the Westbrook's compound were about four hundred feet above the waterline. The horseshoe-shaped inlet, more of a small bay or large cove, provided protection on three sides. Geographically, it was one of the most natural strongholds I'd ever seen. Without coming directly toward the Westbrook's property by water, the easiest way to get there, aside from a helicopter, would be by floatplane.

If I didn't want to be seen from the lodge, the plane would have to land in the bay to the north or south. Then I'd need to hike up one of the steep hillsides until I reached the top of the ridge. It wouldn't get any easier after that because there didn't seem to be a level pathway going back down to the Westbrook's lodge.

The hike would be less difficult on a sunny day, but the upper part of the hillside was covered in thick, waist-high brush that would provide little protection from being noticed during the daylight hours. I would be seen coming from a mile away. At least I confirmed that any attempt to get to their property undetected needed to happen at night.

Hiking at night, on unfamiliar terrain, especially with so many crevasses and slopes, wasn't something I looked forward to. Taking off and landing a floatplane at night wasn't the smartest idea either. It could be done, but the risk of hitting an object in the water, or even a small patch of shallow water was something I needed to think about. I doubted if Chief Carmichael or Pilot Bob would take the risk.

The lodge overlooked the compound, maybe sixty or seventy feet above the main dock, which was large enough to hold a commercial fishing boat on one side. Steps led down to a lower level where several smaller boats could be moored on the other.

The Westward Flyer, a thirty-two-foot charter boat, was docked on the lower level. I'd already known about the charter boat, but I hadn't seen it until then.

A separate floatplane dock and ramp led up to a small hangar a short distance from the main dock, and a cabin and a few sheds were on the south side of the property. The old lodge dwarfed the other buildings in size and scope.

I glanced up and down the shoreline and noticed two spots less than a quarter mile away from the inlet, where Pilot Bob could drop me off without being seen by someone near the lodge. I considered taking a few photos, but I didn't want Lacy to tell the brothers about it and I didn't want to seem overly curious to her, either.

I looked closer at the ridgeline surrounding the compound. The vegetation on the slope was thicker in some areas and sparser in others. It was almost bare on the rocky bluffs—just a few patches of grass and smaller brush—but there were knolls, cliffs, and drop-offs, too.

The tree line started about halfway down the ridge, and there were thicker areas of brush which would be difficult to navigate. The deciduous trees covered the lowlands, almost to the water's edge. I didn't say another word as we passed by the inlet, but that twenty second flyby made the entire trip worth the time and trouble.

I felt satisfied with the outing, and everything was calm until we got about a mile past the inlet. A gust of wind blew the aircraft to the side and the sudden shift made me feel unsteady. Then the plane shook and dipped forward. Whoosh! The plane rose back up as Hannah hit the throttle. The engine roared. We angled higher and my back pressed against the seat, my stomach in my throat. The wind blew the plane to the side again. Whoosh! Hannah hit the throttle and climbed one more time before she lowered our ascent and leveled it out. It was over quickly, but I felt like we'd just finished a theme park ride.

"Looks like some turbulence," Hannah said, her voice shaking. "I hope you had enough sightseeing."

"I've had plenty," I said. "Are you OK?"

"Yeah, I'm fine," she said, "but I'm heading up to five thousand feet."

Lacy didn't seem concerned at all. She leaned forward. "I told you…Jim's a better pilot."

TWENTY-TWO

After we landed at Trident Basin, Lacy invited me back to her place for dinner. We picked up egg flower soup, shrimp stir fry, and some lo mein noodles from *Peking Charlie's*, a restaurant near the harbor. I offered to buy, but she put a card and a coupon on the counter and told me I needed to think twice about my line of work, and that maybe I should go back to the construction industry. She tried to say it in a nice way, but it was obvious to her that photography wasn't a profession that suited me.

The owner of the restaurant came over to the counter while the cashier was giving Lacy her receipt.

"Hey Charlie," Lacy said.

"You saw Walt today, didn't you?"

"Yeah, why?"

"Did he mention me or the duck?" Charlie asked.

"Duck? No, what duck?"

Charlie pursed his lips, said something in Chinese, threw up his hands, and left.

Lacy shrugged. "Walt and Charlie are brothers," she said. "They've had this feud going on for years. I don't speak Chinese so it's hard to know what it's about, but I think it has something to do with their stew."

I smiled. "Their stew?"

Lacy laughed. "I don't know. Nobody knows. Look at this." She grabbed a menu and pointed at two of the items:

Charlie's Stew—14.99
Walt's Stew—Not available and never will be

"I'll bet you've never seen that before," she said.

I chuckled. "Nope."

Lacy led me by the hand outside. "Don't ever get into a discussion with them about their stew, especially their brother's stew."

I laughed. "I'll remember that."

I could tell Lacy still believed my cover story—hook, line, and sinker, so whatever concerns the Westbrooks might have had about me hadn't influenced her. Not being suspicious of me was a good sign. To me, it meant she didn't have anything to hide. She knew the Westbrooks, and she might have known where Kyle was staying, but I was confident she hadn't been involved in any illegal activities with them; up until that evening I hadn't been sure.

***

Lacy's apartment was a second story loft, a stone's throw from the ferry terminal, and only a few blocks from the harbormaster's office. The gift shop underneath her place was called *Kodiak's Treasures*, and she used a private entrance in the back alley where two parking spaces were nestled between a brick wall and the staircase that led up to her place.

"Not a bad work commute," I said. "Do you walk?"

She looked at me. "When my car breaks down, I'll walk," she said, "but don't hold your breath." She took a lighter and a pack of cigarettes out of her purse and lit one up before we went up the stairs and inside. "I haven't hiked like that in a while. My legs are sore."

"I'm tired, too," I said, "but I'm even hungrier. Good call on the stir fry and noodles. It smells great."

Her bedroom and bathroom faced the alley, but her apartment had a huge great room toward the front with a row of windows that overlooked a small section of the harbor.

"This used to be Tagura's headquarters," she said. "My dad worked for them before I was born." She pointed toward the harbor. "I don't remember, but my mom tells me they docked their crab boats right over there."

"Tagura?"

"They had a cannery ship and three fishing boats. In the early eighties, crabbing died off around here, so Tagura left Kodiak, and eventually sold off their operations to another company. My parents bought the building from the owner and started the gift shop. My dad worked here in the store, and my mom and I stayed in Larsen Bay where she worked at the cannery."

She took a couple of drags from her cigarette and continued. "My dad and I didn't spend much time together when I was growing up. He tried to be around. He'd fly back and forth when he could get a ride and we'd come here when my mom wasn't working. After I got married, my mom left the cannery and moved here. They were happy, and business was pretty good back then, but it has slowed down over the years. She still owns the gift shop, and now she has a house up on Hillside Drive, about a mile from here."

"How about your dad?"

"He died in 2012. Heart attack. Probably smoked too much." She put out her cigarette in a tray. "I need to quit." She grabbed two plates from a cupboard and some silverware from a drawer.

"Sorry about your dad."

"It's OK. My mom's getting by, and I'm able to help her out with the payments. I wasn't as close to my dad."

"When did you get divorced?"

"Married at eighteen, divorced at thirty," she said. "My ex was ten years older, and I thought he was really something back then." She smiled. "We split up and I moved here after the divorce was final. It's been twelve years. Best thing I ever did. I started working at the harbormaster's office two years later."

"That makes you forty-two, if my math is right."

"Just turned," she said. "I'm no spring chicken, but what I lack in stamina I make up for in experience." She smiled.

"It's been a long day," I said. "I'm exhausted, so let's eat and then you can drive me back to the hotel. I had a good time today. It was fun. It was a good call because I couldn't have done it without you. Thanks for taking time off work."

"Are you sure? You could stay here if you want."

"Not tonight. I'm probably even more tired than you." I smiled. "Aren't you hungry? Let's eat."

***

After Lacy dropped me off at the Buskin, I scrolled through my messages. Don finished the fence, and he was planning to stain it in the morning. Chris was able to get a list of all the employees who worked for Westbrook Holdings and Special Agent Carmichael was upset at me for not getting my flight to Uyak Bay approved by her office. I was glad. There was nothing that couldn't wait.

I took a long, hot shower, brushed my teeth, and silenced my cell phone. I slept for nine straight hours and didn't have one dream.

***

Knock, Knock, Knock. "Housekeeping."

"I'm here!" I yelled, still half asleep. I sat up too quickly and got light-headed for a second. I rubbed my eyes. The clock showed 7:25 am. Crap! I wondered why housekeeping had come so early. I opened the door and looked up and down the hall. Nobody. I chuckled. *I'm here*, I'd said. Nice. I had slept hard, really hard. I needed a few minutes to get my bearings.

I loaded up on bacon and scrambled eggs at the breakfast buffet. The blueberry muffins smelled fresh and tasted even better. I drank two cartons of chocolate milk and ate a banana to finish off what I had loaded onto my two plates. My eyes had been bigger than my stomach. I was stuffed.

I looked outside the window as I sipped my coffee. A steady drizzle fell as low clouds made the start of the morning seem dreary. I had been lucky the day before. The weather was supposed to be nicer than what I was seeing outside the window, but weather forecasts on Kodiak can't be trusted. I sat and read through my texts.

Chris sent a message about not being able to identify three workers that had been on the Westbrook's payroll during the past year. I went back to my room and called her.

"You said you were able to get information on nine of them," I said. "What about the other three?"

"I was able to cross-reference online sources and social media profiles," she said, "but I couldn't find anything about the three names I sent you. They're all men, but they don't have driver's licenses or credit reports. They're all using the same address, though; the PO box that belongs to Westbrook Holdings."

"That's interesting, but I'm not sure what it means. You know as well as I do, some people come up to Alaska to get away from everything."

Chris sighed. "Yeah, I'll keep trying to get more information about those three men." She paused. "Brad, Chief Carmichael filed a complaint about you for flying to Uyak Bay yesterday."

"Yeah, I saw that. Don't worry, I've had complaints filed about me before. I should tell you about the group of bears I saw."

"You mean a sloth?"

"No, bears."

"No," she said. "A group of bears is called a *sloth*. A sloth of bears."

"What's a group of sloths called?"

"I don't know."

I laughed. "Well, remind me to tell you the story about the sloth of bears when I get back."

"So, it sounds like you had a good time. Maybe Lacy and you can follow each other now. Start a snapchat streak."

"Chris…"

"It doesn't matter to me, but you need to stay focused if we're going to find Westbrook."

I had been looking at the three names on the list: Rodney Davis, KJ McCord, and Dan Skoval. I hadn't noticed something when I first looked at the list.

"... KJ McCord!" I exclaimed. "Kyle's on the island!"

"Are you sure?"

"Kyle's middle name is James. Jason's is Jeremiah, and Pete's is Jonathon. JJ, PJ, and KJ. I'll bet McCord is some old family name! See if you can find the McCord link, just to make sure, and then tell Chief Carmichael. She might have more information about KJ McCord. That should make her happy."

"Are you sure you want to tell her?"

"Yes," I said. "We still need her. I have to get her approval to use Pilot Bob on Sunday."

***

I spent most of the morning on the phone or driving between the harbor and Trident Basin, trying to find a place where I could park the Jeep on Sunday. I needed a spot where it wouldn't be seen, and the bright orange Jeep wasn't exactly a vehicle that could be camouflaged well.

There was a gravel parking area, enough for three or four cars, on Near Island, at the far end of a quarry, but it was at least a half mile walk to where the floatplanes were docked. I knew I'd be tired when I got back from Uyak Bay early Monday morning. I probably wouldn't feel like walking another half mile, but I couldn't think of another option.

I needed to talk to Don, so I pulled into the far end of the inner harbor's parking lot and called him.

"Hey Donny," I said. "I got Lefty's message."

"I covered the Walker's grass with plastic," Don said. "They seemed happy this morning and Mrs. Walker told me she liked the cedar color."

"It's not about their side of the fence," I said. "Lefty had you stop staining because their neighbor called them and said some of the spray came through the boards and got onto their plants. Didn't he tell you?"

"I went over there and looked, but it was just some tall grass that got covered."

"Don't worry," I said. "Lefty told me the guy complains about everything."

"Should I go over there? I have the power washer with me."

"No," I said. "We worked out a deal with him. After you finish staining the Walker's fence, go stain the neighbor's side too. It shouldn't take very long. That section of the fence is only about fifty feet long. If the grass is high, just push it down with the tarps. Make sure to always cover the other side of the fence when you spray."

"OK, I will."

***

I leaned forward and looked up at the sky through the windshield of my Jeep. The clouds were light gray, and the drizzle had stopped. I had some time, so I decided to walk over to *Kodiak's Treasures* and check out the gift shop that Lacy's mom owned. A large window display had various trinkets, from rocks to jewelry, and a wide variety of native Alaskan carvings.

"Welcome to Kodiak," Lacy's mom said, after I came through the front door and stood near a long glass counter. I knew it was Lacy's mom because the two of them could have been twins. Her mother might have been older, but she dyed her hair and styled it in a youthful way, and she stayed fit. "Where are you from?" she asked. She was even more chatty than Lacy.

"I'm from Washington State," I replied, "and I'm looking for souvenirs."

"You came to the right place."

"I can see that."

The shop was filled with typical gift shop merchandise, and I was the only customer there. I noticed a large rack near the far end of the glass case, and Lacy's mom followed me from behind the counter. "I need one of these dream catchers," I said.

"Need?"

"I didn't dream at all last night," I said. "Maybe if I buy one of these big ones, I'll get some action."

She laughed. "I don't know about *action*, but they say the dream catchers will catch the bad dreams as they pass by. The good dreams will flow right through."

"Do you have any "dream starters?"

She smiled. "Someone once said that true happiness is to live your life as if it was a dream."

"I might have to sleep on that," I said. She laughed. "I'll take this fancy one and hope for the best. Do you have any calendars?"

"Oh, yes."

We made our way around the shop, and I added items to my shopping spree along the way: An expensive Alutiq carving, a T-shirt, a sweatshirt, a belt buckle, and even some jewelry that I thought Chris would like. Lacy's mom seemed happy with the sale: $598.25. I pulled out the agency's cash from my wallet. "How about an even six hundred?"

"Here, I'll just give you the two smaller calendars you were looking at, too." she said. She placed everything into two bags. "And don't forget to come back to Kodiak!"

"I will," I said. "Orrr, I won't, I guess. Forget that is." We laughed.

***

I called Chris from the parking lot. "Did you find out anything about KJ McCord?" I asked.

"Chief Carmichael doesn't think your theory about KJ makes sense."

"What's that supposed to mean?"

"She thought the Westbrooks wouldn't have a good reason to put Kyle on the payroll. She said she'd check into it, though, but I get the feeling it isn't her top priority."

"Check into it?"

"Yeah. That's what she said."

"Does she still think her agent was killed by Kyle?"

"She didn't say. I'm serious, Brad, they're fighting us on everything. I filled out the digital request forms like they asked me to do, and now they want me to write a daily report on each of our tracking chips. They already have the GPS locations. Why do they need me to write a report?"

"What about Sunday?"

"Chief Carmichael said that since you gave her notice, they'd provide the transportation like you asked, but Sunday evening and Monday morning will be the last time Pilot Bob will fly you anywhere on the island. He won't land the seaplane in Uyak Bay at night, so you need to figure out your timeline for your flights with him in more detail. She said she wants to have you removed from the case by Tuesday."

Tuesday, I thought. "OK, Chris, we can do this. If Kyle is KJ, or if he's using a different name, that means he's either working on the barge or with Pete. I'll be there when the barge gets into port on Sunday, so by Sunday night or Monday morning we should know if he's on the island or not. If he's not here, it won't do us any good to stick around anyway." I paused. "Still, I'd like to know what Chief Carmichael knows."

"I think the DEA has something planned for next week," Chris said. "Probably Wednesday or Thursday. They might be bringing in extra agents for a drug bust, and that could be the reason Chief Carmichael wants you out of there by Tuesday."

"I could care less about the DEAs so-called drug bust. Have they ever seen that compound up close? They could bring in thirty helicopters and two hundred agents and not find Kyle, or even a milligram of fentanyl. The Westbrooks might only have five acres, but they're surrounded by mountains and wildlife refuge, and there are so many waterways and tree covered areas in the lowlands where someone could hide. If helicopters start coming and going from the Coast Guard base, everybody will know about it. Give Kyle a five-minute head start, and they'll never find him. One or two agents might have a chance to catch him, but thirty agents have zero chance."

"Don't worry about the DEA, Brad. The agency is still in control. Pilot Bob will get you there on Sunday evening. Just place the tracking chips, confirm that Kyle's there, and get back. Let the agency deal with him. They can decide what to do about Pete, the DEA, and Chief Carmichael. I hope you're listening to me: Let the agency worry about Kyle!"

"You're preaching to the choir," I said, "but I've got plans for Kyle."

"Brad, you're starting to worry me. Let the pros take care of him."

"Pros? You mean Chief Carmichael and Driver?"

"The agency has more resources on Kodiak than you think."

"What makes you say that?" I asked.

"I told you, I have contacts."

"Don't hold back with me, Chris. If I need to know something, you should tell me."

"From what I hear, the agency won't make a move until after you locate Kyle. Right now, Chief Carmichael is in charge."

"That's what worries me," I said.

"Oh, by the way, a group of sloths is called a snuggle. I looked it up."

"A snuggle? A murder of crows, a gaggle of geese, and a pride of lions. And now a *snuggle* of sloths."

"I've never heard the term used before," Chris said, "but it beats a *parliament* of owls."

"Or a *shitshow* of government agents," I said. Chris laughed.

***

After Chris's call, I thought about taking a break and visiting Lacy at work. I could see the harbormaster's office from where I was parked. The Jeep's engine was running, and I sat there for a few minutes. I wasn't sure. Chris and I seemed to be getting along better, but whenever I had tried to get close to her in the past, she backed off and seemed more distant.

Chris would never have been *the other woman*, no matter how much she had cared about me when I was married. I guess I would have never cheated on my wife either, even though my marriage had been a disaster.

I wondered why Chris never called me after John died. I couldn't blame her. I tried to give her some space. Maybe I just needed to accept the fact that she wasn't interested in being more than just friends. I didn't want to lose that friendship now by making a move that she didn't want.

I left and stopped at Charter Burger. I probably just needed something to eat. My blood sugar gets out of whack when I don't eat, or when I have too much sugar, and then I can't think straight.

I picked up a Brown Bear Burger with curly fries and a Coke and drove back toward the Buskin. I didn't stop at the hotel. I kept going on Rezanof Drive, until I reached a large gravel turnout close to Kodiak airport's runway. I ate my food and watched the planes take off and land. For some reason seeing airplanes defy gravity always helped me think.

Three employees were on the list, but KJ was the only name that stood out to me. Sunday night was a go, and my plan seemed to be in place. I felt confident we'd find Kyle Westbrook, but I had to wait. Funny how plans change.

TWENTY-THREE

A PFTs job is a lot like private eye work, but so much different. A PFT gets paid to locate targets, confirm identities, and then allow others to track their movements. Private eyes bill by the hour and they get paid to share what they find. The real work of a private eye, in most cases, is to document the actions of the targets. Private eyes get hired to find people, too, but they rarely find anyone who doesn't want to be found.

Kyle Westbrook was on Kodiak Island. I was sure of it. Everything and everyone pointed in that direction. The agency thought the same thing, but they needed confirmation and they needed a precise location. Speculation was worthless. When the agency sent in their other resources, they wanted to be sure the target was there. I needed to locate Kyle and I needed to see him with my own eyes.

***

I was at the Buskin Hotel and had just gotten out of the shower when Don called.

"The fence is all finished," he said.

"Lefty texted me earlier," I confirmed. "He and Cheyenne Rose were excited. He said you did a nice job on it. Even his cranky neighbor was happy."

"I had to get another gallon of stain, but you can take it out of my pay if you want."

"Nonsense, Donny, you're my best employee."

Don laughed. "I think I'm your only employee."

"That's true, but you're still the best. Thanks again for helping me out this week. When I get back, remind me to tell you the story about a group of bears that I saw."

"You saw a sloth of bears!? In the wild!?" Don seemed excited.

"Yes, and how does everyone but me know what a group of bears is called?

"How close did you get!?" Don asked. "Were they the big Kodiak Brown Bears?"

"Yep," I said. "I don't want to say I was scared, but I was so close I could smell their breath."

"I watch the Kodiak Bears online," he said. "They're my favorite bears, even more than polar bears. People get close to them sometimes, and they don't seem to mind. I saw a mother sow with her cubs walk right past some people on a beach! Did you see them eating fish?"

"I didn't see them eating, but they were near a stream. The whole group, or sloth I guess, didn't seem aggressive toward me. Maybe one of the cubs."

"You saw a little cub!? Oh my gosh! I can't believe it!"

"It wasn't all that little, but yes, I saw two cubs."

"Wow!" Don said. "Did you get any video?"

"I got a few photos, from a distance, but no video." I paused. "Oh, here's something I learned. A group of bears is a *sloth*, but do you know what a group of sloths is called?"

Don whispered, "It's a *snuggle*."

"What!? How did you know that!?"

"Well...I was able to vote on it," he said. "I belong to a group." He paused. "Don't laugh. It's an

International Sloth Conservation Group, and I'm a member."

"I think that's cool Donny. Why would I laugh?"

"Sloths are my favorite mammals," he said, "and all the members of the conservation group got to vote. I had to fill out a form online and they totaled up all the votes in England. Some people chose *slumber*, but…" he paused and whispered again, "…I chose snuggle."

***

I hung my dreamcatcher on the headboard and went to bed early. I kept hearing noises in one of the adjoining rooms, which kept me awake for a while, but by ten o'clock I was out. I had a vivid dream that showed me fly fishing on a stream. It must have passed through the dreamcatcher because it was a good dream, and I began to float and watch what was happening in the dream, from above. I was on the Situk River with Boggs, and he was fly fishing and wearing a tuxedo. He was eating a corn dog too, and I was telling him to be careful and watch out for the bears. And then a large boar came up to him and smiled. Then the bear stood up on his hind legs and had a rifle in his paws. His face changed into Kyle Westbrook…"NO!"

I woke up, dazed and confused. My shirt was soaked, and my heart raced. I slid through the sheets and put my feet on the carpet and sat there for a few minutes to calm down. Then I looked at the large dreamcatcher. I had to fold it twice to get it into the small garbage can. I went to the bathroom, took a quick shower, and got back into bed. I slept straight through, until 6:30 a.m. I had another dream, but I didn't remember what it was about.

Chris had texted me to call her, so I unplugged my phone and tapped the screen. She answered after the first ring.

"You were right," she claimed. "McCord showed up in the Westbrook's family tree. Caleb McCord. I found a death certificate from 1884 on a genealogy website, but the McCord name ended with him in 1884."

"Did you find out anything about KJ McCord?" I asked.

"No," Chris yawned. "I spent all night going down the rabbit hole on the genealogy site. I sent all the information to the agency this morning. Aside from Kyle's new name, I didn't see anything else that would help us."

"Did the site have any other information about the name change, or who Caleb McCord was?"

"Not really. The Westbrook name showed up later. I did find out some information about my family, at least on the Hoffman side. They came from Hessen, Germany. Some relatives posted information I'd never seen about my great, great, great grandfather."

"Really!? You're German? That's hard to believe."

"Don't be such an ass," she said, then laughed. "Did you get any sleep?"

"More than you, but I can't remember the last time I wasn't tired. I have that dart tournament tonight. Maybe Kyle Westbrook will show up and make things easy."

"Don't drink too much," she said. "You know how you get when you drink. You need to stay focused and try to gather as much information as you can about the Westbrooks."

"I don't plan on it. I can't imagine the tournament is that important if they're having me in it."

TWENTY-FOUR

I wasn't sure what to expect when I arrived at The Standing Bear Pub, but I certainly didn't expect the crowd to be as large as it was. I picked up a program of the *Monie Marie Dart Tournament* at the front entrance and shimmied my way through the bodies to an area at the far end of the bar, which was still crowded, but at least I could move around without constantly bumping into people.

The pub seemed dark inside, and there was a smaller room close to where I stood with a sign made of stained driftwood. The burnt lettering read, *Sea Gars & Bourbon,* and hung above the room's entrance. I assumed it was a place where people could smoke cigars and drink whiskey, but I knew the indoor smoking laws had changed in Alaska, so I peeked inside to see what was happening. Nobody was smoking, but the mahogany and leather furniture looked expensive, and even smelled expensive. I imagined the whiskey was, too. I could tell immediately that the pub's clientele was different from those I'd seen at The Whiskey River Saloon.

The program had several photos of a crab boat, its captain and crew, and a short story that had been written to honor them: *The sinking of the Monie Marie.*

At the end of king crab season, in 1977, two low pressure systems churned up the waters in the Gulf of Alaska. One came from the southeast and the other from the southwest. A rogue wave formed at the northern center of the dueling storms, a wall of water twice the size of any sailor's worst nightmare. It developed from the south and quickly gathered height, momentum, and volume, on its collision course with The Monie Marie, which measured 120 feet from bow to stern, on its voyage home to Kodiak.

The sea can give, and the sea can take away, and it does so without warning. The crew wasn't prepared for the mountain-sized destructive force that came from the darkness. It wouldn't have mattered anyway. There was no time to panic and nothing to be done.

On that fateful night, The Monie Marie sat low in the water, just twenty miles from Kodiak's coastline, loaded with crab, and weighed down by the pots that were stacked on its deck. Too many pots and too many crabs, some had speculated, but what sunk her was just too much sea.

The rogue wave slammed into The Monie Marie and showed no mercy as it sent her to the bottom of the Gulf of Alaska. A salvage attempt had been made, but the nine souls from Kodiak who had died onboard were never found. The sea had claimed its bounty.

In 1978, the First Annual Monie Marie Dart Tournament was held as a memorial of the disaster. Money raised from the event helped start the Kodiak Maritime Disaster Relief Fund, a non-profit organization dedicated to assist families of the Kodiak Archipelago when their loved ones were lost at sea. Disaster happens far too often in the frigid waters off the coast of Alaska.

We thank The Standing Bear Pub and The Whiskey River Saloon (formerly Blake's Tavern) for their continued support of the relief fund. May you and your loved ones always have a safe voyage home. Signed,

Paul Applegate, President, Kodiak Maritime Disaster Relief Fund.

"Brad!" Lacy called out as she came over to meet me. A man using a walker with large wheels followed her as she cleared the way for him. He was probably in his mid-seventies, and he was dressed like the singer/songwriter Willie Nelson, complete with a scruffy beard, ponytails, and a thick red headband. "This is Willie Nelson, the owner of The Whiskey River," she said.

I smiled. "Hi Willie." I looked around at the people who were in earshot. I wasn't sure if Lacy was serious or not, so I just went with it. "I hope I do well in the tournament. I didn't realize there'd be so many people here."

Willie scoffed. "Randy said you were good, but he didn't know if you'd want to be the team's anchor or not." Lacy chuckled, and I wasn't sure why. Willie reached his hand out and squeezed my bicep. "You look strong enough."

I didn't mind going last, so before Lacy started feeling my bicep, or any other part of me, I said, "I'll be the anchor, but I can't promise you anything."

Willie laughed and coughed at the same time, like he'd gotten too much fresh air and needed a smoke. He leaned forward, grabbed a handkerchief out of his back pocket, and wiped his mouth.

"Are you OK?" I asked.

"I just need my medicine," he said. "Lacy, could you get me my medicine?"

Lacy looked around then raised her hand in the air. "Hey Sid!" she yelled at one of the bartenders. "Can we get a double shot of Jack for Willie?"

"Make it a triple," Willie said.

"Make it a triple!" Lacy shouted.

I turned to look at the bartender, who was looking at us. His eyes met mine as he pulled a bottle of Jack Daniels off a glass shelf and poured what looked like a quadruple, but who was counting? We recognized each other immediately. He smiled like he was expecting to see me, but I was shocked to see him.

"And how about you, sir?" he asked me.

I didn't know what to think. The bartender knew who I was, and he knew I had once worked for the agency, but why was he in the pub, and why was he working as a bartender? I was sure about one thing. I could trust him to keep a secret.

"I'll have a bottle of Budweiser," I said.

Lacy smiled. "Make it two bottles, Sid," she yelled, louder than she needed to. "And keep 'em coming!" She was all fired up and ready to party.

So, it was Sid these days, I thought. I watched him get the beers and Willie's glass of whiskey and bring them over to us. "I don't think we've met," he said to me. "I'm Frank Sydney, but my friends just call me Sid."

Yep, I knew he could keep a secret. "Hi, Sid," I said. We were still friends after all. "My name's Brad Kelso, and I'm the anchor for the Whiskey River tonight."

Sid laughed. "Well, you look strong enough," he said.

What? Everyone thought I was strong enough. What did me being strong enough have to do with darts?

Sid and I nodded at each other, an understanding that it wasn't the time or place for a reunion, and he went back to work. I followed Willie and Lacy to the far side of the pub where an area had been cordoned-off for the tournament. Thick manila nautical rope was pulled through several waist-high metal stands, and it circled around the dart section, which included two tables and eight chairs that had obviously been set up for the dart throwers who were competing.

At the end, two old-style dart boards were attached to the wall, a section of solid wood panels with a dark walnut stain that looked like it had been brushed on before I was born.

A thin strip of wood was fastened to the floor, measuring the correct throwing distance, and it too had been worn down after, what looked like, decades of use.

The dart area was a sharp contrast to the two electronic boards at The Whiskey River, where a piece of gray duct tape had been stuck on the floor. I was happy because I threw steel-tipped darts at home in my shop, so I was used to the shorter distance, which is officially two and three-quarters inches closer than with soft-tipped darts. I could throw the soft tips, but with the way the weight was distributed, I wasn't as accurate with them. I usually threw twenty-four-gram darts, which was a common weight, so if they allowed me some time to practice with a new set, I felt good about my chances in the tournament.

My competitive side started to come out, and with the large crowd in attendance, I was beginning to get excited—not as much as Lacy, but I was starting to get into the moment and forget the real reason I was there. Maybe Chris had been right; I needed to focus more.

Randy came over to where I stood and introduced me to the other three members of the Whiskey River team, which included Bud Taylor, Mick Eberhardt, and Hannah Jones, the pilot from Island Tours.

"It's great to see you again, Hannah," I said. "And nice to meet you Bud and Mick."

The four of us sat down at one of the tables and Bud and Mick started talking about their grandkids, while Hannah flagged down a waitress and ordered us a round of drinks.

Bud taught physical education and coached baseball at the local high school. He volunteered at the Tsunami Warning Center, which was just a desk that had been set up in the Kodiak Harbormaster's Office, so I knew he and Lacy must have been friends, or at least knew each other.

Mick was the owner of *Shady Nights*, a company that sold "Shutters, blinds, and shades," and provided "a good night's sleep" to its customers. Dark shades are used in bedrooms throughout Alaska, when the summer months bring almost twenty-four-hour sunlight in some places. "Shady Nights," he said, "provided the best value for your money," in both vertical and horizontal window coverings.

I found out Hannah was a full-time bush pilot who flew her own plane from Kodiak to several villages in southwest Alaska, and she worked part-time for Island Tours when they needed an extra pilot. She knew the Westbrooks, or at least had dealt with them, so I began to feel like playing in the tournament wasn't a complete waste of time.

After our brief introductions, we chatted about strategy, rules, and the throwing order. I asked my teammates if any of them would rather be the anchor, but they all just smiled and told me I was probably the strongest of the four of us.

Before we started, Paul Applegate, president of the charitable organization, gave a lengthy speech about the Monie Marie and the Relief Fund, and how people could contribute. It occurred to me as I looked around the room that people were there for a variety of reasons; some were probably interested in watching us throw darts, and some were just there to drink, but a few of them had lost family members, or loved ones, in one of the dozens of boating accidents that happened in Alaska each year.

Lacy came over to wish us luck. "Hey Bud, hey Mick," she said. "Take care of my boy."

They both looked at me, then they looked at each other and laughed.

"Hey Lacy," Hannah said.

Lacy smiled at Hannah, a crooked smile, like she'd stepped in something that smelled, "Hey, Hannah Banana."

I could feel the tension between them rising. Lacy had been so different when she was alone with me, but around the crowd she was more brash and intense. I wasn't sure why, but tension was something we didn't need. People tend to clam up when there's tension. "Wish us luck," I said to Lacy.

"Good luck," she said, then went back to her table where Willie and another couple were sitting.

"I guess everybody already knows each other," I said. "What's the story with Willie Nelson? Is that really his name?"

Hannah chuckled. "That's his name, alright," she said. "William T. Nelson, not Willie H. Nelson, like the singer. As you can see, he's a big fan, too. He bought Blake's about fifteen years ago and changed the name to Whiskey River, his favorite Willie Nelson song.

"He's dressed like that as long as I've known him," Bud said.

"He's a great guy," Hannah said. "He gave me a job when I first came to Kodiak four years ago. I worked at the saloon for a year before I got my pilot's license. I think he misses managing the bar, but Randy does a good job."

"Randy's great," Bud said, and they all nodded in agreement.

Mick leaned in and whispered, "I saw Willie sober one night, and he told me he'd been abducted by aliens, and the only reason they brought him back was because his blood alcohol levels were too high."

"Willie was *sober*?" Bud asked, laughing.

We laughed even harder. I supposed being abducted by aliens was a possibility, but any story about Willie being sober was a stretch.

Bud brought an extra set of darts, that happened to be twenty-four grams, and from my first practice throw with them, I'm not sure why, but I couldn't miss. Even so, we split the first two matches, but we won the two out of three games when I hit a double sixteen to finish out the third match.

The place erupted in cheers after my final throw, and The Whiskey River Saloon's regulars, most of whom had walked the twelve blocks to The Standing Bear Pub, began to sing *Take Me Out to the Ballgame,* with the words "dart game" substituted for ballgame and Whiskey River substituted for home team. I had no idea why, but it must have been a tradition for the winning team because nobody from The Standing Bear Pub joined in. "…for it's one, two, three darts you throw for the Monie Marie!"

After the song, Paul read a poem that had been written years earlier by a daughter of one of the crewmen of the Monie Marie. Then, he presented all the "throwers" with certificates for competing in the tournament, and gold ribbons for the four of us on the winning team. Shortly after the ribbons were passed out, I found out what being the anchor for the team really meant.

Two guys, who were probably international strongman competitors, took out an anchor from a large glass case in the front of the bar. It had been salvaged from the Monie Marie. The whole scene gave me an uneasy feeling, probably because the place went quiet, and my teammates began to move away from me like I was contagious.

Paul smiled, then looked down and read from his notes. "Brad Kelso, the winning anchor for The Whiskey River Saloon this year, has invited all of you in attendance to accompany him on his voyage home. The Standing Bear Pub and The Whiskey River Saloon have offered to donate all of tonight's drink receipts to our Kodiak Maritime Disaster Relief Fund." Paul looked up and smiled as the whole place erupted in applause.

"Thank you all for coming and thank you for your contributions! No matter how far you go, or where your voyage may take you, may you always return home." Everybody lifted their glasses and took a drink.

I stood up as Lacy came over to congratulate me with a hug. "Not bad," she said. "I knew you had it in you."

"What's up with the anchor?" I asked.

"Since the team won, you have to carry it back to The Whiskey River," she said.

"*Me?!*"

She laughed. "Yep, the team's anchor has to do it alone. They have a strap and a pad, so you can load it onto your back if you want."

Crap. It was twelve blocks to the Whiskey River Saloon, uphill and downhill. Twelve blocks would be a long way to haul anything that weighed as much as that anchor.

Sid walked over to where we were standing carrying a tray with three shot glasses of whiskey filled to the rim. "Anchor's away!" he called out.

"Anchor's away!" the rest of the crowd yelled, just before I downed each one.

After the third shot, the crowd parted like the Red Sea and the only thing standing between me and the anchor was my pride, which gave away a few minutes later when the two burly men strapped the anchor onto my back. It seemed heavier than I'd first thought, much heavier. I had trouble believing all the dart players, who were anchors of the past tournaments, carried it the entire way. Apparently, I was wrong.

"Nobody has ever failed to get it home," Lacy said, "but Stanley Sherman dropped it a few times, and it took him two hours to drag it back to Blake's; but that was a long time ago and he was drunk."

So much for looking strong enough. Maybe being sober was the key. I already had a good buzz because I wasn't used to drinking whiskey. The first few steps to get outside were difficult, but the crowd was certainly encouraging me as we walked along the street, and then I got a short stretch of downhill, which helped quicken my pace. The crowd that followed me loved it, and they cheered even more the faster I went. Then the street leveled out and began to go back uphill. I stopped for a moment, halfway to the top as the crowd went silent. I was ready to be done, but I glanced to the side and saw Tony Lee standing behind Lacy and Willie. He was with another man I didn't recognize.

Our eyes met and Tony Lee smiled at me like he knew I was finished. I just smiled back, took a few short steps, grunted, and rearranged the anchor before continuing forward. When I got to the top, the crowd howled even louder like I was an Olympic distance runner on my last lap. I could finally see the sign in front of the Whiskey River Saloon as I made my descent for the final four blocks. I looked back around, and Tony Lee and his friend were gone.

The steps going up to the saloon were the hardest, but they unstrapped the anchor when I got inside and Randy gave me a tray with three more shots, which went down much smoother than the first three. I yelled, "Anchor's away!" before each drink to a very jubilant crowd.

Apparently, scenes of the event had been live streamed on one of the social media sites, because when I finally got seated in one of the booths, after a long congratulatory kiss from Lacy, I checked my phone and found out that Chris had been watching the event from her home office in Camas. "Nice dart throwing!" she had texted earlier. But when her last text came through, it only had two words, but I felt like her message was clear: "Anchor's away."

TWENTY-FIVE

Lacy had driven me back to the hotel that night, not that I had remembered it, thanks to all the shots of whiskey I'd consumed after the tournament, but there were two clues to support my assumption. The first was the fact that I woke up in Room 112 at the Buskin, and I knew I wouldn't have driven there, or walked six miles in that condition, no matter how drunk I was. The second clue, and probably the one that gave it away, was that Lacy was sleeping next to me.

My back ached, my head pounded, and my mouth was drier than the Sahara. Other than that, I felt like crap. And the last thing I remembered was Lacy asking me if she could stay the night at the hotel instead of driving home.

Lacy started out in the other bed but by morning she was snuggling against me like a group of sloths. I don't know what made me feel so guilty about it. We hadn't done anything, but I kept thinking about Chris and how she'd react. In all the time we'd known each other, Chris and I had never officially dated, but I still felt like I had done something wrong. Maybe I had. The future squeeze play with Lacy had almost turned into a current squeeze play, and the last thing I needed were more complications during the mission.

It didn't make me feel any better knowing Chris knew my exact location, along with where Lacy's car was parked. There was no way she didn't already know about her staying with me. What should I tell her? Maybe I just wouldn't say anything about it. I didn't need to bring it up. It's not like I owed her an explanation.

I rolled to the side of the bed and looked at my phone. No messages from Chris. She always sent me messages in the morning. Crap.

"You're up early," Lacy moaned. She was lying on her stomach, with her face buried in her pillow. "Today is Sunday, you know."

I yawned. "I'm going down to get some coffee. Do you want anything?"

"No," she growled, "and take your time."

The fog made it seem even darker as I looked out the windows of the breakfast area. Since Alaska is so far north, the daylight hours change drastically throughout the year, but in late September, the difference isn't as much as it is in the summer and winter months. It was 6:50 am, and the sun would rise at eight o'clock. Then it would stay light until almost 8:00 pm. Twelve hours of daylight and twelve hours of darkness.

If Pilot Bob dropped me off just before sunset, I'd have the entire night to complete the mission and get back to a place where he could pick me up in the morning. *Plenty of time*, I thought, *with hours to spare*. I knew where I was going, and I knew what I was going to do. I just didn't know how I was going to do it yet.

"You're up early," Sheryl said as she grabbed a cup of coffee and sat down next to me.

"That seems to be the consensus," I said, "but I'm used to getting up early. The light is better in the morning, and when I worked in construction, I would've already been at the jobsite by now." She grinned at me, and I smiled. "Look who I'm talking to. You're the manager of a hotel."

"I'm always here," she said. "I have a place in town, but sometimes I use a room here when I need to. Is Lacy still sleeping?" she asked. "Her car is in the parking lot."

"She seemed to think Sunday morning was a good time to sleep in," I said, "so I'm giving her some space."

Sheryl smiled. "You learn fast," she said. "Lacy likes her space."

"That was my take this morning."

"Congratulations on last night."

I was pretty sure she meant the dart tournament. "Thanks."

"It's too bad you'll be leaving soon. I know Lacy will miss you."

"Yeah, the magazine won't pay me to stay on Kodiak and take photos forever, but who knows? Maybe someone will write an article about the sinking of the Monie Marie, along with the dart tournament. I could get paid to take a few selfies. They could even write a song about it, like they did with the *Edmund Fitzgerald. Gitche Gumee* might be a big lake, but it has nothing on the Gulf of Alaska.

She smiled. "I can see why Lacy likes you. She hasn't had much luck with men, but she's a fun person to be around. She's lived on Kodiak forever, and she's great at her job…"

"Hey!" I interrupted. "I understand! She's sleeping in my room right now, so you don't need to sell me on her." We both chuckled. "I like her, but we don't need to worry about tomorrow, or the next day. I did that once. What's that old saying? Yesterday is history, tomorrow's a mystery, but today? Today's a gift. That's why they call it the present."

Sheryl got up, grabbed her coffee, and slid her chair under the table. She smiled. "I've got to get back to work. Like I said, I can see why Lacy likes you."

***

Jason Westbrook was scheduled to come into port with the barge at 11:00 a.m. which gave me a few hours in the morning to gather information and plenty of time in the afternoon to get ready. Even if Kyle was onboard, the only thing I planned to do was follow him. If he stayed in town Sunday night, it would make my job easier, but I didn't expect him to stick around. Whether he was on the barge or not, I was probably only down to one option: hiking over the lower ridge to get to their compound in the dark.

I hoped to complete my mission by Monday morning. If I was lucky, I'd be sleeping in my own bed on Tuesday. Yeah, I still needed some luck. One way or another, the day and night were going to be long, and I needed to relax and stay focused.

The Buskin had a nice breakfast spread on Sunday mornings. Several stainless-steel trays were on a table, against the wall. I watched one of the guests pick up the lid and saw the pan filled with round sausage patties. The other pans had scrambled eggs, bacon, and hash browns. Everything smelled good, but my head still ached, and the caffeine hadn't kicked in yet. Maybe I'd just have yogurt and a bagel with cream cheese. I'd heard yogurt is easy to digest, and even though my stomach felt OK, I didn't trust it.

I was standing there with a thick paper plate in my hand trying to decide where to start when I heard a woman scream "No!" from what sounded like the front desk area. I ran towards her.

Sheryl had her cell phone pressed against her face and was crying, just about as hard as a person can cry. Only one thing can make someone cry like that. Someone she loves was either dying or dead. She didn't even look up at me before she ran toward the back office.

"That didn't sound good," I said to the girl standing next to me. She had been working in the breakfast area and looked concerned, too. We didn't say anything else to each other. The girl looked like she'd just gotten out of high school, and she wasn't sure what to do. I'd been out of high school for almost forty years, and I didn't know what to do, either. We just stood there, listening to Sheryl, who was on another call, crying from the back room. Then Sheryl came out. She looked pale, but under more control. Then she saw the girl and me and started sobbing again.

"My son is...on his...way... to the hospital," she said, barely coherent. The girl and I waited as she kept crying. "Philip will be...here in...an hour." She kept pausing to cry. "Can you watch... the front desk...until he ...gets here?"

The girl and I looked at each other. Was that even a question?

"Of course," I said. "Uh..." I pointed toward the girl.

"Alisa," the girl said.

"Alisa and I will be here," I said. "Is your son OK?"

What a stupid question. I always ask stupid questions when women are crying. Sheryl just started crying again.

"Don't worry," I said. "Are you OK to drive?"

Sheryl nodded. She turned off the computer and told us not to worry about checking people in or out. Just write down their names and take their keycards if they bring them to the desk. If anybody wanted to check-in early, they'd need to wait until Philip got there. One maid was already working on the second floor, but the others wouldn't arrive until nine. Then she grabbed her things and hurried out the front door.

I looked at Alisa and she shrugged. "You should probably just keep taking care of the breakfast buffet and I'll stay here, OK?" I didn't have to ask her twice.

I grabbed a coffee, a Greek yogurt, and a banana, and sat on a tall stool behind the front desk. A few guests wandered around the lobby after they finished breakfast. They looked at me as I sat there and ate, probably wondering what I was doing behind the counter. I had my sweatpants on, flipflops, and an old Seahawks T-shirt that read, *24 Beast Mode*. My hair was a mess, and I hadn't showered. I probably smelled like the bottom of an old whiskey barrel and who knows what else.

At first, waiting behind the front desk was even worse than a stakeout because people watched me even more than I watched them. It was only for an hour, though, and I had some time to kill. I looked at the fake fireplace and the couch in the center of the room. It was tempting. In all the time I'd been at the Buskin, I'd never actually seen anybody sit on the couch. I finished my coffee and went to get a refill in the breakfast area. Alisa and I nodded at each other. We had this.

I went back to my stool and called Lacy on the hotel's phone. She picked up the receiver. "I'm still sleeping!" she hollered and hung up. I hadn't said anything. Did she think it was me or Sheryl calling?

More guests walked through the lobby and the breakfast area. I sat there for over ten minutes before anyone said anything to me. A woman, who looked showered, fully dressed, and ready for the day, came up to the counter.

I could tell she wasn't sure if she should ask me, "Do you work here?"

"No."

She seemed bewildered. I would've explained the situation to her, but I was bored and wanted to see where the conversation was headed.

"Is there someone I can talk to who works here?"

"Not right now, but you can talk to me. I'm a good listener. What would you like to talk about?"

"I called guest services, but nobody picked up."

"Well, you're here now. What can I help you with?"

"I thought you didn't work here."

"I don't"

She got a disgusted look on her face, like I was wasting her time. "May I speak to the manager?"

"No."

She just stood there, looked at me and waited. This wasn't as much fun as I'd hoped. I sighed. "The manager got a call a few minutes ago," I said. "She had to run to the hospital, and the assistant won't be here for another…," I looked at my phone, "…49 minutes. Give or take."

"So, who are you?"

"My name is Brad and I'm a guest who's helping out. I'm in Room 112. And you are...?"

"I'm in Room 146, and I'm leaving for a few hours. I'd like maid service before I get back here at ten. Will you let someone know?"

"Please?"

"Pardon me?"

I just thought she should've been more polite. Not only was she no fun, but she didn't have any manners. I waited for it too, but after a few seconds I gave up. "OK," I said. "One forty-six. Maid service by ten. I'll pass it on."

The woman left and another man came up to the counter.

"I'd like to check out."

"Name and room number?"

"Larry Andrews, Room 208."

"Do you have your keycards?"

"Oh, yes, he said. Just the one." He took his keycard out of his front pocket and set it on the counter. I wrote his name and room number on a sheet of paper.

"The computer is down, so we'll send you a receipt. Same credit card?"

"Yes, that's fine."

"You're all set. Have a great day!"

"Thanks."

I was getting more comfortable behind the counter by the time Philip showed up, at 7:45. I walked back to Room 112 and quietly opened the door.

"Where have you been?" Lacy barked. She was fully dressed and had just finished putting on her shoes. "Sheryl's son, Adam, is in the hospital," she said. "We need to go." She looked up at me. "Can you hurry?"

I thought about telling her, but it wasn't worth the effort. "Sure."

After I took a quick shower and got dressed, Lacy drove us from the Buskin to a medical center in downtown Kodiak. "Adam is only seventeen," Lacy told me. "He's a senior in high school. The doctor told Sheryl it was an overdose of some kind, but she didn't even know he was taking drugs. He's awake now, so that's a good sign, don't you think?"

"Being awake is always a good sign," I said.

We sat in a waiting area with several other people who all looked like they'd rather be doing something else. I could relate. Sheryl was able to stay with her son in his room, but we weren't allowed to visit him. Sheryl came out twice to give us updates, and Lacy kept referring to us as "we," like "Don't worry, we'll stay here," and "We can get you something if you need it."

By nine thirty, I was done with the "we" business. I was sorry I hadn't driven the Jeep to the hospital separately because I had to get to the port before Jason came in with the barge. I'd never met Adam, and I barely knew Sheryl. I didn't want to seem heartless, but I still needed to find Kyle Westbrook and figure out how to kill him.

"Lacy, would you mind taking me to my Jeep?" I asked. "I can give you a call this afternoon."

"OK, but let's wait until Sheryl comes back out."

I looked at my phone. "OK."

"I can't believe you woke up so early," she said. "Didn't you have a hangover?"

"Still do," I said. I rubbed my temples. "The last thing I remember is when you asked me if you could stay the night."

"I didn't think it meant sleeping in the other bed, but I suppose I was just as tired as you were. It was nice for me to just hold someone. It's been a while. Most men aren't like that."

A police officer walked in and spoke to one of the nurses briefly. He was in uniform and was carrying a clipboard. He looked at Lacy and me, then walked over to where we were sitting. "You're here for Adam?" he asked.

"Yes," Lacy said.

"His mom is with him," I said. "Down the hall, Room 114."

"I'll wait here for a few minutes if you don't mind." He looked around. "I'm Officer Dunning. Is anybody else here from the party?"

"What party?" Lacy asked. She was concerned and didn't realize he was just trying to gather information.

"The party from last night," he said. "Didn't you see Adam last night?"

"No," Lacy said. She looked at me.

"I've never met Adam," I said. This is Lacy Miller. She's a friend of Adam's mom. Did you find out what happened?"

"We're still gathering information," he said. He opened the clipboard. "Lacy Miller," he whispered as he wrote down her name. "And you are?"

"Brad Kelso," I said. I leaned forward in my seat. "So, Officer Dunning, you're telling us Adam was at a party last night. We heard from his mom that he overdosed on something. Have you got any idea what it was, or who gave it to him?" My investigative mode kicked in.

"I can't say yet."

"Can't or won't?"

Dunning smirked. "We're still trying to piece together what happened."

A nurse came over and nodded at Dunning. "Take care," he said to Lacy and me, and walked down the hallway.

"What do you think he took?" Lacy asked.

"Something he shouldn't have," I said. "I think Officer Dunning will be talking to Sheryl and Adam for a few minutes. Do you mind taking me back to my Jeep?"

TWENTY-SIX

After Lacy dropped me off, I didn't have time to stop by the Buskin, so I drove the Jeep to the pier and parked a short distance away, right in front of a restaurant called *The Angry Growler*. I suppose it was more of a pub, but the sign outside said they served Sunday brunch, so maybe if anyone drove by and saw the Jeep, they'd think I was inside having a meal.

I ordered a coffee to go and sipped it as I walked toward a long dock where the barges unload. The coffee was an organic Sumatra blend, and it tasted as good as it smelled. I was still hopeful I'd get lucky and see Kyle Westbrook get off the barge with his brother, Jason. Maybe Jason would fly back to Uyak Bay this afternoon and Kyle would remain in town for the night. He'd stay at the Buskin Hotel, right across the hall from me, in Room 113. Wouldn't that be something? I tended to fantasize when I had too much time on my hands. Maybe that was the real reason I didn't like stakeouts. None of the fantasies ever came true.

I could see the barge in the distance when I finally received a text from Chris. It wasn't what I'd expected: "Leave now and call me when you get to your hotel."

If there was one thing I'd learned as a PFT, it was to trust my handler. I didn't think about Chris's motives for wanting me off that pier. I just left.

I called her from the Buskin's parking lot. "What's going on?"

"I should ask you the same question," she said. "You're an asshole, but that's beside the point. There's been a development. Chief Carmichael wants you off the island tonight. She's sending Pilot Bob to pick you up at Trident Basin at five."

"What does that mean?" I asked. "Tonight's the night we've been waiting for. Everything is in place."

"It's not my decision," Chris said, "and it has nothing to do with last night. It's an official call from Chief Carmichael's office."

"That's a bunch of crap! I only need one more day, twenty hours tops. Can't she wait until I get back from Uyak Bay?"

"She wouldn't tell me what's going on, but I think they plan to raid the compound tomorrow morning."

I scoffed. "Carmichael was worried about *me* messing up *their* investigation. She told me on the flight to Kodiak that they almost had enough evidence to convict Pete of distributing fentanyl. I can't believe she doesn't see what's going to happen. It's like they've never done field work before. I've got a better chance of catching Pete with fentanyl than they do, and I'm not looking for it. I don't think their drug bust should be more important than locating a murderer."

"You're not listening, Brad. She was very specific. You need to be in Anchorage tonight. Since the timeline was changed by the agency, she said they'll pay us the full amount of the contract. This wasn't a negotiation. Those were her orders."

"So, we're done? They're just pulling the plug?"

"Yes, Brad, well said. We're done! Be there at five." *Click.*

"Crap!"

This was shaping up to be the second worst day of my life. Chris was mad at me, and what was I supposed to tell her? That Lacy spent the night with no funny business? She probably wouldn't believe me, and how could I blame her?

Chief Carmichael didn't even trust me to be on the island, let alone allowing me a little more time to complete my mission.

Kyle Westbrook was out there somewhere, and our best chance to locate him was in the hands of the DEA. I wouldn't have given Chief Carmichael a ten percent chance of finding him. And what if they did? The DEA has rules. What would they do? Arrest him and try to convict him in a court of law? No prosecutor would bring a murder case to trial with such flimsy evidence.

I had a headache still, and my back was sore from hauling a damn boat anchor through the streets of downtown Kodiak. Even Lacy was miffed at me for leaving the hospital early. Now I had to tell her I was leaving at five, for good. That was the least of my concerns, and she never expected anything from me, but I still needed to tell her. I owed her that much. All in all, it was already a crappy day, and it wasn't even lunch time.

I went to my room and packed my bags and suitcase. I'd never felt so bad about how I'd handled myself during a mission. I hadn't found the target, and I managed to get everyone upset with me, for one reason or another.

I drove down to the southern harbor and parked the Jeep in a small gravel lot. The fog was starting to lift, and the birds seemed more active. I walked down to a landing and across the wooden planks until I reached the *Northern Sky*. I didn't see anybody, so I yelled, "Ahoy Skip!"

He came outside. "Brad Kelso," he said. "You've been busy." He paused. "Heard about your shenanigans from last night."

"Permission to come aboard?"

"Yeah, yeah, I'm too tired to come up with another riddle. So, I guess you're starting to become quite the celebrity."

I climbed over the rail. "My fifteen minutes of fame," I said. "I thought I had more time on the island, but I'll be flying out this evening."

"Well, you were never one to stick around," he said. "Heard tell you and the little filly from the harbormaster's office were getting cozy last night."

"Little filly, Skip? Do you know everything that goes on around here?"

"I talked to her mom, Nancy, this morning. Nice lady. We've known each other for years. She said you were a great customer, but she thinks her daughter deserves someone who'll stick around. I put in a good word for you. Not sure you needed it. I said you were honest, never asked for anything, and you'd never let an old man go thirsty." He had obviously been looking at the six-pack cooler I brought with me.

I pulled out two bottles of Budweiser and twisted off the tops, then handed one to Skip. "You're a damned liar," I said.

"I guess you do ask for things once in a while, but I'd vouch for you anytime," he said.

"I might need it."

Skip laughed and raised the bottle. "Here's to friendship, and to those who deserve it." The bottles clanked together, and we took a drink.

"You're leaving this evening, huh? I suppose you want your bag back."

"Yeah, did you look inside of it?" I asked.

"Hell yes!" he said. "That type of lock box makes me think of a gun. With ammunition it seems about the right weight."

"You put your old metal detector on it, didn't you?"

"Long enough to know it wasn't gold or silver," he said. He took a drink. What was I supposed to do? A ship's captain can never be too careful about what's stowed on board." He took another drink.

"I should have saved you the trouble," I said. "It's a 9mm Glock. All legal. Sometimes I carry it for protection, and sometimes I just use it to shoot old bastards."

"Figured as much," Skip said, "and I'm not that old!"

TWENTY-SEVEN

Skip and I finished off the six pack below deck. It didn't take as long as it should have. I was feeling better by the time I drove back to the hospital. Most of the cobwebs in my head were gone and I was hungry again.

Lacy and her mom were sitting next to each other in the waiting room when I arrived. They didn't seem upset, so I imagined Adam was doing better.

"I was starting to think you wouldn't come back," Lacy said.

"I'm only stopping by for a few minutes," I said. "I just found out my company is sending me on another assignment. I'm going back to Washington State this evening. My flight leaves at five."

"You're leaving today?" Lacy asked. She shook her head. "That figures."

"When do you plan to come back and visit," Nancy asked. She seemed less surprised.

"I don't know. I wasn't expecting to leave so soon, but I had a nice time on the island. I think I even managed to get some photos that the magazine can use. I have Lacy to thank for that."

"Yeah," Lacy said. "A nice time, blah, blah, blah." She stood up. "I'm going out for a smoke." She walked through the front doors. I thought she needed a minute, so I sat down.

"How's Adam doing," I asked Nancy.

"Sheryl says he'll be fine. He was at a party, and someone gave him a pill, so he tried it. It was supposed to be something kids are taking called *Ecstasy*, but the doctor said it had a substance in it called fentanyl. I've heard of fentanyl before. It's an opioid. The doctor told Sheryl that Adam only took one pill. The police officer said the drug dealers are making fake pills with fentanyl and they're even selling them as prescription medications now. They can make them look like any drug, even over the counter medicines."

"I've heard that, too," I said. "Someone told me that more people under the age of thirty-five have died in the last couple of years from fentanyl than from suicide, cancer, and homicides combined."

"That's scary," Nancy said, "but at least Adam will be OK. They think he must have had a strong reaction because he's never taken drugs before. I'm sure he's learned his lesson, but it's hard to believe just one pill could've killed him."

"We think of people who overdose as junkies," I said, "but sometimes people like Adam, who don't know how dangerous the drug is, can die from taking one or two pills. Even people who've used drugs in the past and have been clean and sober for a long time are overdosing. I read something that said the most dangerous time for an ex-addict is the first time they go back to using. Their system isn't ready for the same quantity of drug, and the first relapse can kill them."

"Back in the day, I smoked a joint or two." Nancy said, "but that was it." She smiled. "Lacy's dad would get it sometimes, but when I smoked too much pot, I just fell asleep. I never heard of anybody dying from it."

Lacy came back inside and sat down. She was cordial. "Are you all packed yet?"

"I didn't have very much to pack."

Nancy put her hand on my forearm. "Lacy told me about your trip to Uyak Bay." She smiled. "I miss living on that part of the island. It's been years since I've been back there. We had some good times when she was a young girl. She said Pete Westbrook was giving you a bad time at the saloon. She and those Westbrook boys were as thick as thieves back in the day, especially little Kyle."

"Mom," Lacy said. "Brad doesn't want to hear about it. He probably needs to go."

"Kyle was two years younger, and the three of them would build forts in the rocks. They'd just disappear. Nobody knew where they went."

"The three of them?" I asked.

"Lacy, Kyle, and Pete," Nancy said.

Lacy started warming back up. "It took me almost an hour to go from Larsen Bay to the Westbrooks in a skiff," she said, "and that's when the water was calm. Mom exaggerates, but we did have fun. One of the forts was inside a rock formation, really well hidden, just above the tree line. We used to pretend there were pirate ships out in the bay, and we'd hide our gold and precious gems in the fort every time a boat or a plane passed by. We had a chest we filled with rocks from the shore." She smiled. "It was more of a cave, but the three of us built walls inside, and a slanting roof on top of it, then covered it all with dirt and rocks and grass. It was on a steep slope, so it was really well hidden. Their parents didn't even know it was there. That was thirty years ago."

"Thirty years," Nancy said. "It's hard to believe."

"What about Jason?"

"Jason was older," Lacy said, "so he was doing his own thing. He helped with the fort, and he packed the lumber up the hill for us. When he was around, they'd always fight, and sometimes he'd beat up Kyle and Pete."

"He was always a mean boy," Nancy said. "He broke Pete's leg once and little Kyle would have bruises up and down his arms. I didn't like it when Lacy was over there when he was around."

"He never touched me," Lacy said, "not once. But he did have a bad temper. He'd be calm one minute and then he'd just snap for no reason."

"Why did Kyle leave?" I asked Lacy. "You told me he left a long time ago."

Lacy and her mom looked at each other. Nancy shrugged.

"You might as well know," Lacy said, "everybody else does." She paused. "Kyle went out with Amy Pearson, who was Ethan Beverley's girlfriend. Kyle was twenty-two and Amy had just graduated high school. I know Kyle and Ethan had a fight, but Kyle didn't kill him. He told me that, and I believe him. He would never lie to me. Anyway, Ethan and his brother, Evan, were found in the water. The police said they were probably murdered." She paused. "Blunt force trauma, they called it. Kyle was the main suspect, and he left because Mr. Beverley threatened to kill him. Some people say Beverley hired a hitman and paid for it in advance."

"That must have scared Kyle. Where did he go?" I asked.

Lacy hesitated. "He lived on the mainland, up in Pedro Bay, for a while and worked for one of his uncles, but he didn't like it. He was in Montana for a few years, and then he moved back to Alaska and…" She paused. "I don't think anyone is looking for him anymore. The police never charged him, and they didn't have any evidence. How could they have any? He didn't kill anyone."

Lacy didn't know him as well as she thought. He probably left Montana after he killed Boggs. But she seemed to know exactly where Kyle had been living in the past. I was sure she knew where he was now.

"So, does Mr. Beverley still think Kyle did it?"

"Mr. Beverley died quite a few years ago, but like I said, Jason and Pete still think there's someone out there who wants to kill Kyle." Lacy's eyes narrowed. "I don't want to talk about Kyle anymore. We had fun as kids, but we're all grown up now."

"Well, they sure have a nice place on Uyak Bay," I said. "Kyle should just live there. I can't imagine anyone is still looking for him. Especially if he didn't kill anybody."

"I tell them the same thing." Lacy said "It's so stupid. All three of them are so paranoid. They're scared of their own shadows. There's nobody out there hunting down Kyle."

Lacy was certainly wrong about that. If she only knew…I started thinking about the DEA's drug bust. If they couldn't catch Pete with drugs, and they couldn't find Kyle, maybe I'd fly back into town the following week, or the following month. I didn't need the DEA's permission, and the agency wouldn't care if I came back. I wouldn't be on the payroll, so I wouldn't have to worry about Chief Carmichael, or anybody else.

Lacy shook her head and looked at me. "Men are such idiots sometimes."

Nancy laughed. "As you can tell, Lacy doesn't hold back."

I smiled. "I think that's what I like about her."

"You see, mom, every time I find a guy who likes me, and can tolerate me, he has to leave."

I stood up, leaned over, and gave her a hug while she remained in her chair. "Thanks for everything."

She smiled. "If you ever come back to Kodiak, you know where to find me."

"I know."

I was glad I stopped by the hospital. I'd learned more about the Westbrooks in those fifteen minutes than the previous five days. I was glad to hear Adam would be OK, too. I couldn't imagine how scared Sheryl must have been.

***

I stopped by The Standing Bear Pub on my way through town. The man behind the bar was about my age, but taller, maybe six feet, and he could pinch more than a few inches. I'd seen him at the dart tournament pouring drinks and not saying much. He had a thick mustache that matched his eyebrows, or *eyebrow* was more like it. He wore a Standing Bear Pub apron, probably the same one he'd had on the night before.

"Is Sid in?" I asked.

He smiled. "Brad Kelso," he said. "How's your back?"

I laughed. "Not as good as it was yesterday afternoon."

He chuckled and pulled out an envelope from the register. "Sid thought you might stop by. He left this note for you."

The envelope was sealed. "Thanks," I said. "Maybe next year, The Standing Bear Pub will win, and your anchor will get to haul that thing back here."

The man chuckled again as I walked toward the door. "Maybe."

I sat in the Jeep and rolled down the window. Some birds were squawking a short distance from where I was parked. The air was chilly and damp, and the afternoon wind had picked up some. Kodiak smelled like a harbor town, but the air was still fresh, not stale. I opened the envelope and unfolded the letter. *Gone today, here tomorrow* was written with a Sharpie. Good old Sid. He always knew how to make me smile.

TWENTY-EIGHT

I loaded my gear into the Jeep when I got back to the Buskin. The wind had picked up throughout the afternoon. I checked my weather app. A cold front was forecast to pass through Kodiak sometime during the night, but it wasn't supposed to leave any snow at the lower elevations. I called Chris from the parking lot.

She answered the phone by asking me a question—really it was two questions: "So, are you all set? Did you say your goodbyes?" She already knew the answers.

"You've been tracking me, haven't you?"

"That's what I get paid to do, Brad, worry about you, what you're doing, and who you're spending time with. It's the chapter titled, *stupid is as stupid does*, in the handler's manual."

"I'm sorry, Chris. "I feel bad about last night, but nothing happened."

"You don't owe me an apology, or anything else," she said. "Why do you feel bad? You're free to do whatever you want. I think you're an idiot, and you risked screwing up the mission, but I'm a big girl. I know how you are. It was a good reminder."

The worst part of Chris being mad at me was her saying she knew how I was, and that it was a good reminder. What did she mean by that? That I had no self-control, and that I was being stupid? Maybe she was right.

"Nothing happened," I reiterated. "I let her stay the night. I have another bed."

"She slept in the other bed all night?"

"Well, mostly. If it makes you feel any better, I feel like crap."

She scoffed. "You *should* feel like crap."

"You know I'd never lie to you, Chris. Nothing happened."

"Nothing, Brad? I'm not going to get into a discussion with you about the definition of *nothing*," she said, "but you're either an idiot, or an asshole, or both."

"Aside from me being an idiot, then, I did find out some interesting information about the Westbrooks, but I'm not sure if..."

"Hang on a second, Brad," Chris interrupted. I waited. "I just received a new message. It says that Pilot Bob will meet you at the airport, not at Trident Basin. You can meet him where you picked up the Jeep."

"What's going on, Chris?" I looked at my phone. 4:30 p.m.

"I'm not sure," she said then paused. "The message says that Pilot Bob landed at Trident Basin, and he told Chief Carmichael that one of the Westbrooks was there. He said their plane is getting ready to leave from one of the docks, so it must be back in service already. The water is getting choppy too. Chief Carmichael doesn't want you to go anywhere near there right now."

"Which Westbrook is there?"

"The message doesn't say. Chief Carmichael wrote that the DEA has a car parked in Trident Basin's lot. Pilot Bob will use it to drive to the airport and meet you."

"They must have another plane."

"There's one more message," Chris said, then paused. "Oh, it just says that when Pilot Bob gets to the airport, he'll explain everything."

"Try to find out if it was Jason, Pete, or Kyle at Trident Basin."

"I will, but don't worry about it. Just get to the airport and wait."

***

I arrived at the airport at 4:45 p.m. The place looked different in the daytime. There was more activity where the small aircraft and rental cars were parked. Nobody paid much attention to me. I supposed they were used to the bright colored Jeep being parked there.

I texted Chris. "At the airport now. Anything new?" She didn't text back. I waited until 5:00 p.m. before I called her. "What's happening?"

"I haven't heard anything yet," she said. "I'm just waiting. They haven't sent me any more messages. Pilot Bob is probably on his way, but their locator map isn't working right now."

"Did they ever say which Westbrook was at Trident basin?"

"No, does it matter?"

"It might. I should have just waited for the barge," I said. "Dammit! It's probably Jason heading back to Uyak Bay, but it could be Kyle, especially if their plane needed to be picked up."

"It doesn't matter now," she said. "Let me know when Pilot Bob arrives."

"I will."

***

Pilot Bob was late. Too late. At 5:30 p.m. Chris called me back. "Any sign of Bob?"

"Nothing," I said. "It's only ten or twelve minutes from here. I'll drive over there. Something isn't right. We should've heard from him by now."

"No, Brad, wait a few more minutes."

"Why? If I see him on the way, I'll just turn around."

"You need to wait!" Chris exclaimed.

"For what?" I asked. "Jason must be gone by now. That goes for any of the Westbrooks. "I'll call you when I get there."

I thought I'd arrive and see Pilot Bob standing near the open hood of a car, his battery dead, or maybe even a tow truck driver there trying to assist him. But as I pulled up to Trident Basin's upper parking lot, there was no activity whatsoever. The area around the floatplanes seemed lifeless. The only noise was the flapping sound of the flags near the docks.

It *was* a Sunday evening, so maybe it was normal for the place to be empty. The wind had picked up and the weather was iffy but not seeing anybody there hadn't been what I'd expected. The whole scene made me feel uneasy. Pilot Bob wasn't around, and I hadn't passed him on the road. I looked down at the docks and saw his Cessna. I had no idea what the Westbrook's plane looked like, but there were seven floatplanes docked there.

I called Chris. "I'm at Trident basin right now, and there's nobody here."

"Did you talk to Bob?"

"No," I said. "He's not here. I'm looking at his plane right now. Do you know what vehicle the DEA parked here?"

"Let me check," she said. "I'll call you back."

I waited a few minutes and looked around. I saw a small bag on the dock near Pilot Bob's plane, but I didn't want to go down to look at what was inside of it yet. Both Bumble Bee planes were there. I only saw three cars besides the Jeep, two in the upper lot and one closer to the water.

Chris called back. "I'm looking at an agency's locator map right now, in real time. It shows all of the tracking devices we have in that area. The DEA's car should be there. It's a white Chevy Malibu. License number XCV…

"No need," I interrupted, I'm staring at it right now." I went up to the driver's side door and looked inside. I felt the front hood. "Nobody has driven this car in the last few hours," I said. "I checked the door and was surprised when it opened.

"The door's unlocked," I said, "but there doesn't seem to be anything inside."

"Wait!" Chris said. "Pilot Bob's location is showing up on the screen. Do you see him?"

"No."

"Go down toward the water. Is there a building, or some other structure to your right?"

"Hang on," I said. I closed the door to the Malibu, opened the back of my Jeep, and grabbed the bag with the lockbox inside of it. After I put in the combination, I took out the 9mm Glock, screwed on a silencer, and inserted a full magazine into the gun. I turned off the safety, pulled the slide, and released a round into the chamber. I was scanning the area at the same time. "OK, now I'm ready."

"The map shows a structure to your right, down near the water, in front of the last dock."

I walked slowly. "Do you know what the Westbrook's plane looks like?" I asked.

"Never mind," Chris said. "You're getting closer to a building, aren't you?"

"There are two small buildings," I said. "Do you see where I'm at?"

"Yes, I'm picking you up. Pilot Bob is to your right, maybe twenty or thirty feet past the buildings."

A mixture of sand and rocks were along the shoreline, and I kept walking. A black object was five or six feet from the water. I picked it up. "Looks like an iPhone 8," I said. "He needs an upgrade."

"Do you see him?" Chris asked.

"No, but you're not going to like this, I see two sets of footprints, heading down the beach. It looks like they were running. And they haven't come back yet."

"Let me call this in," Chris said. "I don't want you down there alone."

"Too late," I said. I kept walking along the shoreline, following the prints. "There's a ramp up ahead, but it looks like they headed up the hill. Hang on. Do you still see where I am?"

"Yes, but stay there. This mission isn't worth you ending up in a body bag."

"Relax, Chris. If the Westbrooks catch me, they'll probably just throw me into the ocean."

"Nice, Brad. That makes me feel better."

"You still love me, don't you? Admit it."

"You're an ass, and you have no idea what love is."

After a few hundred feet, the footprints turned away from the water, and continued up a small bluff. I climbed to the top.

"I'm on a paved road now," I said. "I don't see any more tracks. This road goes back toward the floatplane docks, parallel to the beach. Do you see me?"

"Yes, you're just below an area that looks like a quarry. Do you see the piles of sand and gravel? That paved road goes all the way back to the upper parking lot."

"Yeah, there's some equipment above here, and…oh, wait…"

An area of grass, on the other side of the paved road, had been trampled down. I saw a small patch of what looked like blood, about the size of a silver dollar, on the ground, and it looked fresh. Several large stones were on the slope and one of them had obviously been moved because it had left an impression in the soil. I felt my gut sink.

I looked at the pavement again. I noticed several tiny areas of smeared blood and a few droplets that led back toward the parking lot. I followed the trail all the way back to the Malibu. It's funny how a person only sees certain things when they're looking for them. I hadn't noticed the blood near the car until that moment. I opened the Malibu's door again and reached down to open the trunk. I walked back and raised the hatch. "Crap!"

"What is it?" Chris asked.

"Bad news," I said. "My flight to Anchorage has been delayed."

TWENTY-NINE

Pilot Bob's body had been crammed into the trunk of the Malibu. The back of his head was bashed in, and he had been placed face up, on purpose. His wallet and keys had been tossed onto his chest. A card, with his photo, was sticking out of his mouth. I took a closer look at his ID. It was his DEA badge. Whoever killed Pilot Bob had killed before. No first timer made statements like that.

"Are you sure he's dead?" Chris asked. She didn't have the benefit of a visual.

"Yeah, Chris, he's dead. Do you want me to send you a photo?"

"That's OK," she said. "You need to get out of there. Do what you need to do, and I'll take care of notifying people on this end. I'll contact Chief Carmichael first."

"There's a bag on the docks, near his plane," I said. "I'd like to see what's inside of it."

"You don't have enough time. Drive back to the airport and park in the same spot you parked before. I'll book you on the next flight off the island. We'll let the agency deal with the local law enforcement."

I looked down at the bag. It would've only taken me two or three minutes to go down there, grab it, and run back up to the parking lot. I thought about it, but I realized the police would get it when they came. Chris could find out from the agency what was inside of it.

The sound of a ship's horn rang out from the other side of Near Island. It was a reminder for me that I was close to town, but I still hadn't seen anybody near the floatplanes. The hill obstructed most of my view. If I couldn't see anyone, they couldn't see me. Chris was right, though. I needed to leave.

I wiped down the Malibu's door handle and the back latch with my sleeve, then closed the trunk. I scanned the area again before I got back into my Jeep and left. I didn't pass by any cars on Near Island, so I kept driving over the Alimaq Bridge and took a left on Rezanof, toward the airport. A police car was in the distance coming toward me. Its lights were on full tilt, so I turned down the next street toward the harbor.

The police car passed by. I watched it in my rearview mirror. I drove a few more blocks and turned onto a familiar street, then parked in front of the Whiskey River Saloon. I glanced around and then pointed the rearview mirror toward myself. My face looked worn and hollow. I hadn't realized how much I'd been sweating. I looked like crap. I really needed to get in better shape.

After I gathered myself, I wiped my face with a T-shirt that I had pulled out from one of my bags. It was one of the shirts I had bought at Nancy's gift shop, *Kodiak's Treasures*. I held it up. The shirt was royal blue, and *Welcome to Kodiak* was written on the front. It had an outline print of three bears fishing in a stream. I wondered how many bears were needed to be considered a sloth. Two—three—more? I had no idea.

I heard more sirens in the distance, and I knew where they were headed. I called Chris back.

"Police are all over the place! What's going on?"

"I contacted Chief Carmichael," she said. "I told her you needed a few minutes to get out of there, but she must have already called it in. Where are you now?"

"I'm OK, but it was close. If I would have waited another thirty seconds, I'd be at the police station right now, getting asked questions that I can't answer. Is there any chance I'll be able to leave?"

"I've been checking for flights, Brad. The airlines don't have any more going out today, but there's one to Anchorage tomorrow at 7:30 in the morning."

"What about chartering a helicopter or a small plane?"

"I'll check. Do you have a place you can go for an hour or two?"

I looked up at the Whiskey River sign. "Yeah, just text me when you have something."

***

I waited fifteen minutes, until the sirens died down, before I went inside.

"Hey, look who's here," Mick called out from across the room. "Anchor's away!"

Mick, Bud, and Hannah stood near the electronic dart boards. A few people I'd recognized from the tournament waved as I made my way toward my teammates.

"Have a seat," Bud said. He pointed toward a booth where two pitchers of beer were half full.

"I'll get another glass," Mick said. He walked toward the bar.

"Let's get a couple of orders of those barbecued wings," I said. "My treat."

"Now you're talkin," Mick said. He stopped. "How are you feeling after last night? You look a little pale."

"I'm here," I said.

"At least in spirit,' Bud said. We laughed.

"You're hungry, so you must not feel too bad," Mick said, then continued to the bar to order.

"How often do you come here to play darts?" I asked.

"Our dart league meets here on Sundays," Bud said. "But we don't have any matches today because of the tournament last night. I think it'll just be the three of us this afternoon, or four now with you."

Bud, Hannah, and I sat down. "Did you hear about the pilot over at Trident Basin," Hannah asked.

The question caught me by surprise. How could they know about it? "Uh, no."

Bud looked serious. "Randy picked up something on the scanner a few minutes ago," he said. "It didn't sound good."

"It wasn't anyone from Island Tours," Hannah said. "All of the pilots posted that they're OK on the group text."

"What happened?" I asked. "A crash?"

"No," Bud said. "From what Randy told us, a pilot was killed in the parking lot. They think he was murdered."

"The owner of Island Tours just texted," Hannah said. "Their planes weren't damaged. I guess whatever happened occurred in the parking lot. I thought about going down there to check things out." She looked at me. "You'd probably like to take some photos. You can come with me if you want."

"I don't take those types of photos," I said.

Randy came out from the back and looked upset. "The man was a pilot from Anchorage, guys. They found him in the trunk of his car. The whole place is cordoned off, and they're not letting anyone down there right now."

"Well, there goes your plan," I said to Hannah. "They'll probably shut down that area all night."

"Maybe," she said.

"So, where is Lacy?" Bud asked. He smiled. "You two seemed to hit it off."

"We said our goodbyes today," I said. "I was supposed to fly out this evening, but the company called and said there was a cancellation."

"From Trident Basin?" Bud asked.

"No," I said. "I was scheduled to fly out from the airport. I don't know what happened. I think the company messed up. Now, they're trying to schedule a flight to Anchorage for later tonight. Actually, I wanted to spend another day over at Uyak Bay, but the company set up another assignment for me in Washington State."

I don't know why I mentioned Uyak Bay. I'd been thinking about the Westbrooks, the raid, and I suppose it just slipped out.

"I could give you a ride," Hannah said. "At least to Uyak Bay. I can't go all the way to Anchorage because I have plans, but I could get you over to Uyak Bay, and pick you up tomorrow afternoon. I'll give you a discount, let's say three hundred for the round trip." She looked at her watch. "But we'd have to leave here by seven. Seven fifteen, at the latest."

"Isn't your plane at Trident Basin?"

"No, my plane is parked at the airport right now. I only use the bumble bees when I'm flying for Island Tours. Mine is amphibious. I have both wheels and floats."

I looked at my phone. 6:15. I had no place to stay, no flight to Anchorage, and no idea what the DEA had planned. Hannah wouldn't just drop me off near the

Westbrook's inlet at sunset without an explanation. I wasn't sure what to do.

"Is Walt still around?" Hannah asked.

Of course! Walt's Bear Camp. I could figure out how to get to the Westbrooks later.

"I think his daughter gets into town on Tuesday," I said, "so he should still be there. I'll ask him."

The air seemed colder and dryer when I walked outside. The wind howled through the streets. I looked at my phone and hit the call button.

"Are you OK?" Chris asked.

"Aside from being cold, I'm OK. Any word from Chief Carmichael?"

"Not directly. I don't think we're a priority right now. I can see from the GPS map that you're still in town. Are you secure?"

"Yeah, I'm fine. Have you found any flights?"

"Not yet, but I have you booked on that commercial flight tomorrow at seven thirty. We might be able to get you on a transport from the Coast Guard base earlier in the morning. I've been blocked from using any of the charter companies tonight, and Chief Carmichael has rented every helicopter on the island for the next twenty-four hours."

"Every helicopter?"

"Don't ask me. The companies are all saying the same thing. They're booked until Tuesday."

"What did you mean by 'blocked' from using charters?"

"Yes, blocked. Since you found Pilot Bob, they're trying to eliminate traffic on the island tonight. They haven't told me an exact time, but the raid is planned for tomorrow morning. The agency has already taken over the murder scene at Trident Basin. They have two US Marshals down there right now."

"That was fast," I said.

"The DEA has a field office set up at the Coast Guard base. They plan to coordinate the drug bust from there. They've had it set up for a couple of days, and agents are coming in from all over, even the lower forty-eight. They'll probably have twenty or twenty-five agents go out on the raid in the morning. I don't know why the US Marshals were there. Maybe they were still gathering evidence from Pulte's murder."

"If I can get a pilot to fly me somewhere, will they let me takeoff from the airport?"

"I don't know. Like I told you, Chief Carmichael doesn't want anyone to use private charter services tonight."

"What if we tell her it's to leave Kodiak and get out of her way?"

"What pilot are you thinking about? Hannah Jones?"

"Yeah, I'm having a beer with her right now. She said she's available."

"I don't think that's a good idea, Brad."

"Why not? Doesn't the DEA want to get rid of me?"

"Brad, you don't understand what's going on there. They're sending out new protocols."

"New protocols?"

"It means there are three or four agencies working together on this drug bust tomorrow morning. I'm sure they'll be using a Coast Guard vessel, and maybe some helicopters and floatplanes. We know the US Marshals are already there. There could be FBI agents, and even some of the local law enforcement might get involved."

"What about me? Was Chief Carmichael specific about my role?"

"You're not considered an asset anymore, but you haven't been officially released from your assignment yet either. Pilot Bob's murder has complicated things and they're not worried about you right now. They know you're still on the island, but we don't fit into their plans. Like I said, you're not a priority to them. I think they've written you off, but at least Chief Carmichael is still answering my calls and texting me back."

"So, they haven't scrubbed my mission yet?"

"Not technically," Chris said.

"Do you think Chief Carmichael would allow me to leave Kodiak if I asked her nicely. Pretty please with sugar on top?"

"Brad, what are you thinking about doing?"

"My job."

"Brad, we're already getting paid. If you try to find Kyle, the only thing you're going to do is mess things up."

"Listen Chris, this raid won't work. I don't care what kind of protocols they have in place. It's been less than forty-five minutes, and everyone on this island already knows about what happened to Pilot Bob. Do you think the Westbrooks are going to sit there and wait for the DEA to show up in a Coast Guard Cutter or a helicopter? Kyle will be gone, and the drugs will be gone, too. We've got one shot at finding Kyle. He's the man who killed Boggs, remember? I'm fifty-six years old, and I'm not afraid of the Westbrooks, the DEA, or even the agency."

"That's not a plan, Brad. You're just running on emotions right now."

"I don't think you understand what I'm saying, Chris. Listen to me closely! I'm not asking you for permission, I'm asking you for help! I care about you more than any other person in this world. I messed up last night and I'm sorry. I don't want you to be involved with this if you think they'd come after you later. But this is my decision. I'm asking you officially: Will Chief Cassandra Carmichael allow me to use a private charter to leave Kodiak this evening?"

There was a long pause before Chris replied. "When I ask her, do you still want me to say pretty please, with sugar on top?"

THIRTY

When I went back inside the saloon, Bud, Mick, and Hannah were devouring the chicken wings, their fingers and lips all lathered in barbecue sauce. I couldn't help but think about Pilot Bob in the trunk of the Malibu, his badge stuffed into his mouth like a barbecued wing. I lost my appetite. He didn't deserve to die that way. It was such a lousy way for him to be remembered. Kyle, or whoever had killed him, would certainly deserve everything that was coming to him.

"We should get another order," Mick said after he wiped his face. Bud didn't say anything. He just held up two saucy fingers. Hannah was chuckling and eating at the same time. They seemed to be having a good time. The day had been a real roller coaster. I wasn't sure if things would ever settle down.

Walt emailed me back. He said he could have a room set up for me if I came for the night. If we couldn't make it, he understood, but I needed to let him know if my plans changed. He'd already heard about the *Trident Basin Killing,* as it was now being called, on the radio. News traveled fast on Kodiak. I was sure the Westbrooks had been following the reports, too.

I laid down four one-hundred-dollar bills on the table in front of Hannah. "My company said they'll pay you four hundred dollars if you take me to Uyak Bay this evening and pick me up tomorrow."

She nodded. "I think we have a deal."

"I had to convince them it'd be worth it," I said. "Now, they expect a cover photo." I smiled.

"No pressure there," Hannah said. "But that's up to you." She picked up the cash, grabbed her coat and smiled. "Thanks for the bonus."

Before we left, Randy came out from the back office to give everybody an update of the *Trident Basin Killing*. One of his friends on Kodiak's police force told him the feds were in charge of the investigation now, and that local police had been removed from the crime scene. "They had been placed in a supporting role," he said.

The agency hadn't wasted any time. I wondered what the following day's news headlines would be. Would the agency make up a story about Pilot Bob, or blame his death on drug dealers? Were they waiting for the outcome of the raid? As long as the words, "Brad Kelso, former freelance photographer" weren't in the headlines, I didn't care about the DEA's plans. Maybe I should have.

When I paid for the wings, I glanced above the bar and smiled. I took a sharpie and wrote on a dollar bill. I taped it right next to a bill that read, "Wouldn't you like to know—LM."

I laughed when I first saw Lacy's dollar. What I wrote was less than profound, but it sort of rhymed. "Anchor's away—you owe me a beer, BK." I didn't know how long it would take before Lacy noticed it, but I knew she'd smile when she did.

I began to feel like my luck had changed for the better. Maybe I'd be able to complete my mission after all. Kyle, Pete, and Jason were the prime suspects in Pilot Bob's murder, but the only evidence the agency had was a few texts from Pilot Bob, and he hadn't specified which Westbrook he'd seen. My money was on Kyle, but from what Lacy and her mom had said, Jason was the most dangerous Westbrook, at least when they were younger. I couldn't get past how the killer had placed Pilot Bob's DEA badge into his mouth. That was a psychopath's move. The only Westbrook who fit that type of profile was Kyle. He was the outlier, the lone gunman, the quiet neighbor that Lacy would never have dreamed could be a murderer. Of course, I knew something she didn't. He murdered Boggs and he'd almost gotten away with it. Almost.

Maybe a badge in the mouth was just an indicator that Kyle had evolved as a killer over the years. I had never studied psychology, but any motive for leaving a body like that seemed messed up to me. Most of the people I'd tracked were criminals of one kind or another, but there was always a method to their madness. And why would Kyle have chosen a DEA agent? Did Kyle have some involvement in the distribution of fentanyl? The DEA had been focused on Pete. And what role did Pete and Jason play in all the killings? Were all three of the brothers involved in everything?

I had so many questions that needed answering, but I needed to stay focused. My job had been to find Kyle and to provide the agency with a way to locate him. As far as Chief Carmichael was concerned, my mission had already ended, but as long as the agency hadn't sent me an official order, I planned to finish what I'd started.

I tossed my cell phone into my suitcase and pulled out the extra phone from my bag. I didn't think it was being tracked by the agency, but I wanted to make sure. I called Chris on my way to the airport.

"You'll be happy to know," she said, "Chief Carmichael was very pleased to hear you'll be leaving Kodiak."

"That's what I thought. So, she said I could charter Hannah Jones's plane as long as I promised to leave Kodiak?"

"I didn't tell her it was Hannah Jones. I just told her you planned to leave Kodiak with a private aircraft if she would allow it. She said yes."

"That works."

"There's just one problem, Brad. You don't have any intention of leaving Kodiak Island. Lying to the DEA, and the agency, is not a very good way to make friends. They won't like it."

"Wait, Chris, I think you misunderstood me. I'll be leaving the *City* of Kodiak this evening, not the island."

There was a long pause. "Hang on, let me check my messages," she said. I waited. "Yeah, I never said anything besides *leave Kodiak*, which could be taken either way. They're not going to like it when they find out, though; especially Chief Carmichael."

"You're saying I could get on her bad side because she thought I was referring to the island, not the city, when I said I'd leave Kodiak?"

"Pretty much."

"I've been on her bad side before. She'll get over it."

"She may not be your boss, but she outranks you, and she could make your life miserable. She could probably find a way to arrest you if she wanted."

"My life is already miserable," I said. "One more person who's mad at me won't make any difference. Listen, Chris, I don't have much time. How does my location show up on your screen?"

"It shows you on Rezanof, about three miles from the airport."

"What trackers are being used by the program to locate me?"

"The Jeep and the other phone. Are you planning to use this phone from now on?"

"Is the agency tracking it?"

"It doesn't show up on my screen," she said. "But that also means I won't know your location after you drop off the Jeep."

"I'll take some tracking chips with me, so you'll have my phone and the chips if you really need to find me. Don't activate them before tomorrow morning. If you do, Chief Carmichael and everybody else will know where I am, and I need some time."

"How much time?" she asked.

"Give me until sunrise."

"What should I tell Chief Carmichael, if she asks?"

"Tell her I said she doesn't need to worry about me, and I left the phone in the Jeep. She's got a big drug bust to focus on, and I wanted to wish her luck. She's going to need it."

"Oh, before you leave, I wanted to tell you, she asked me what your shoe size was, and if one of the sets of tracks in the sand was yours."

"I didn't even think about the tracks I'd left in the sand. What did you say?"

"I said you wore a size 10, and that yes, you had followed the other tracks, and that's how you discovered Pilot Bob's body in the trunk.'

"Did she thank me?"

"Not exactly. She was too upset about Pilot Bob getting murdered to thank anyone. But I don't think she blames you. She directed most of her anger toward our Lord and Savior. She did tell me something interesting, though, that the extra shoe prints, that weren't Pilot Bob's, were size eleven."

"What are the Westbrooks' shoe sizes?"

"Some bean counters researched credit card receipts, and they found out both Pete and Jason had purchased size eleven shoes in the past. They don't have any idea what Kyle wears, but his size could be eleven, too."

"So, that doesn't help us."

"No, but it eliminates most of the other people who worked for the Westbrooks. Tony Lee wears a size fourteen."

"What size do you wear, Chris? They're like gunboats."

"For your information, I'm a size twelve in women's shoes, and you're an ass."

"I didn't mean anything by it. Having large feet is a good thing. It makes you more stable when you're standing."

"I can't believe I still care about what happens to you," she said. "I must be delusional."

"I'm pulling into the airport now," I said. "If something happens to me…"

"Don't give me that!" she exclaimed. "I'm going to light up those tracking chips at sunrise, tomorrow morning, and I expect you to be back, having coffee at Walt's Bear Camp. If not, I will be extremely put out."

I smiled. Chris and I always used quotes from our favorite movies. *The Princess Bride* was a classic. I simply responded, "As you wish."

***

Hannah's De Havilland Beaver was painted white with red trim. Its four small wheels, two underneath the floats, were used to land the aircraft on either a paved runway or in the water. I was glad her plane was set up to be amphibious since Trident Basin had been locked down because of the murder. Aside from taking four hours on a boat, I felt like she was the only way I could get to Walt's that evening.

"Do you like flying your own plane more than the bumble bees," I asked her as I put my bags inside.

"I guess so, but Island Tours has been a great side job for me. Taking tourists around the island is more fun than transporting merchandise to remote areas. I don't really care though. I just like to fly."

"I guess that makes me a tourist."

She smiled. "You lost your tourist status when you carried the anchor of the Monie Marie back home last night."

I laughed. "So, I'm a local now?"

"No," she said. "You're just not a tourist."

I smiled. She didn't realize how right she was.

THIRTY-ONE

Days, hours, minutes, and seconds. Throughout my life I've thought about various jobs, events, and experiences in terms of how much time they took. I might calculate seventy-three hours of labor when I'm making a bid on a bathroom remodel. How much time will it take to drive forty-eight miles on the freeway? I'd usually guess forty-eight minutes. How long before my patience dries up when I'm on the phone and being put on hold? About thirty seconds.

Did it matter if the time spent turned out to be more or less? At the end of the day, if the remodel took ninety hours to complete, if traffic added ten minutes to the drive, or if I waited on hold for fifteen minutes before hanging up, I tried not to dwell on it. Agonizing over time that has been wasted only wastes more time.

But memories are important. The difference between remembering something and dwelling on it can be significant. Recalling an experience that might have lasted hours, minutes, or seconds, only takes a moment. An instant. The fraction of a second that it takes to have a thought. Memories are the great equalizer of time, either well spent or wasted. The same holds true for forgetting something; but the opposite of remembering isn't forgetting. It's living in the present.

For government agents working undercover, being in the present is critical, but taking those extra moments to remember details, even if those details seemed insignificant at the time, can be the difference between life and death.

I was tired and worn out. The entire day had been broken up into what seemed like short, forgettable moments of time. I didn't feel like remembering anything, but that was dangerous. I was still on a mission, and I was still working undercover. As Hannah and I flew toward Uyak Bay, something dawned on me. I looked at my backpack and my bag in the back seat. Crap! I realized I'd forgotten something. Something important.

On my way to the airport, I had thought about what to take with me and what to leave in the Jeep, but it had completely slipped my mind when I loaded my bag and backpack onto the plane. There was no way around it. I was in trouble, and there was nothing I could do about it. At least I'd only be seeing Hannah and Walt over the course of the next few hours, so I thought I still might be able to pull it off. I had messed up though, big time. I had forgotten my camera.

I picked up a few pointers during my brief time as a professional photographer. One of the things I'd learned was to have the right lenses with me and to know when to use them. Another little tidbit was to view a shot looking through the viewfinder of the camera. Shadows and lighting can change significantly when seeing them through a wide angle or a zoom lens. But the most important rule of all—*rule number one*—is something even most amateur photographers wouldn't screw up. To take photos, I needed a camera!

I laid my head back and closed my eyes. What a frickin' nightmare. I was asleep before I could even start to worry about what I was going to do about it.

***

"KELSO!"

Adrenaline rushed through my veins. "Huh!? What?"

"Kelso!" Hannah shouted again. Maybe she didn't actually shout my name, but it sounded like it over the headset. "We're getting ready to land."

I'd only been asleep for about thirty minutes, but it seemed like several hours. I was glad because I needed the rest, but my brain hadn't caught up to my mouth yet.

"Where are we?" I asked.

Hannah laughed. "I don't know where you're coming from, but we're getting ready to land on planet earth."

I could barely muster a smile. "Sorry."

Hannah laughed even more. "I accept your apology," she said and kept laughing.

"I was out."

"Ya think?"

I became more coherent as we circled twice, before landing in front of Walt's Bear Camp. Hannah slowly maneuvered the plane to the dock. Walt reached up and grabbed the rail beneath the wing when we were close enough, then Hannah got out and tied us off.

"Back for more?" Walt asked me.

"I guess I can't get enough of Uyak Bay and the rest of Kodiak's natural beauty," I said.

Hannah smiled. "Yeah, Brad was a real chatterbox the whole way here. He couldn't stop talking about the landscape." She looked at me and we both laughed.

"I have a room ready for you in the lodge," Walt said. "Room number five."

"Is that the red room?" Hannah asked.

"No," Walt said. "Red room is two. Green room is five."

I grabbed my bag and backpack and hoped nobody noticed my camera bag was missing.

"I need to get back," Hannah said, "so I'll pick you up tomorrow afternoon. How does around two o'clock sound?

I looked at Walt and he nodded. "Two o'clock," I said.

"Don't forget to get that cover shot," she said.

I chuckled. "I won't."

Walt and I waved at Hannah as she taxied her plane away from the dock and took off against the wind. I looked up at the ridge. There was only one practical way for me to get from Walt's Bear Camp to the Westbrooks without being seen. I needed to hike, and I needed to do it at night without Walt knowing about it.

The skiffs were out of the question and there were too many spots along the shoreline that were impossible to hike around. Since I was a photographer who was there to take photos, a nighttime cruise on Uyak Bay would have seemed suspicious. Walt probably wouldn't allow his skiffs to be taken out at night anyway.

I yawned. "Are you as tired as I am," I asked Walt.

"I'm not tired at all," he said. "It's early. I made stew and biscuits if you're hungry. My daughter isn't coming until Tuesday, so it will be nice to have some company. I told you, I'm usually in Victoria by now. It's been a strange week being here all alone."

"You're telling me."

We walked toward the lodge. "If you want, I could stay in one of your cabins instead of inside the lodge. I snore really loud."

Walt shook his head. "The rooms have extra insulation, so I won't hear you. But the floor might creak a little if you walk around."

"I'm a sleepwalker, too. I should have said something."

Walt put his arm around my shoulder and laughed. "You're a funny guy. Are you hungry? Do you want some stew?"

Actually, I *was* hungry. But *stew*? When we got inside, I could smell the biscuits first. Walt led the way up to the second floor to a large bedroom. It had been painted lime green with white trim. The bed sheets, the carpet, and even the blankets were green.

"This is definitely not the red room," I said.

"Would you prefer the red room?" he asked.

I looked out the green room's window. There was no good access, just a ten or twelve-foot drop from the window onto a patch of grass and rocks. The ground looked really hard, too.

"Where do you sleep?" I asked.

"Down the hall," he said. "Room number one."

That meant we were divided by room number three, and maybe he wouldn't hear me when I left.

"No, I like green," I said. "I might wake up early tomorrow morning, before sunrise, and go for a long walk along the beach or do some hiking. Is there a trail leading up to the ridge?"

"Yes," he said. "The trail goes all the way up to the top of the lower ridge, and there's a good place to view the sunrise if you like to get up early. It takes, oh, maybe twenty minutes to get to the top."

"Are there any good paths along the ridgeline?"

"No, the trail ends close to the top. It's rocky up there, but people sometimes walk on the rocks too. Are you just going to hike, or do you plan to rent a skiff tomorrow?"

"I'm not sure yet, but I'll leave you a note if I go for a hike."

"I'd appreciate that. You can take one of the two-way radios with you. I'll show you how to use it before you go to bed."

***

The distance to the Westbrook's compound was about two miles, including the hike up to the top of the lower ridge. At an average pace of a little over a mile an hour, assuming I didn't run into any obstacles, I'd be hiking for about two hours each way. It might take another two or three hours once I was on the Westbrook's property to make sure Kyle was there and to place the tracking chips. If I had an opportunity to get my revenge, I would, but I didn't have a good exit strategy planned out yet.

Walt and I sat across from each other at a large oak table that could seat twelve. The dining room was long and narrow with several prints of Kodiak Island's wildlife hanging on the walls. It felt awkward being so far apart from each other while we ate. We even had our own salt and pepper shakers. He drank wine, and I nursed a Budweiser with the stew, which tasted as good as any stew I'd ever eaten.

"This stew is really something," I said. I waited for him to say something about Charlie, the duck, or his brother's menu, but he didn't. "And the biscuits are great, too! Do you cook most of the meals for your guests?"

"No, I have a cook and a housekeeper during tourist season, but I like to make my stew. It's an old family recipe, but I have a secret ingredient." He chuckled. "All the guests get my stew and biscuits for one night during their stay. They like it, and it gives the cook a day off." He smiled.

He seemed to be in a good mood, so I didn't dare ask him anything else about the stew. "You said your daughter is coming this week. Where does she live?"

"British Columbia, near Vancouver. It's been two years since she's visited here, but I see her during the winter sometimes. She lives three hours away from Victoria, by ferry." He smiled at first then looked sad. "Her mother and I divorced a long time ago." he paused. "Are you married?"

"Divorced," I said. "Eight years." Both of us shrugged. There wasn't much else to say about the subject.

I think Walt was a little disappointed when I said I wanted to go to bed, but I told him I liked to get up early. I knew I had a long night in front of me. It was nine o'clock when I locked the door to the green room and got my backpack ready. I took a sweatshirt out of my bag, along with a black stocking cap and a pair of gloves. I wrapped my Glock and two extra magazines in the sweatshirt and stuffed them into the backpack next to a bottle of water and a fitness drink. I had two small LED flashlights, fully charged, so I put one in the pack and one in my pocket. Walt's two-way radio went into the backpack's side pocket, and I made sure it was turned off. I drank a five-hour energy drink, extra strength, and hoped it would work for six or seven. Then I wrote out a note for Walt, placed it on the bed, and waited.

At nine twenty, I heard Walt go into the bathroom. When he turned on the fan, I opened the bedroom door. It was only the two of us there, but I still looked up and down the hallway before I stepped out of the green room. I gently closed the door and left it unlocked, which was a risky move, but if I needed to come back, I didn't want to make any noise or have to wake him up. If Walt checked the door in the morning, he'd see the note and not expect me to return for several hours.

I felt better when I finally got outside, and I didn't have any trouble finding the first part of the trail leading up to the ridge. I shined a flashlight periodically on the way, only when I needed to use it. I wanted to conserve the battery life and I didn't want to be a beacon on the hillside, especially when I was so close to Walt's.

When I reached the top of the ridge, the breeze picked up, and the wind came at me, head on. I started hiking south. My face was numb, and I used the hood of my coat to block as much of the cold as possible, but with the wind and the darkness, hiking on the rocks was harder than I'd expected. I still made good time, but my whole body was getting tired from going through the brush, or up and down over the rocks.

When I was far enough away from Walt's, I used the flashlight, and my pace picked up in some areas where the rocks were smooth. The wind eventually died down which made it more comfortable to navigate, especially around the steeper slopes and cliffs.

It was eleven o'clock when I finally reached the ridge that surrounded the Westbrook's compound.

THIRTY-TWO

The Westbrook's property looked eerie at night from the top of the horseshoe-shaped ridge. Two pole-mounted lights were at the far end of the docks, and they lit up the area near the water. I could see the trail which led from the main dock all the way up to the lodge.

It looked like several lights were on inside the lodge, but I wasn't close enough to see anything through the windows. Nobody was moving around outside and there was a thin layer of fog covering the lowlands.

The footholds between the rocks allowed me to move down the slope without too much trouble, but the brush thickened the lower I went. I was glad I'd brought the gloves with me. My coat protected my body from the taller brush, but I spent quite a bit of time grabbing onto the rocks and branches, and whatever else I could find to stabilize me. The rocky terrain was steep, but not technical, and the areas that didn't have rocks were covered in thick foliage.

The faint glimmer coming from the dock lights allowed me to see where I was going until I reached the trees. Then the shadows darkened the lower portion of the hillside which slowed my descent. My eyes soon adjusted, and I was able to see a narrow path that ran just below the tree line in both directions. I walked to the right, toward the bay, and another path split off and headed lower. I took that fork and meandered down until I approached a large clearing which included the lodge and several outbuildings.

A covered area for wood storage was about sixty feet from the lodge and about the same distance from the docks. Five or six cords of split firewood had been stacked underneath a framed lean-to which had no front or back. The metal roofing was large enough to keep all the wood dry, and some small logs and rounds that still needed to be split were there, too. I took up a position behind the wood pile. I could smell the aroma of freshly cut firewood as I knelt in the darkness.

From that vantage point, I could remain hidden, yet I was able to see the lower part of the compound with clear lines of sight all the way up to the lodge. It was a perfect spot for a stakeout. The Westbrook's floatplane and a small skiff were docked, but when I looked out toward the bay, I saw the light of another vessel coming into the inlet.

I waited. I recognized the charter boat when it got closer. It was the *Westward Flyer*. I was curious to find out who the captain was, especially so late at night.

Whoever was on the boat appeared to be alone and I could tell, even from a distance, it was a man at the helm. He maneuvered the *Westward Flyer* toward the lower dock like he'd probably done it a thousand times before, then reversed the engine at just the right time. The boat nearly stopped, then slowly drifted toward the wooden edge. He jumped out quickly and tied the ropes around the metal cleats. He didn't hesitate as he began to unload several of the plastic containers he'd brought with him. Once he was under the lighted area, I recognized him immediately. It was Pete Westbrook.

As I watched Pete continue to unload, the lodge's porch light came on. A man walked down to the docks and picked up one of the containers. My heart raced. The man helping Pete was the same man whose photo I'd memorized. His smug, bearded face had been etched into my brain. It was Kyle Westbrook.

"Any trouble?" he asked Pete.

"Hey KJ," Pete said. "No, no trouble. What's going on at Trident Basin? I heard a report that a pilot was killed."

Kyle shook his head. "It was a DEA agent."

Pete looked surprised. "The pilot was a DEA agent?"

"Yeah. He had a badge with him. Jason found out the DEA set up shop over at the Coast Guard Base."

"Who told him that?"

"Mac."

"Who killed the agent?"

"You need to talk to Jason about that."

"Dammit!" Pete exclaimed. "Are they coming here?"

"Jason thinks they're planning somethin'. He doesn't know when it's gonna happen yet, but it could be as early as tomorrow."

Pete sighed. "What about the fent?"

"The fent's in the fort," Kyle said. "Jason doesn't want Ivanoff to come here, so he plans to meet him tomorrow morning in Pedro Bay. He's inside talking to Mac right now."

"How's the plane?"

"No leaks," Kyle said. "I looked it over. They did a good job."

There was no doubt about it; all three brothers were involved in the distribution of fentanyl. I still didn't know who had murdered Pilot Bob. Pete hadn't killed him. Kyle didn't act like he'd killed him either. Kyle said he checked-out the plane, so maybe he was the Westbrook who Pilot Bob saw at Trident Basin. *Who was Mac?*

Then I heard a noise. "Wroff! Wroff! Wroff!" A large German shepherd shot down the path, from the lodge, toward the docks. My heart nearly stopped.

"Hey girl," Pete said as he knelt on the wooden decking. The dog ran toward him. He rubbed its neck and head.

"Bella, come here!" a man yelled from the lodge's front door. It was Jason. I was about sixty feet away from all three Westbrooks.

Pete smiled. "You're such a good girl," he said. He kept petting her.

There were no two ways around it, I was in trouble. One sniff from that dog and I was toast. I looked up at the trees. The gentle breeze was blowing toward me. I was lucky

"Bella!" Jason yelled again.

The dog left Pete and began to move quickly toward the lodge before stopping suddenly, about halfway. She looked in my direction. Bella's back went upright and stiff. Her ears pointed upward, and her growl showed her large canine teeth. *Crap.*

"Bella!" Jason yelled even louder. "Come here!"

The dog looked toward her master, then she put her nose out in front of her and sniffed toward the ground. She went back inside the lodge and Jason closed the door. I breathed again. I heard one last bark coming from the other side of the door; just a little reminder of how lucky I had been. Jason walked down to meet his brothers.

"What's going on?" Pete asked Jason.

"Mac says the DEA will be here in the morning." Jason said. He snickered. "Coast Guard vessel, choppers, the works. He's going to call when they leave the base. Tony's down there with him right now. I'm meeting Ivanoff tomorrow in Pedro Bay instead of having him come here."

Jason didn't seem worried at all. It was the first time I'd ever seen him in person. He seemed more calm, cool, and collected than his brothers.

"That's what KJ said. Did you talk to Ivanoff about my share?"

"Yeah. He said nothing's changed. Maybe next time."

"What did you say to him?" Pete asked. "I could've been stopped yesterday. Five thousand isn't worth the risk."

"That's up to you, brother. You agreed to it."

"That's bullshit."

"Don't get greedy, Pete! Do you think it should come out of my share?"

"No."

"Then shut your mouth!" Jason said, "or I'll shut it for you!"

In an instant, there went Jason's calm, cool, and collected demeanor. Lacy had been right about his temper.

"I don't want to fight with you about it. I just think the situation has changed for us."

"What's changed, Pete? A couple of DEA agents thought they were smarter than me? Ivanoff told me he doesn't trust you. He thinks the pressure will get to you. I told him you could handle it, but now I'm starting to wonder."

"I'll be fine."

"You better be!" Jason bellowed.

"Tell him about the pilot," Kyle said.

Jason chuckled. "Mac was right. The guy had a badge. I took care of it. Ivanoff pays us to take care of things. He said if everything goes well, the next shipment could be a lot bigger. He said he's been having trouble with his supply chain, and I could become his primary."

"I'm done after this shipment," Pete said.

"Don't give me that," Jason said. "I'm just getting started."

"I don't want to risk it," Pete said. "We're not using my boats anymore."

Jason grabbed Pete by the collar and tossed him to the ground. Then he whispered loudly, "You'll be done when I say you're done. I'm not going to run a fuckin' barge business for the rest of my life. I'll take out the *Ho* or the *Flyer* anytime I want."

Pete got back up. "The deal was you get the barge business and I run the fishing operations."

"Deals change," said Jason. He laughed. "Ivanoff says we could be supplying the entire state, and parts of western Canada in a couple of years. Do you realize what that means?"

"You don't own me," Pete said. He walked toward the lodge.

"Dammit, Pete!" Jason yelled. "Don't be like that!"

Pete stopped and turned around. "I'll keep my mouth shut tomorrow. Tell Ivanoff he doesn't have to worry about me, but I'm out."

The DEA had been more concerned about Pete, but it became obvious to me that Jason oversaw the drug operation. A guy named Ivanoff was even more important and controlled at least some of the market. I looked at Kyle Westbrook, who stood sixty feet away from me. I'd let the DEA worry about the drugs. My focus needed to be on Kyle.

"What time are you leaving?" Kyle asked Jason.

I'll take off as soon as I hear from Mac or Tony, but I don't think the DEA will leave the base before daybreak." He looked at his watch. "I'll shoot for around seven forty-five. You haven't heard of any activity around the Larsen Bay Airport, have you?"

Kyle shook his head. "No."

Jason chuckled. "So, they'll all be coming from the base. I wish I could be here with Pete to see it."

"What about me?" asked Kyle.

"You can come with me to Pedro Bay. If you take the Flyer out, they'll wonder where she's at. You can just stay at the cabin for a few days."

I had been right about the DEA's drug bust. It was definitely going to be a bust. But if I put trackers on the plane, and somehow let Chris know, the DEA could probably arrive in Pedro Bay before Jason and Kyle got there. At least Chief Carmichael and the DEA could get their drug arrests. I needed to let Chris know, but I still had the option of taking care of Kyle right there.

I pulled out the Glock from my bag and screwed on the silencer. I pointed it directly at Kyle's head. I was a good shot, but from sixty feet away, there was no guarantee. If I killed him, then what? Would I be willing to take out Jason, and maybe even Pete, and then claim their deaths as collateral damage? They were distributors of fentanyl, currently the most dangerous drug on the market; but did Jason and Pete deserve to die? I needed to focus and be patient. The tracking chips had to be placed first. I waited until all three of them had gone inside the lodge. Then I waited even longer.

THIRTY-THREE

Timing is everything.

Normally, I would have waited behind the wood pile for a few hours, then leisurely gone out to the docks and placed tracking chips in the plane, the skiff, and the *Westward Flyer*. Most of the time it would've been safer to wait, to ensure the Westbrook brothers had gone to sleep. In this case, however, there were two issues that concerned me. The first one was that I didn't know if the brothers would actually go to bed. They knew a drug bust was coming in the morning. If I were in their shoes, I wouldn't have been able to sleep. The second issue, and the one that worried me the most, was Bella, and more specifically, the German shepherd's potty habits.

At my house, from ten o'clock at night until six in the morning, Jenny was good to go. But if I didn't let her out by six fifteen, six thirty at the latest, I'd have to suffer the consequences. And if I let her out earlier in the evening, she'd wake me up earlier in the morning. She was a well-regulated machine as far as her potty schedule—her being the machine, and me being the one who was well-regulated.

But, as far as Bella was concerned, I had no idea what the German shepherd's habits were. If the Westbrooks let her out at any time while I was out near the docks, I'd be more vulnerable than if I waited behind the wood pile. I didn't want to be forced to kill the animal. I like dogs, even if they're a little mean. I would've just as soon taken out Jason and Pete, two men I hadn't planned on killing, before doing anything to hurt Bella.

The Westbrook brothers certainly weren't innocent, having contributed to the fentanyl problem I'd heard so much about. Maybe they deserved to die. But Bella? I had my gun out, and I would've killed her, but as Chris liked to say, I would have been very put out.

The more time that went by, the less concerned I became about Bella being let outside. I also started to get cold just sitting on the damp ground behind the woodpile. When I finally thought the coast was clear, I looked at my phone. It was one forty-five. I waited until two o'clock and slowly got up. My knees were stiff from squatting so long.

I moved toward the floatplane as quickly, and as quietly, as possible. I tiptoed a short distance on the wooden planks, then stepped off the dock onto one of the plane's floats. I gently opened the pilot's door and placed three of the tracking chips underneath a rubberized mat, directly behind the pilot's seat. When a PFT couldn't communicate with their handler, three chips in the same location meant that a plane, car, boat, or residence was critical to the mission. Two tracking chips were more important than one, but three chips meant the location was a priority.

Once Chris activated the trackers, I thought the agency would see where the plane was headed and could follow Jason and Kyle all the way up to Pedro Bay. It would take them at least a couple of hours to get there in the floatplane. If the agency acted fast enough, they would find the drugs with them. I also placed a tracking chip in the *Westward Flyer*, and one in the skiff, just in case.

After I was finished, I made my way back behind the wood pile. Since I hadn't been seen or sniffed out yet, I was more confident than ever that the mission was going to be successful. The only thing I needed to do was make a decision: Should I hike back to Walt's or stick around and be an idiot?

I decided poorly.

If I would have been a hundred percent sure the Westbrooks would've been caught in Pedro Bay, I would have left. I had done my job; but there was one thing I couldn't get out of my mind: The *fort*. Kyle said it clearly. "The fent's in the fort." I smiled and repeated it to myself as I made my way back up the hillside. "The fent's in the fort." I couldn't get the thought of this hidden fort out of my mind. It was like waiting in line at Disneyland and listening to the song, *"It's a small world after all,"* before going on the ride. I was in a trance and, for better or worse, there was no going back. "The fent's in the fort." I needed to find this hidden fort that Lacy had talked about. It was obviously the place where the Westbrook's had stashed their fentanyl. What other fort could there be?

I recalled Lacy telling me it was just above the tree line, so when I got up to the main path, I stopped and did the math. The inlet, at that level, was roughly six or seven hundred feet across. The diameter, multiplied by *pi*, and subtracting the open area of the bay, meant my search area would encompass a little over one thousand five hundred linear feet and probably within a band of around twenty or thirty feet in height. Fifteen hundred feet is a little over a quarter mile. Hmmm...a quarter mile? I could do that.

I looked up toward the ridge and felt a few light flurries melt on my cheeks. The cold front wasn't supposed to leave any accumulation. If I left right then, I'd probably be back at Walt's and sleeping in the green room in two hours. Walt and I would listen to the radio in the morning and hear the shocking news about the drug bust. For lunch, Walt's stew and biscuits would probably be available.

I would tell him about how I had dropped my camera down a deep crevice near the top of the ridge while I waited for the sunrise. Yeah, it sounded plausible, but who was I kidding? I wanted to find the fort. I decided to give myself some time to locate it. I felt like I could spend a few hours searching for it before I needed to start hiking back.

I stayed in the shadows and slowly made my way around the hillside. The path that circled the property was just below the tree line, and along the way, several paths led down, some to the lodge and others toward the other outbuildings. Even the main path wasn't very wide, and areas of dense brush covered portions of it. I used my flashlight whenever I couldn't see the lodge. I figured if I couldn't see them, they couldn't see me.

Hiking on the slope and trudging through the brush took its toll on my legs. The vegetation thinned out where rocky knolls had prevented its growth, but those areas were steeper, and the layers of stone and loose gravel were just as difficult to traverse. Lacy had mentioned the fort was in one of those rocky areas, so I searched each one and came up empty. Nothing. I took off my backpack and placed it on top of a large rock to make it easier to move. I planned to go another hundred feet or so, then turn around. I'd just pick up my pack on the way back.

I had already traveled around most of the inlet, but it began to seem like a waste of time to keep going. I climbed on top of one of the rocky knolls, just above the tree line. The brush had thinned out, and even with the light flurries I looked over the trees and could see the water shimmering on the bay. I had given it an effort, but I was tired. Maybe I'd search one more area of rocks, then call it a night. That's when I saw a plastic water bottle on a small flat area just below me. I went down a few steps and picked it up. The Westbrooks not only distributed illegal narcotics, but one of them was a litterbug too. I looked around, but I didn't see anything else at first. The layered rocks all looked the same.

I put the bottle in my coat pocket and climbed back up a few feet onto the edge of the rocks. That's when I first saw it. A two-foot-wide dark space between one of the rock layers. I was only a few feet away from it. I got up and shined my light. There it was—the fort.

It was so well hidden, even Lacy's description hadn't done it justice. The wooden door was less than twenty inches wide, and it had been painted black. From above it, below it, and to one side, the entrance could not be seen, and I could have easily climbed right past it. The doorway was more like a crevice, and even when I shined the flashlight, it just looked like a shadow unless I was directly in front of it. If one of the painted hinges hadn't been scuffed, I might have never seen the door.

Before I entered, I stopped and glanced out toward the bay again. I imagined a pirate ship cruising up and down the coastline searching for the place where a treasure had been hidden. I smiled as I recalled Lacy's description. The door latch was sticky, and I had to use some leverage to pull it open.

When I shined my flashlight inside, I realized the fort wasn't very big, only about seven feet deep and six feet wide. It was less than five feet high too, so I had to duck to go inside. I guess it would have seemed large to a few young kids, but I just felt cramped and claustrophobic, so I left the door open. There were no chairs, but what looked like a small end table had been placed in one corner and a wooden shelving unit took up about half of the rock wall on the other side. I had to admit, even though it was small, it was a pretty cool fort.

On top of the end table was a large dark gray suitcase. It was nothing fancy, it looked like any one of the larger suitcases you'd see in baggage claim. I unzipped the case and opened the flap, then pulled off a thick foam cushion from the top. Glass vials containing a white powdery substance were separated by soft foam in dark plastic trays. There were four trays in the suitcase, and fifty vials could fit into each one. The case and trays had been designed well because they fit perfectly, and the two cushions provided plenty of protection for the vials. I slid three tracking chips into an area behind the liner. They stuck really well to the case's shell and couldn't be seen.

I didn't know how much fentanyl the suitcase contained, but with the weight of the vials and the case itself, I would have guessed between ten and fifteen pounds of the drug. That amount would've valued the suitcase at roughly a hundred fifty thousand dollars on the street. Fentanyl is cheap, compared to other narcotics, but it's extremely potent and deadly.

After I closed the case and zipped it back up, I thought I heard a noise outside. I stopped to listen. Nothing. I left everything where I'd found it and closed the door to the fort. When I turned to leave, a bright light nearly blinded me before my knees buckled from the blow to my head.

THIRTY-FOUR

My temples throbbed when I finally woke up. The pressure felt like my skull had been caught in a vise and my brain would explode at any moment. My hands were zip-tied behind my back, and I was lying on my side. A rope, which was wrapped around a small tree, bound my feet together. I wasn't going anywhere.

The bitter taste of my own blood made me queasy as I took shallow breaths. I couldn't see anything except a faint light coming from the sky and the damp soil where my face was planted. My left eye was sore and there was a sharper pain above my left ear from whatever I had been hit with. Maybe it was from the fall. My whole body ached. The cold ground against the side of my face relieved some of the pain.

My stocking cap must have come off when I'd been hit. Even with my coat on, I shivered from my head being exposed. At least I recognized where I was lying. It was the flat area between the fort and the path where I'd found the plastic water bottle. *Wait!* Somebody was there.

I heard the crunching sound of loose rocks above me and two voices coming up the path. The three men met on the flat area and stood above me.

I was nearly blinded when one of them shined a flashlight directly on the side of my face. Not being able to squint was difficult, but I remained still.

"Has he moved?" Jason asked.

"Not yet," Kyle answered.

"We can't wait much longer. He's still breathing. I need to find out who he works for. He didn't get here from the bay, so he must have hiked along the ridge."

"He's a long way from Walt's," Pete said. "That's not an easy hike in the dark."

"Walt has that trail that goes all the way to the top," Jason said. "If he just followed the ridge line, it wouldn't have taken him too long, maybe a couple of hours to get here."

"That's a four-hour round trip," Pete said. "Why would he be hiking all alone, at night, for four hours?

"Maybe he didn't plan to go back," Jason said. "If he's with the DEA, he might be part of the raid."

"What if he's *not* with the DEA?" Kyle asked.

"Then he's still a problem for us. Maybe even a bigger problem. He can't be one of Ivanoff''s guys, but he must know about the shipment. Why else would he be here? And how did he know about the fort?"

"How is he communicating with anyone?" asked Kyle. "His phone won't work here."

"Who knows?" Jason said, "but that's a good question to ask him when he wakes up."

The three men climbed past me up to the fort with Jason leading the way. I opened my eyes and watched them. Each of them was carrying a rifle. It became obvious that Jason was running the show.

Light flurries continued, but the flakes were melting as soon as they hit the ground. The sky kept getting lighter, so I knew it was getting closer to morning. I must have been knocked out for a couple of hours, but a concussion was the least of my worries.

The brothers came back down to the flat area. I felt a large boot kick my thigh, but I didn't move. "You should have told me about him." Jason said.

"He was just another photographer, and you were gone." Pete said. "Lacy has a thing for him, and he doesn't act like a DEA agent."

"Don't be an idiot," Jason said. "He found our fort." He paused and kicked me again, even harder than the first time. "In the dark, no less. He knew exactly where it was."

I barely opened my eyes and could see Kyle set his rifle down. He shined his flashlight on my wallet. "He doesn't have a badge," he said, "and his ID says he's a photographer. Maybe you're wrong about him."

Jason grabbed Kyle's shirt and threw him against the rocks. "So, now you're Mr. know-it-all!" he hollered. "What should we do with him?! Let him go?! You've got to be kidding me. How in the hell did he know about the fort?"

"Lacy must have told him," Pete said. He scoffed. "That bitch never could keep a secret."

"What else did she tell him?" Jason asked.

"Who knows?" Pete said. "She probably got excited and told him all about our childhood." He chuckled.

"Is this funny to you?" Jason asked.

"No."

"I don't think this is funny at all," Jason barked. "This is about as *not* funny as it gets!"

"Why don't we just toss him into the bay?" Kyle suggested. "The tide's going out."

"Are you brain dead?" Jason asked. "His phone has GPS. Whoever he's working for already knows he's here." He looked at Pete. "Are you sure he's staying at Walt's?"

"Yeah, I talked to Walt this afternoon. He told me Kelso was coming there to take more photos. Walt said he was supposed to get picked up by Hannah Jones tomorrow. It just doesn't make any sense. I still don't think he works for the DEA."

"Maybe he went for a hike and got lost in the dark," Kyle said.

Jason mocked his younger brothers in a high-pitched voice. *"Maybe he went for a hike and got lost in the dark. He can't be with the DEA."* He shook his head. "Are you kidding me? The two of you should have your own reality show. You could call it *Clueless on Kodiak*. I don't give a shit if he sleepwalked here. There's no way in hell he's just a photographer. Where is his camera? Does he even have a camera?"

They looked around briefly. "He must have a bag or a backpack around here somewhere," Pete said. "Maybe he has a SAT phone."

"It doesn't matter right now, but you need to find it," Jason said. "Here's what's going to happen. When he gets up, try to get some answers from him. Find his camera and pack, then take him up to that spot on the ridge where the drop off is. When they find his body, it'll look like he was on his way back and fell. If he doesn't have a SAT phone, the GPS on his cell phone will confirm where he's been."

As I laid there and listened to them, I realized that none of the brothers seemed very concerned about my well-being.

"I'm not hiking up there in this weather," Kyle said.

Jason scoffed. "We need to get that phone as far away from here as possible. Like I said, it'll look like he came here and planned to go back over the ridge. What can they prove? They'll waste all their time trying to figure out how he fell."

"I'm still not hiking up to that ridge right now," Kyle said.

Jason started to get angry. "What do you think this is, a game? If he puts up a fight, you might have to knock him out. It's going to take both of you to throw him off the cliff."

"You could do it," Kyle told Jason. "Why do I always have to do the hard work?"

I could hear Jason grab Kyle and throw him against the rocks again. This time, the two men struggled.

"That's enough!" Pete pleaded, trying to break them up. "That's enough!"

I found myself rooting for Kyle, but I wasn't sure why. Maybe they'd kill each other. With Pete in the middle, they eventually stopped fighting.

"Dammit, Jason," Kyle said, "I think you broke my rib."

"Stop your whining," Jason said. He wiped his mouth and mocked his younger brother in a high-pitched voice again: *"Why do I always have to do the hard work?"*

Kyle went after Jason, this time, and they crashed against the rocks again. Pete tried to break it up, but then he and Jason started fighting. They finally separated.

"This is bullshit," Pete declared.

Jason was breathing heavily. "Kyle, I'll tell you what." He wiped his mouth and grabbed a stone, about the size of a softball, from the ground. "You kill Kelso with this rock, and I'll go with Pete. I'll even carry Kelso's body up the hill."

There was a moment of silence, then Jason started laughing. "Go ahead, Killer, let's see what you got."

Jason gave the rock to his younger brother. Kyle took it but didn't come towards me at first. Jason kept egging him on. "Come on Killer. He's already half dead. One more blow to the head and we'll get to see some of his brains squirt out, like a squashed tomato." Jason shined the light on my face and kept laughing.

The hardest part about playing possum is right near the end, when the urge to yell and scream is almost overwhelming. I didn't feel very good about my situation at that exact moment, but I continued to lay motionless.

Kyle must have hesitated, but I couldn't see what he was doing. I barely opened my eyes when Jason directed the light toward his younger brother. All I could see were Kyle's boots, probably a size nine. I was pleasantly surprised when I heard him drop the rock.

"I knew it," Jason said. Just like in Montana. You can't kill him. I had to bail your ass out that night. You were just rolling around on the ground with that guy. Heck, he almost killed *you*, and you still couldn't shoot him." He spoke in a high-pitched voice again. *"Why do I always have to do the hard work?"* He scoffed and spoke like Jack Nicholson in *A Few Good Men*. "Because you can't handle the hard work."

"That's right, Jason," he said. "You bailed me out in Montana. But you forget; that guy wasn't after me. He was telling the truth."

"How was I supposed to know that? Both of us thought he was there to kill you, so don't put that on me. He lied about the postcard you found, didn't he? It's not like he was just some tourist."

Montana? Wait! Was he talking about Boggs? *Woah!* Jason killed Boggs!? I wasn't sure what to think, but I immediately felt like Jason was the one the agency should be after, not Kyle.

"What about the Beverley brothers?" Kyle said. "Who took the blame for killing them?"

"You're the one who was chasing after Ethan's girlfriend," Jason said. "What was her name? Amy? I wasn't going to watch those two idiots beat you up because you had a crush on some floozie."

"She wasn't a floozie!"

"And ever since then, I'm the one who has to hide," Kyle said. "Mr. Beverley has been dead for years, and I'm still supposed to do whatever you and Pete want me to do. I'm tired of it."

"Come on Kyle," Pete said. "That's not fair."

"Fair?" Kyle said. "Is it fair that I have to live in Pedro Bay or Dutch Harbor most of the time? I had to change my name just to get a job working for the family business. I haven't killed anybody. Jason's the one who's been killing everyone. I'm tired of running away from things I didn't do."

Jason's voice was more serious. "What's that supposed to mean?"

"Now's not the time to argue about it," Pete said. He looked up. "It's almost morning."

"I'm staying here at the lodge with Pete," Kyle said. "I'm done running."

"Don't be such an ass," Jason told Kyle. "Do you think this guy works alone? Hell, this place will be crawling with DEA agents tomorrow morning, and they're going to be really pissed off because of that pilot." He laughed. "I knew he was a DEA agent. Mac told me he saw him a few days ago when they set up their camp at the Coast Guard base. I can tell you one thing; he could run for a guy who looked like he was out of shape" He chuckled. "I wish I would've had my rifle with me."

"So, you killed the pilot?" Pete asked. "Is that why they're coming here tomorrow?"

"They've had this raid planned for a long time," Jason said. "Don't blame me. Mac and Tony think it was you who messed up. They think you might have said something to Lacy about the shipment."

"Lacy doesn't know anything," Pete said. "Why would I tell her about it?"

"I don't know," Jason said, "but if Kelso is missing someone will be looking for him. If he's with the DEA, they'll want someone to blame." He looked at Kyle. "Sorry little brother, but if you're here you'll be the one they accuse."

Kyle picked up the rock. "You want me to kill him right now?" he asked Jason. "You want me to squash his brains out all over the ground?! Is that it?!"

"Whoa there!" Pete said as he held Kyle back. "We have time. Let's find out who he works for first."

Kyle dropped the rock. "Maybe I'll just tell them the truth tomorrow. I've got nothing to hide."

"Don't ever say that again," Jason said loudly, "or I will personally kill you and throw you into the bay. They won't be looking for you." He paused. "And I'm not kidding."

"We need to just calm down," Pete said.

"I haven't got time for this," Jason said. "If he doesn't wake up soon, haul him up to the cliff. It won't do us any good to shoot him. Just make sure he's knocked out before you untie him. I'll go down and get everything ready to go."

"I don't want to kill him," Kyle said.

Pete shook his head. "We don't have a choice."

Jason smirked and then spoke as he started walking down the trail. "You two can decide who kills Kelso, but he needs to be at the bottom of that ravine with all of his gear in the next thirty minutes. If not, you'll be joining him."

***

Pete poked me several times with the butt of his rifle. Then he unscrewed the lid of a plastic bottle and poured water on my face. I moaned a few times and opened my eyes.

"Brad Kelso," he said. "Welcome to hell." He and Kyle laughed.

This time, I squinted when they shined the flashlight on me. "What time is it?" I asked.

"Let's get him up," Pete said. They tried to sit me up, but I played heavy, like a wet noodle. The only thing I could do was try to delay my own death until reinforcements came, which I knew would be too late.

"I'm not going to drag him all the way up there," Kyle said.

"You're going to have to help, Kyle." They continued to struggle with me, and I pretended not to fight them.

"Screw Jason!" Kyle exclaimed. He stood up and backed off. "Why do we always have to do what Jason tells us to do? I'm tired of it. He's the only one who's killed anybody."

"Be quiet, KJ!" Pete whispered loudly.

"I don't care who knows!" Kyle yelled. He raised his arms in the air. "I'll tell everybody! Hello DEA agents! I'm Kyle Westbrook. I'm not the one you're after! My brother, Jason, is the one who killed your agents. Not only that, but Jason killed…"

Pete turned to look at me, probably to see if I was coherent and listening, and he missed two things that I saw. The first was a faint flash of light coming from the top of the ridge, and the second was part of Kyle's head being blown off by the rifle shot. I saw them both before I heard the sound. Pete turned to see his brother fall onto a large bush.

"What the fu…"

"Jason," I rasped, unable to fully understand why I said his name or what it meant. I was still tied up, and I knew I would be a dead man soon. For whatever reason, I yelled his name again. "Jason!"

The next word that came out of Pete's mouth changed everything.

THIRTY-FIVE

"Jason!" Pete yelled.

Maybe he was just repeating what I'd said, or maybe I had given him an idea that I hadn't even fully considered.

With ridges on three sides, along with the trees and the rocky slope, it would've been nearly impossible to pinpoint the location of the shooter since only one shot had been fired. Pete looked around in every direction trying to see where the blast came from.

"Jason!" he yelled again. "Dammit, Jason!"

Pete ducked behind a small bush near me. His rifle moved toward the path Jason had taken.

"He's coming to kill you next," I whispered loudly.

"Shut up!"

"You're not a killer. I heard Jason and you arguing earlier. The murders were all committed by Jason, and I'd be willing to tell the DEA you weren't any part of this after they get here." Pete looked confused so I kept talking. "That is, if he doesn't kill us first."

"Shut up!" he yelled again, but with less conviction. He squinted and kept looking toward the trail and just above and below the tree line.

The flurries had stopped. The air was still as the sky grew lighter with every passing moment.

"You're the only one who knows the truth," I insisted. "If you keep me alive, I'll be able to confirm that you had nothing to do with it. The murders, the drugs; it was all Jason."

Pete pointed his rifle at me. I shook my head. "You're not a killer."

Pete didn't say anything else. He stood up and took off down the trail, the opposite direction of where Jason had gone. I looked up toward the ridge and saw nothing, but I knew what *one shot, one kill* meant. It meant the shooter had left and I was alone.

The game I was playing was my only chance. I struggled to sit up as my head throbbed and my legs tingled from the numbness, or just the lack of circulation. A mix of dried blood and dirt covered the back of my head and parts of my face. The zip ties they had used were thick and there were three of them wrapped tightly around my wrists. If they left me there alone for ten or fifteen minutes, I thought I could work my way through them against the rocky hillside. As I considered my situation, things could have been worse.

I pulled against the rope that still leashed me to the tree and I leaned back as far as I could. A small notch was on a rounded stone behind me. I began to rub up and down against the hard surface. The skin on my wrist quickly became raw, but I kept working the ties against the rock. A couple of minutes went by, and my wrists were getting the worst of it, but I knew how plastic weakened with constant pressure and friction, so I kept rubbing.

I stopped suddenly when I heard a noise coming from the trail below.

It was Jason. He looked at me and then climbed up to a clearing next to Kyle's body. The faint light showed his frustration.

"What the fu…"

"It was Pete!" I whispered loudly.

Jason pointed his rifle at me. "What?"

"Pete shot KJ and then left to go after you," I said. "He said something about not getting his fair share, and he told KJ that he'd take the whole shipment himself." I blurted it out so fast I thought I'd screwed it up.

"Bullshit," he said.

"KJ argued with him and that's when Pete shot him."

Jason came over to me and pointed the rifle at my head. He could see I was still bound. "Don't give me that bullshit! What really happened?"

"Listen, I know who you are. You're Jason Westbrook. My name is Brad Kelso. I'm with the DEA and we've been tracking your brother, Pete. I don't know if you realize this, but he and KJ have been involved in the distribution of fentanyl."

Jason's bewildered look turned to a smirk. He lowered the rifle and looked me in the eye.

"Yeah," I continued, "there's a suitcase full of fentanyl up in that fort."

"You're telling me Pete shot Kyle?"

"Yeah. I woke up when they were arguing. I don't know why, but he shot him in the head."

I could tell Jason wasn't sure what to think. Kyle was dead and Pete was gone, and I was tied up. I pressed my luck.

"Lacy told me about the fort. Pete told her he planned to make a lot of money with this shipment." I paused. "We know KJ is Kyle, too, and we think he was responsible for killing two of our agents." I looked over at Kyle's body. "I guess he got what was coming to him."

Jason raised up the rifle and pointed it at my face again. *Crap.* I shouldn't have said that, but I had nothing to lose.

"You're the only one left who can tell us the truth," I said. "Pete doesn't have a choice. Now he needs to kill both of us in order to blame the drug shipment on you and Kyle." I looked down at the trail. "He took off in that direction. You better watch your back. Like I said, he needs to kill both of us before the rest of our agents get here this morning, and he knows it."

Jason paused to think. I wasn't sure if he'd bought my story at first. "I knew you were with the DEA," he said. He lowered the rifle.

"Yeah, if you don't believe me, go up there and take a look. The case of drugs is still there. Pete planned to deliver the fentanyl to someone named Ivanoff. You didn't know anything about it, did you?"

Jason slowly shook his head. He was still thinking.

"If I'm dead, it'll be your story against his," I said.

I looked toward the bay. I needed more time and I needed Jason to believe he only had one option. I doubled down.

"They'll be here soon. We've got GPS trackers on the plane if he decides to take off."

Jason was still thinking, then he looked toward the bay. "What do you know about Ivanoff?" he asked.

"We only know Pete was supposed to meet him soon," I said. "We don't have anything on Ivanoff, but we think he's a big player. Have you ever heard of him?"

Jason shook his head. "No," he said. "I know the name, but I don't keep track of Pete's business. You say Kyle killed two of your agents?"

"Yeah, I understand this could be a shock to you, but we think Kyle killed one of our agents this summer, and another one yesterday at Trident Basin. We know he's been working for Pete."

He looked at me and grinned. An evil grin that showed no remorse for whatever he planned to do. "Wait here," he said, then he got up and left.

"Can you untie me?" I cried out, but Jason had already taken off down the hill. *Crap!*

I started rubbing the zip ties against the rock again. The sky brightened even more. I felt like every second counted. My wrists bled and the cold sweat dripping off my brow stung my eyes. I could barely feel my wrists anymore. I looked out toward the water and the faint outline of a large vessel approached, but it was still nearly a mile away. It seemed to be moving slowly, too slowly, over the calm waters.

I kept working my hands against the rock. "Plick!" One of the zip ties snapped.

I rubbed even harder, knowing I didn't have much time, and that's when I heard two rifle shots, one after another. The sound echoed up and around the entire ridgeline, but I knew where the shots came from. I just didn't know which brother had fired them. Then there was nothing but silence. I waited. I felt too tired to rub and my wrists were bleeding, but I kept going.

"Plick!" The second zip tie broke. Only one more to go. I could barely feel my arms as they moved back and forth over the last tie.

"Plick!"

I looked out toward the bay. The white Coast Guard cutter with its unmistakable red marking kept getting closer. It wasn't a pirate ship, but the agents onboard had certainly come for the hidden treasure that had been stashed in the fort.

The rope that bound my legs was tight, and by the time I finally got free, the cutter had already pulled into the dock. Two large helicopters approached. A coordinated effort, I supposed.

I climbed up to the fort and checked to make sure the fentanyl was still there. Then I went back outside and crawled onto a rocky ledge behind a large bush. I didn't have enough strength to move very far. I leaned my head back against a rock and breathed. I felt the cold and damp air going in and out of my lungs. I finally felt safe. I thought about Chris. *If she could see me now.*

Tears fell down my cheeks. I didn't know why. I wasn't sad or happy. Maybe I was relieved, but I certainly wasn't finished.

THIRTY-SIX

I sat on a round stone in front of the fort, with my arms crossed, while a US Marshal completed his report. He was the second law enforcement officer who had interviewed me. I answered the same questions that had been asked in a slightly different way by a special agent with the DEA. Typical tactics. The digital recorder attached to the marshal's clipboard had a small LED light that went off after he touched one of the buttons. Another special agent had given me a blanket, and provided me with medical attention, but I'd been sitting there for nearly an hour, and I was ready to leave.

"I think that's all for now," the Marshal said. "We might have a few more follow-up questions for you later today. We have some helicopters coming in and Special Agent Carmichael said you could take one of them back to Kodiak."

"Thanks, I have a few errands to run this afternoon, but I'll be in town. Just call or text me if you need anything else and I'll get back to you."

"That's fine," he said. "Oh, before you go, she wants to talk to you. She's down by the docks."

I looked at the pathway that meandered toward the water's edge. Another Coast Guard vessel was coming into the inlet. The fog had thinned out, and the clouds were high in the sky with a reddish tint. *Red sky in the morning*, I thought. It may have been daylight, but I couldn't seem to get warm.

The agent had told me Jason was being questioned below, and that he wasn't being very cooperative. I needed to be careful. Had I given Jason, the man who murdered Boggs, and two DEA agents, a way out?

My legs felt stiff as I followed one of the agents down the hillside. The path looked different in the daytime, much easier to navigate. The air seemed thicker the lower we went. The shade from the trees gave me more of a chill as we slowly snaked down toward the docks.

I saw Chief Carmichael with two other agents standing on the wooden planks in front of the Coast Guard vessel. All the agents wore black jackets with *DEA* screened on the back in large, white lettering.

"Hello, Chief," I called out as I got closer.

She turned around and looked at me, then smiled. "Nice work, Kelso," she said. "I read your first statement. They told me you had a few bumps and bruises, but I have to tell you, you look like shit."

"Now I can call you Cass, right?"

"Not a chance. But maybe I should be calling you Special Agent Kelso. That was nice work."

"What's the story with Jason Westbrook?" I asked.

She pointed toward a bench in front of the lodge, about sixty feet away from us, where Jason and two DEA agents were talking. Jason was handcuffed as he sat on the bench. Both agents were standing near him, one older, one younger.

"He talked to me and my deputies a few minutes ago," she said. She looked down at her clipboard. "Jason said he didn't know about his brother's involvement in the distribution of fentanyl until last night. He confronted Pete about it outside the lodge, and Pete told him Kyle found Brad Kelso on the property and planned to kill him." She looked at me. "That's you."

She shrugged. "Pete or Kyle were going to kill you near the fort, as Jason called it, just above the tree line. Pete told him they'd already tied you up, and that you were a DEA agent."

She paused. "I wonder why they thought that."

"Who knows," I said.

She flipped up the first page of her notes and sighed. "Later, he said Pete shot Kyle up near the fort and that you saw him do it. When you told him about it, Jason came back down to the lodge and tried to convince Pete to let you go, but Pete had a rifle and said he was going back up to kill you."

She flipped up the paper and read from the next page. "Jason kept arguing with his brother, and when Pete turned and pointed his rifle at him, he shot him twice. Self-defense, he says."

I shook my head. "Do you believe all of that?"

"We've got two dead bodies in the right places, and he was standing here on the dock, waving at us when we arrived. What are we missing?"

"Jason murdered Pete," I said, "and he ran the entire operation. He was the one who killed Pilot Bob, and agent Pulte this summer. He probably killed Boggs, too."

"That's not what you told the agents who questioned you earlier."

"I gave them the information they wanted."

She looked at me, and I could tell she understood what I was saying. She wasn't as bewildered as I'd expected her to be. She nodded. "Do you have any evidence?"

"Nothing that would stand up in a court of law," I said, "but I know exactly what happened. You know there's more to this story than what the evidence shows."

She nodded again. "We suspected Jason was involved in the distribution of fentanyl, just because he was running most of the family businesses, but we don't have any evidence that he ever committed murder. Are you sure?"

"Positive."

She paused to think. "He's trying to lawyer up, but he's still talking." She shook her head. "Right now, our hands are tied. He's asked for his attorney. The DEA has rules. We don't have a good reason to charge him with anything right now. I'm not even sure if we'll take him back to Kodiak when we leave." She furrowed her brow. "And I mean the *city* of Kodiak!"

"I'm telling you, he killed Pete, and he murdered both of your agents. You've read my file so you know I wouldn't say something like that unless I was absolutely sure."

She shook her head. "The prosecuting attorney won't file any charges, and the DEA will be more than happy with the drug bust, not to mention the fact that we're bringing back Kyle Westbrook's dead body. Right now, we don't have enough evidence to convict Jason of jaywalking."

I wasn't sure what I could do at that point, but I needed to do something. The place was full of DEA agents, and it was only going to get more crowded as they searched the property. I certainly had no intention of trying to get Jason to talk. Besides, he was too smart for that. I motioned with my head toward Jason and the other agents. "Do you mind?"

"No. We have a few minutes. See if you can get something. You can send the other agents over here. Do you have a recording device?"

"I don't need one."

***

"How long do I have to stay handcuffed?" Jason barked at the deputies. They looked at each other, then at me as I approached.

"Special Agent Carmichael says you can remove his cuffs," I said.

The deputies looked toward the docks where the chief stood. She raised her hand and nodded, then the older deputy shrugged his shoulders. The younger one took a key from his pocket and removed Jason's handcuffs.

Jason smiled and rubbed his wrists. "Do you mind if I go inside now and get a drink? This is the third time I've asked."

"Just sit right there for a few minutes," the young deputy barked. "If you're thirsty, we'll get you something." I grinned. I wasn't sure what Jason had said to them before I got there, but whatever it was must have gotten on the young deputy's nerves. Maybe it was just the fact that Jason didn't seem too concerned about his two brothers being loaded onto the Coast Guard vessel in body bags. He seemed more interested in getting a glass of water, or maybe even…

"I'll get him a drink," I said. The young deputy nodded, and Jason and I looked at each other before I turned away and walked toward the lodge.

"It's about time!" I heard Jason say.

The lodge's kitchen was a large, separate room with two ovens, two refrigerators, and a huge island in the center. It had plenty of cupboard space throughout. I had forgotten that years earlier the place had been used to house and feed vacationing guests, probably eight to ten at a time. It could've used a remodel. With some new cabinets, appliances, flooring, and a fresh coat of paint, the place would've been as good as new. I would've bid eighty-four or eighty-five hours of labor, tops.

Several rows of sodas and fitness drinks were on the bottom shelf of one of the refrigerators. I smiled. I preferred the bottles. I took out three Bevo fitness drinks and unscrewed one of the lids, then reached in my jacket pocket. I felt a small glass vial.

When I walked back outside, I carried the three bottles in a large cloth bag I'd found in one of the kitchen cabinets.

"I never OK'd any of this," I heard Jason tell the deputies as I approached. "I haven't seen a warrant, either. And I haven't been allowed to contact my attorney. I demand to be released from custody, and I want it to be clear that I have requested my attorney to be present several times."

When I got to the bench, the two deputies seemed to be getting tired of Jason's demands. "Do you want me to put the cuffs back on you?" the younger deputy asked. The older one just smiled.

"Special Agent Carmichael said she wanted to talk to both of you," I said.

The deputies left us alone and walked toward the Coast Guard vessel where Chief Carmichael was writing notes and speaking to one of the crew members. Four agents began to move the two bodies onto the dock, one at a time, using a gurney.

"Why am I being held like this," Jason said to me as I sat down next to him. "I haven't done anything wrong."

"That seems to be the consensus," I said. "They're still trying to sort things out. Give them some time. They have two dead bodies on their hands and a lot of questions. They're not interested in holding you for very long."

Jason smiled like he knew the situation. "So, that's it?"

"As far as the DEA is concerned, they'll probably want to get another statement from you, but then you'll be free to go." I looked him in the eye. "Before I leave, I wanted to thank you for helping me out up there. I guess I owe you."

Jason smirked at me as I took a bottle from the cloth bag and set it on the bench. I twisted the lid off another one and took a drink.

"So, you just decided to have one of my Bevo fitness drinks without asking?" he said.

"I'm sorry. You're right, I should've asked. Do you mind?"

"Knock yourself out," he said. I smiled.

I stood up. "I'm heading back to town, then flying over to Anchorage tonight, so I probably won't be seeing you again."

He unscrewed the lid and held the bottle up. "Here's to that," he said.

I smiled as he drank most of it. "Ahh," he said. "That hit the spot."

We stayed there for a while and watched the bodies of his brothers being loaded onto the Coast Guard vessel's deck. I held up my drink. "Here's to your brothers," I said. "I didn't really know them. For all their faults, they were still too young to die." We both took another drink.

His eyes squinted as he looked at me. "You don't act like law enforcement," he said. "I can't figure you out."

"The truth is, I haven't done this type of work in a long time." I downed the last of my drink and put the empty bottle back in the cloth bag. "I recycle," I said.

He finished his drink, so I held out the bag. He gently placed his empty bottle in it. He pulled out the last Bevo, unscrewed the lid, and took another drink. "So, the DEA must be happy," he said. "Is this one of your larger busts?"

"It ended up not being a bust for me," I said.

His puzzled look was followed by a sharp cough. His eyes watered as he laughed and wiped his mouth. "What's that supposed to mean?"

I chuckled. "I don't know. It's been a long week, but I'm almost finished. I'm ready to get back on a plane and go home."

"I'll be glad when you and everybody else are gone," he said, then paused and took another drink. "How did you know about Kyle? Was anybody still after him?"

"After him?"

"Because of those two brothers people thought he killed?"

"Did he kill them?" I asked.

Jason smiled. "I wouldn't know," he said. "He was never charged with killing them, and he didn't talk to me about it. I would never aid and abet anyone who committed murder." He laughed. "My guess is that it was someone else, maybe even their father. That guy seemed like a loose cannon." He took another drink, then coughed again and hunched forward. He screwed the lid back on his drink and placed it on the bench.

"It's not important," I said. "I knew a guy once who was killed for no particular reason. Wrong place at the wrong time. I can't imagine what it must have been like for Kyle. All these years and everybody thinking he was a murderer."

"Kyle was a good man, and he knew his place."

"What about Pete?" I asked. "Did he know his place, too?"

Jason looked up at me with his stone-cold eyes. "Who are you?"

"Just nobody who wants to be somebody. That's what Pete thought. I'd like to think I'm somebody, though, who just wants to be nobody."

Jason coughed again, then he grabbed his stomach and bent over.

"Do you need anything?" I asked.

He shook his head and wiped his mouth again. He seemed puzzled as he looked at the bag I was carrying, then he began to cough again.

"I'll get someone," I said.

He glared at me and was having trouble breathing. Then he threw up in the grass.

"It's too bad that Kyle was blamed for killing the Beverly brothers," I said. "Everyone still thinks he killed my friend, too. His name was Samuel Boggs. You and I are the only ones who know the truth. I don't see any reason to convince them otherwise." I paused. "Kyle protected you all these years. It's kind of ironic, actually. In a roundabout way, he got back at you by not killing me when he had the chance."

Jason was having too much trouble breathing to say anything as I walked away from him. I thought I heard him say "no" once, but I didn't stop to turn around. Chief Carmichael was overseeing things on the dock. As I approached her, I finally looked back and watched Jason fall to the ground in a seizure. Two DEA agents raced toward him. "He didn't tell me anything," I told her.

She glanced at Jason, but only for a moment, then turned toward me as I began to step onto the dock. "You're sure that he ran the operation and killed my men?"

I didn't hesitate. "Yep."

She looked back at Jason, who was on the grass and had stopped convulsing. The agents near him were scrambling and calling for help on their handsets.

"What are we looking at?" she asked.

"Karma," I said. "They say it's a bitch."

She nodded. "We have a final count on the vials found in the case. A hundred and ninety-nine total. Each vial had enough fentanyl to kill several thousand people."

I stopped and turned around. "Is that right? I asked. "I read somewhere that they're putting it into pills and tablets, and many of the people who overdose on it don't even realize they're taking fentanyl."

She nodded again, then started walking toward Jason and the other agents who were attempting to revive him. She stopped and looked back at me. "I was wrong about you," she said, "and I'm sorry about that. Maybe we still need a little old school every once in a while."

"Hey, I'm not that old," I said. She laughed, then turned away and waved.

I smiled, then walked to the end of the dock and looked out at the bay. I sat down and stretched my legs over the edge. Then I dropped one of the two Bevo fitness drink bottles and a small glass vile into the water. They made a small splash and disappeared. I didn't want to be a litterbug, but...

I looked up as a floatplane circled twice before it landed. It pulled up to the dock, a short distance from where I sat. I stood up and grabbed the bar under the wing. Hannah Jones got out and tied the plane's line to a cleat. She looked toward the lodge at all the agents who surrounded Jason Westbrook. They didn't seem as hurried.

"Brad Kelso," she said, "is all of this your handy work?"

I didn't answer as we stood there together and watched.

"So, you're the informant?" I asked.

"Well, I don't always feel informed," she said. "I like flying, but I also get paid by the Southern Alaska Port Facilities, too. They contract with the government to build infrastructure projects in Alaska."

I smiled. "It sounds like a critical infrastructure sector partnership."

"I don't know," she said. "They don't seem to get much infrastructure built, but I've always felt that my job was critical."

I looked at her and smiled. "I can guarantee it."

She smiled back. "CH-163 said you might need a ride. I guess she knows you."

We turned and walked toward the floatplane. "Yep, she knows me."

THIRTY-SEVEN

"Kelso…Kelso…"

"Sorry," I said. I opened my eyes, but I was barely coherent.

Hannah laughed. "Why do you always say you're sorry when you wake up? Is that the line you use on women because it's not a very good one."

I chuckled, "Leave me alone. I'm too tired and sore."

"That's even worse," she said. "You're better off saying you're sorry.' She laughed. "Get ready to land. We're on our final approach."

After we landed, we taxied past the orange Jeep and stopped near several other planes. The Jeep was right where I'd left it. It'd been less than sixteen hours since we'd taken off from the airport in Kodiak, but it seemed like an eternity.

Hannah shut the engine down and looked at me. She seemed concerned. "You should get your head scanned today."

"Is that the line you use on men, because it's not a very good one," I said. She laughed, but I just chuckled. I was too tired to laugh, and my neck was stiff from sleeping on the plane.

After we stopped, I grabbed my bags and got out. We just looked at each other, smiled, and nodded. Nothing needed to be said. I was never great at goodbyes anyway.

When I peeked inside the Jeep, I saw my camera bag in the back seat. I sighed. *Crap.* I forgot about Walt.

"Hey!" I yelled to Hannah. She was still near her plane. She heard me and came over to the Jeep. I held the two-way radio in my hand. "What about Walt?" I asked.

She smiled. "I forgot to mention, I told Walt this morning that you bumped into Sid while you were hiking on the ridge. The two of you did some trekking together before sunrise. You got the photos you needed, so I picked up both of you where Sid's boat was anchored, about a mile to the north of the bear camp."

"What did he say?"

"Walt said to call him, or to pay the bill online before you leave Kodiak. He said he wants his two-way radio back, too." She smiled and grabbed the radio. "I'll get it back to him."

"Thanks."

"I told CH-163 about your bill and she took care of it. You should keep your handler, she's a good one."

"Thanks. She's great, but this was my last mission."

"Too bad." she said. She smiled, then turned and walked away. "See ya around, Kelso."

I just smiled. My phone was almost dead, so I plugged it into the front console of the Jeep and started the engine. I turned on the heater as high as it would go and sat there for a few minutes until it warmed up. I called Chris.

"You should have seen all the messages I received after I activated those tracking chips this morning," she answered.

"Hello to you, too."

"There were nine tracking chips near the same location on that hill. After we picked up the signals, none of them moved for over an hour." She paused. "You had me and everyone else worried."

"Who's everyone else?"

"Well, I was worried."

"I assure you; it was less fun on my end."

"Yeah, I heard you got a little banged up. I suppose you'll want someone to take care of you for a few days."

"Is that a proposition?"

"Who, me? No, I thought you might want to talk to Lacy about it. She's probably devastated right now. She'll need consoling, and I'm sure she'd love to be your nurse for a couple of days. Of course, you'd have to make up some story about what happened to you."

"Chris, I'm sorry."

"Yeah, you've said that before." She paused. "I have two flights, from Anchorage to Portland, already booked. One tonight, and one in three days. You get to decide."

"I don't want to stay here," I said. "I want to see you. What time does my flight leave?"

"It leaves Kodiak at six. With the connecting flight, you'll get into Portland at ten thirty-five."

"Will you come get me?" I asked.

"I suppose Jenny wants to see you, and by the time we get back here it'll be late. I'll make up the spare bedroom. No funny business."

"I've thought about you a lot over the last couple of days. I can't wait to see you."

"Chief Carmichael says you look like a train wreck. I guess I'd at least like to see that."

"So, you knew about Sid, didn't you?"

"I'll talk to you about it when you get back. I'll be there when you land."

***

I had a couple of stops I needed to make before I left Kodiak. The Standing Bear Pub opened at 11:30 am, and I was there at 11:35. The place looked different in the daytime. Rays of sunlight streamed through the windows. Unlike the night of the dart tournament, the place was almost empty. Two guys were in a booth toward the front, drinking coffee; but other than that, the only other person I could see was Sid, who was behind the bar. He watched me as I walked along the old wooden floor and sat down on one of the stools in front of him.

"What can I get for you?"

I was too tired to play games. "Hey Del," I said. "Thanks for being there. I didn't know you could shoot like that."

He smiled. "It's Sid."

"OK, Sid, thanks."

"You should be more careful," he said, "or stick to PFT work. We got lucky."

"Lucky?" Your plane went down in Norton Sound eleven years ago. We buried you. I even said a few words at your funeral."

"That was the agency's idea," he said. "My cover had been compromised during my last mission, so they killed me off. Standard procedure."

"That's standard procedure for someone who does wetwork, not for a PFT."

Sid smiled at me. I knew immediately what that meant. I looked around to make sure the two men couldn't hear us. "And the Westbrooks?"

"You're not the only one who was friends with Boggs," he said. "I told the agency we needed you on this one, and I was right." He paused. "We've been short-handed, and Homeland Security's bureaucratic protocols are making things impossible in Alaska. Sometimes, other agencies, like the DEA, think they run the show."

"What's Carmichael's role with the agency?"

"They gave her a title." He smirked. "She's a good agent, but she was only told what she needed to know."

"I guess it's over now."

"Yeah," he said. "Jason's death was ruled a suicide by accidental overdose. I'm not even sure what that means." He paused and smiled. "I told the agency you wouldn't be interested in doing any wetwork. They asked me this morning. I guess some people were impressed by your resilience. You might not know this, but Boggs told them the same thing before they originally hired you."

"He was right. So are you."

"I thought you might stop by," he said. "I'm glad you did, but I'm going home in a few minutes to get some sleep."

"You look tired," I said, "but better than someone who's been dead for eleven years."

"Have you looked in the mirror lately?" he asked.

I sighed. "It could be worse. A lot worse."

He nodded. "To be honest, I didn't think you'd make it. I hated leaving, but…"

"One shot, one kill," I said. "Protocol fifteen: When two missions collide in the field, complete your assignment first, then assess your own risk." I paused. "I know the drill."

Sid nodded. "I'm glad to hear you say that."

So, you have a boat?"

"Yeah, I need to go back to Uyak Bay and pick it up tomorrow. If you ever come back into town, we'll go fishing."

"I'd like that," I said. I stood up. "I guess I should thank you before I go."

"Let's call it even," he said, "You saved me from having to give a speech at your funeral."

I smiled and knocked on the bar twice before I left. Sid smiled and nodded.

***

It was late in the afternoon when Chief Carmichael met me at the police station in Kodiak. We sat across from each other in a small room that had obviously been used to question witnesses. Three cameras were mounted in the corners, near the ceiling. The white, bare walls added to the overall ambience of the room. Two recording devices had been placed on the table between us.

"Are you sure you don't want an attorney," she asked me. "One will be provided to you at no cost."

"I waive the privilege for now,' I said. "I took a shower and slept for two hours this afternoon so I'm good to go. You said you had some questions?"

"Yes," she said. Her casual demeanor turned official when she turned on the recorders. "The preliminary results lead us to believe that Jason committed suicide. He overdosed on fentanyl. A lot of it."

"Is that right? Those results came back fast."

"We're preparing a statement for this evening's news. The final lab results should be available later today."

"How can I help?" I asked.

She smirked. "Jason must have had some of the drug with him, but we never found any containers. You didn't see him take anything, did you? I need to ask for the record."

"What does it look like?"

"Our assumption is that it was in a powdery form like the vials in the case."

"How much did he take?"

"The preliminary report says at least a tenth of a gram, maybe more."

"Is that a lot?"

"Yes," the Chief said, "we don't usually have people who overdose on that much fentanyl, but I've heard of it happening before. That quantity is enough to kill several hundred people. It's cheap, so people get confused about the amounts, but there's no room for error with fentanyl. Of course, like I said, our theory is that he must have killed himself."

"All I noticed was that he seemed overcome with grief about his brothers, especially Kyle. He kept talking about ways to get out of his situation and wanting to leave, like a person does when they've lost hope. When I sat down next to him, I gave him a bottle of a fitness drink I found in the lodge."

She smiled. "Our deputies confirmed that. We checked out the bottle he drank from, and it was clean. The coroner said the amount he ingested would have had a rapid effect, so he must have taken it while he was sitting on the bench. Just to confirm, you didn't see him ingest anything?"

"Aside from the fitness drink, I didn't see him eat anything. Of course, I was only with him for five or ten minutes, and I spent most of that time watching the bodies being lifted onto the boat."

"I think that's all we need for now," she said. "The DEA appreciates your cooperation." She smiled and turned off the recorder, probably just as relieved as me to be finished.

I shook my head. "Millions of doses of fentanyl, all packaged in a suitcase. It makes you stop and think."

"It's the biggest problem we face right now," she said. "That and the fact they're putting it into pills, and making it look like so many recreational and prescription drugs."

"So, this was a good bust for you and the DEA?"

"Anytime we can keep it off the streets, it's good," she said, "but I don't think it was worth losing two agents. I wanted to let you know, after we notified the Westbrook's crew members, two of them started talking to us. Another one, Mac Dalton, wants to cut a deal. I guess he has quite a bit of evidence about Jason's involvement, really his command over the operation. It turns out, Jason controlled everything, just like you said."

I nodded. "Does anyone know about me?"

"We don't think so," she said. "Your name has never been mentioned and it'll be redacted on the final report."

I stood up. "Is that it?"

"That's it." She reached out her hand. I shook it.

"If you need anything else," I said, "you know where to find me."

"We know."

THIRTY-EIGHT

I stood in line at Anchorage's airport with my carry-on bag and waited to board. I used a plastic spoon and finished off the bowl of clam chowder I'd ordered from the ale house, but I was still hungry.

My mind drifted back to the Westbrook brothers and what had happened. I thought about Boggs, and what he would have thought about the way things turned out. Wherever he was, maybe he was smiling, knowing he wasn't forgotten, certainly not by his friends, but not even by the agency. They never gave up their search for his killer. I wished he was still around to talk with me about it. Even after twelve years, I still missed my friend.

I showed the attendant my boarding pass and walked through the short tunnel. I made my way down the center aisle of the plane until I saw Row 23, Seat D. Seat F had an elderly woman who must have pre-boarded because it looked like she was already settled in. She stared out the window at whatever was on the tarmac.

"Can I help you with your bag, sir?" a flight attendant asked me from behind.

I looked at her, a young woman in her early twenties, who probably weighed less than a hundred and ten pounds soaking wet. Her perfume was light and sweet, matching her demeanor. I thought it was funny that she wanted to help me put my bag in the overhead bin, or maybe she was just being courteous, asking me like she'd been trained to do. I chuckled to myself, imagining her trying to walk uphill with the anchor from the Monie Marie strapped onto her back.

"No thanks, I've got it," I said. She smiled and moved down the aisle toward another passenger who probably needed her assistance more than I did.

My carry-on, the cloth shopping bag I took from the Westbrook's lodge, had expanded with each item I'd placed inside of it. I felt bad for having it with me, but it wasn't like I'd saved it as some trophy or memento from what had happened, like a killer keeping a souvenir. It was just a nice cheap bag, and I could get a lot of stuff into it. I was even able to slide the three calendars from *Kodiak's Treasures* inside of it. As I raised it up and tilted it to get it into the overhead bin, the calendars fell onto my neck and shoulders, then fanned out in every direction before landing in the aisle. "Crap!"

The flight attendant glanced back at me, first with a look of surprise, but then she smiled. I smiled back. Nothing needed to be said.

There was a space between two other carry-ons, so I pushed the bag in and closed the bin before I reached down and picked up the calendars. I grabbed the back of the headrest of the seat in front of me with one hand, allowing other passengers to pass by, then I sat down and buckled my seatbelt. I placed the two smaller calendars into the mesh holder on the back of the seat in front of me, then looked at the third one, which was too large for the holder.

Kodiak Bears was written on the front, and a smaller version of all twelve photos, one for each month, were on the back. *Great photos*, I thought, and I knew what I was talking about, having been a freelance photographer. I chuckled to myself and set the calendar on my lap.

"Are you coming from Kodiak?" The woman sitting in 23F asked me. I nodded. "My husband and I used to live there before he passed away. Now I have a small house in Anchorage. I guess it's been five years now. My name is Dee."

"I'm Brad," I said. "Is Portland your final destination?"

"I hope not," she said and chuckled. "My daughter lives in Beaverton, and I'm staying with her and her husband for three weeks. I have two grandkids now, seven and five, and a third on the way."

I pulled out the two calendars from the mesh holder and gave them to Dee. "These are for your two grandkids," I said. "One has photos of Kodiak's harbor seals, and the other one shows marine life in Uyak Bay. It has killer whales and sea otters."

"I can't take these," she said.

I looked at the calendar in my lap. "They're for your grandkids," I said, "plus, this calendar has Kodiak bears, and the person I'm giving it to will like the bears."

"Well, thank you," she said and smiled. She looked at the calendars. "I think they'll like these. She stuffed them into the mesh pocket in front of her. "What happened?" she asked.

I pointed at my wounds. "You mean this?" I asked.

Dee nodded.

"I got caught stealing calendars," I said. She had a shocked look at first and then we both laughed

I looked at the photos on the back of the larger calendar again. Kodiak bears. I liked bears too. They looked bigger in real life. Much bigger. More powerful, too. The photos didn't do them justice.

"Do you know what a group of bears is called?" I asked Dee.

Dee hesitated. "I think it's a sloth," she said.

"That's right, and do you know what a group of sloths is called?"

She laughed. "I have no idea. What?"

I whispered, "a snuggle." She smiled.

***

After we took off and gained altitude, I leaned my seat back as far as it would go and closed my eyes. I thought about Chris and how nice it would be to see her again. I wondered what she thought of me, with all my faults and how sometimes I was such an idiot. Would she ever go out with me on a date if I asked her? A real date. I faded off...

"Excuse me sir!" a woman said, as she grabbed my shoulder and startled me awake.

"Sorry," I said before I became coherent.

It was the same flight attendant who asked if she could help me before. "Is your name Brad Kelso?"

"Yes."

"We have a call for you on our communications network. Could you come to the front of the plane, please?"

"OK." I looked around at the other passengers, but the only one paying attention was Dee.

I shrugged. "Must be the dealership wanting to sell me that extended warranty," I said. She laughed.

I followed the flight attendant to the front of the plane, and she handed me a receiver, closed a privacy curtain, and left. I had no idea who was calling.

"Hello?"

"Is this BK-643?" The woman on the phone asked.

"Yes."

"One moment please."

A man came on the line. "Brad Kelso?" he asked.

"Yes."

"You need to get back to Alaska. We've just spoken to CH-163 and she's agreed to the contract. We have another job for you and it's urgent!"

Author's Notes

I had so much fun writing *Whitefish*! The idea came to me after listening to a friend of mine, named Brad, talk about his adventures in Alaska when he was younger. That's Brad's silhouette on the front cover.

Whitefish has little to do with any of his stories but listening to them gave me the idea for this novel.

So, why Kodiak? I've always been fascinated with Kodiak Island, mainly because of the Kodiak brown bears, so I did some research about the island in 2021.

I contacted Robin Barefield, a fish and wildlife biologist who lives with her husband, Mike, near Uyak Bay. It's the remote area of Kodiak Island where some of the story takes place. Mike and Robin run *Munsey's Bear Camp*, where people can vacation by fishing, hiking, and watching wildlife in their natural habitat (including whales and the Kodiak brown bears). If you're interested in the adventure of a lifetime, search for *Munsey's Bear Camp* online!

Robin is also an author, and she has written several mystery novels and a fantastic reference book called *Kodiak Island Wildlife.*

Robin was happy to help me with some of the details of the island, including what it's like to live there. I took some "artistic liberties," but Robin was very adamant about me getting any information about the bears right. In her own words: "PLEASE GET THIS RIGHT!!! Kodiak is considered the model for bear management (or big game management) throughout the world!"

One of the fascinating things I learned while doing research was the "false charge" that many bears will do when confronted by humans. Sadly, many bears get shot by people who don't realize what's taking place.

Aside from Brad and Robin, there are so many people to thank, but my list starts with my wife, Sara. It took me over ten months to finish this novel, and that includes hundreds of hours of not doing other things. My honey-do list seems to get longer the more I write.

A shout out to my editor, Russ. Editors are always important for authors like me to produce a quality manuscript and Russ did a remarkable job.

I have some friends who agreed to let me use their names in the story. I won't mention all of them, but I'll have to throw some darts with Bud and Mick soon. And Chris? She's a great handler!

Of course, *Whitefish* is a work of fiction and every line written was from my own imagination.

When I wrote the last line, even before it was edited, I felt like I wouldn't be seeing my friends again for a while, so I wrote a short outline and a chapter and a half of *Miss, the Target*, another Brad Kelso novel. More than anything, it was to keep the characters alive and in my thoughts.

Should I write more Brad Kelso novels? You tell me! Go to Amazon and Goodreads and give this book a rating or write a review. I'm anxious to see and hear your thoughts. Feedback will be very important for me as I decide whether to continue writing Brad Kelso novels, so spread the word! My honey-do list still has room to grow!

Thank you for your support, and I hope you enjoyed reading *Whitefish*!

KELLER CONSTRUCTION

Whether it's nailed or screwed, I'm the dude!

Made in the USA
Middletown, DE
11 April 2022